TEN
TOMORROWS

TEN TOMORROWS

Edited by

ROGER ELWOOD

A FAWCETT GOLD MEDAL BOOK

Fawcett Publications, Inc., Greenwich, Conn.

TEN TOMORROWS

Printed in the United States of America
September 1973

CONTENTS

TEN
TOMORROWS

MS. FOUND IN AN ABANDONED TIME MACHINE
by
Robert Silverberg

If life is to be worth living at all, we have to have at least the illusion that we are capable of making sweeping changes in the world we live in. I say *at least the illusion.* Real ability to effect change would obviously be preferable, but not all of us can get to that level; and even the illusion of power offers hope, and hope sustains life. The point is not to be a puppet, not to be a passive plaything of karma. I think you'll agree that sweeping changes in society have to be made. Who will make them, if not you and me? If we tell ourselves that we're helpless, that meaningful reform is impossible, that the status quo is here for keeps, then we might as well not bother going on living, don't you think? I mean, if the bus is breaking down and the driver is freaking out on junk and all the doors are jammed, it's cooler to take the cyanide than to wait around for the inevitable messy smashup. But naturally we don't want to let ourselves believe that we're helpless. We want to think that we can grab the wheel and get the bus back on course and steer it safely to the repair shop. Right? Right. That's what we want to think. Even if it's only an illusion. Because sometimes—who knows?—you can firm up an illusion and make it real.

The cast of characters. Thomas C——, our chief protagonist, age twenty. As we first encounter him he lies asleep with strands of his own long brown hair casually wrapped across his mouth. Tie-dyed jeans and an ECOL-OGY NOW! sweatshirt are crumpled at the foot of the bed. He was raised in Elephant Mound, Wisconsin, and this is his third year at the university. He appears to be sleeping peacefully, but through his dreaming mind flit disturbing phantoms: Lee Harvey Oswald, George Lincoln Rockwell, Neil Armstrong, Arthur Bremer, Sirhan Sirhan, Hubert Humphrey, Mao Tse-tung, Lieutenant William Calley, John Lennon. Each in turn announces himself, does a lightfooted little dance expressive of his character, vanishes, and reappears elsewhere in Thomas's cerebral cortex. On the wall of Thomas's room are various contemporary totems: a giant blowup photograph of Spiro Agnew playing golf, a gaudy VOTE FOR McGOVERN sticker, and banners that variously proclaim FREE ANGELA, SUPPORT YOUR LOCAL PIG FORCE, POWER TO THE PEOPLE, and CHE LIVES! Thomas has an extremely contemporary sensibility, circa 1970–72. By 1997 he will feel terribly nostalgic for the causes and artifacts of his youth, as his grandfather now is for raccoon coats, bathtub gin, and flagpole sitters. He will say things like "Try it, you'll like it" or "Sock it to me," and no one under forty will laugh.

Asleep next to him is Katherine F——, blond, nineteen years old. Ordinarily she wears steel-rimmed glasses, green hip-hugger bells, a silken purple poncho, and a macramé shawl, but she wears none of these things now. Katherine is not dreaming, but her next REM cycle is due shortly. She comes from Moose Valley, Minnesota, and lost her virginity at the age of fourteen while watching a Mastroianni–Loren flick at the North Star Drive-In. During her seduction, she never took her eyes from the screen for a period longer than thirty seconds. Nowadays she's much more heavily into the responsiveness thing, but back then she was trying hard to be cool. Four hours ago, she and Thomas performed an act of mutual oral-genital stimulation that is illegal in seventeen states and the Republic of Vietnam (South), although there is hope of changing that before long.

On the floor by the side of the bed is Thomas's dog

Fidel, part beagle, part terrier. He is asleep too. Attached to Fidel's collar is a day-glo streamer that reads, THREE WOOFS FOR PET LIB.

Without God, said one of the Karamazov boys, everything is possible. I suppose that's true enough, if you conceive of God as the force that holds things together, that keeps water from flowing uphill and the sun from rising in the west. But what a limited concept of God that is! *Au contraire,* Fyodor: With God everything is possible. And I would like to be God for a little while.

Q. What did you do?

A. I yelled at Sergeant Bacon and told him to go and start searching hooches and get your people moving right on—not the hooches but the bunkers—and I started over to Mitchell's location. I came back out. Meadlo was still standing there with a group of Vietnamese, and I yelled at Meadlo and asked him—I told him—if he couldn't move all those people, to get rid of them.

Q. Did you fire into that group of people?

A. No, sir, I did not.

Q. After that incident, what did you do?

A. Well, I told my men to get on across the ditch and to get into position after I had fired into the ditch.

Q. Now, did you have a chance to look and observe what was in the ditch?

A. Yes, sir.

Q. And what did you see?

A. Dead people, sir.

Q. Did you see any appearance of anybody being alive in there?

A. No, sir.

This is Thomas talking. Listen to me. Just listen. Suppose you had a machine that would enable you to fix everything that's wrong in the world. Let's say that it draws on all the resources of modern technology, not to mention the powers of a rich, well-stocked imagination and a highly developed ethical sense. The machine can do anything.

It makes you invisible; it gives you a way of slipping backward and forward in time; it provides telepathic access to the minds of others; it lets you reach into those minds and c-h-a-n-g-e them. And so forth. Call this machine whatever you want. Call it Everybody's Fantasy Actualizer. Call it a Time Machine Mark Nine. Call it a God Box. Call it a magic wand, if you like. Okay. I give you a magic wand. And you give me a magic wand too, because reader and writer have to be allies, co-conspirators. You and me, with our magic wands. What will you do with yours? What will I do with mine? Let's go.

The Revenge of the Indians. On the plains ten miles west of Grand Otter Falls, Nebraska, the tribes assemble. By pickup truck, camper, Chevrolet, bicycle, and microbus, they arrive from every corner of the nation, the delegations of angry redskins. Here are the Onondagas, the Oglallas, the Hunkpapas, the Jicarillas, the Punxsatawneys, the Kickapoos, the Gros Ventres, the Nez Perces, the Lenni Lenapes, the Wepawaugs, the Pamunkeys, the Penobscots, and all that crowd. They are clad in the regalia that the white man expects them to wear: feather bonnets, buckskin leggings, painted faces, tomahawks. See the great bonfire burn! See the leaping sweat-shiny braves dance the scalping dance! Listen to their weird barbaric cries! What terror these savages must inspire in the plump suburbanites who watch them on Channel Four!

Now the council meeting begins. The pipe passes. Grunts of approval are heard. The mighty Navaho chieftain, Hosteen Dollars, is the main orator. He speaks for the strongest of the tribes, for the puissant Navahos own hotels, gift shops, oil wells, banks, coal mines, and supermarkets. They hold the lucrative national distributorships for the superb pottery of their Hopi and Pueblo neighbors. Quietly they have accumulated vast wealth and power, which they have surreptitiously devoted to the welfare of their less fortunate kinsmen of other tribes. Now the arsenal is fully stocked: the tanks, the flamethrowers, the automatic rifles, the halftracks, the crop-dusters primed with napalm. Only the Big Bang is missing. But that lack,

Hosteen Dollars declares, has now been remedied through miraculous intervention. "This is our moment!" he cries.

"Hiawatha! Hiawatha!" Solemnly I descend from the skies, drifting in a slow downward spiral, landing lithely on my feet. I am naked but for a fringed breechclout. My coppery skin gleams glossily. Cradled in my arms is a hydrogen bomb, armed and ready. "The Big Bang!" I cry. "Here, brothers! Here!" By nightfall Washington is a heap of radioactive ash. At dawn the acting president capitulates. Hosteen Dollars goes on national television to explain the new system of reservations and the roundup of palefaces commences.

Marin County District Attorney Bruce Bales, who disqualified himself as Angela Davis's prosecutor, said yesterday he was "shocked beyond belief" at her acquittal.

In a bitter reaction, Bales said, "I think the jury fell for the very emotional pitch offered by the defense. She didn't even take the stand to deny her guilt. Despite what has happened, I still maintain she was as responsible as Jonathan Jackson for the death of Judge Haley and the crippling of my assistant, Gary Thomas. Undoubtedly more so, because of her age, experience, and intelligence."

Governor Ronald Reagan, a spokesman at the capitol said, was not available for comment on the verdict.

The day we trashed the Pentagon was simply beautiful, a landmark in the history of the Movement. It took years of planning and a tremendous cooperative effort, but the results were worth the heroic struggle and then some.

This is how we did it:

With the help of our IBM 2020 multiphasic, we plotted a ring of access points around the whole District of Columbia. Three sites were in Maryland—Hyattsville, Suitland, and Wheaton—and two were on the Virginia site, at McLean and Merrifield. At each access point, we dropped a vertical shaft 600 feet deep, using our Hughes fluid-intake rotary reamer coupled with a GM twin-core extractor unit. Every night, we transported the excavation tailings by truck to Kentucky and Tennessee, dumping them as fill in strip-mining scars. When we reached the 600-foot level we began laying down a 36-inch pipeline route straight to the Pentagon from each of our five loci, employing an LTV molecular compactor to convert the soil castings into semi-liquid form. This slurry we pumped into five huge adjacent underground retaining pockets that we carved with our Gardner-Denver hemispherical subsurface backhoe. When the pipelines were laid, we started to pump the stored slurry toward the Pentagon at a constant rate, calculated for us by our little XDS computer and monitored at five-hundred-meter intervals along the route by our Control Data 106a sensor system. The pumps, of course, were heavy-duty Briggs & Stratton 580's.

Over a period of eight months, we succeeded in replacing the subsoil beneath the Pentagon's foundation with an immense pool of slurry, taking care, however, to avoid causing any seismological disturbances that the Pentagon's own equipment might detect. For this part of the operation, we employed Bausch & Lomb spectrophotometers and Perkin-Elmer scanners, rigged in series with a Honeywell 990 vibration-damping integrator. Our timing was perfect. On the evening of July 3, we pierced the critical destruct threshold. The Pentagon was now floating on a lake of mud nearly a kilometer in diameter. A triple bank of Dow autonomic stabilizers maintained the building at its normal elevation; we used Ampex homeostasis equipment to regulate flotation pressures. At noon on the Fourth of July, Katherine and I held a press conference on the steps of the Library of Congress, attended chiefly by representatives of the underground media, although there were a few non-freak reporters there too. I demanded an immediate end to all Amerikan overseas military adventures and gave the president one hour to reply. There was no response from the White House, of course, and at five minutes to one, I activated the sluices by whistling three bars of *The Star-Spangled Banner* into a pay telephone outside FBI headquarters. By doing so, I initiated a slurry-removal process, and by five after one, the Pentagon was sinking. It went down slowly enough so that there was no loss of life: the evacuation was complete within two hours, and the uppermost floor of the building didn't go under the mud until five in the afternoon.

Two lions that killed a youth at the Portland Zoo Saturday night were dead today, victims of a nighttime rifleman.

Roger Dean Adams, 18 years old, of Portland, was the youth who was killed. The zoo was closed Saturday night when he and two companions entered the zoo by climbing a fence.

The companions said that the Adams youth first lowered himself over the side of the grizzly bear pit, clinging by his hands to the edge of the wall, then pulling himself up. He tried it again at the lions' pit after first sitting on the edge.

Kenneth Franklin Bowers of Portland, one of young Adams' companions, said the youth lowered himself over the edge, and as he hung by his fingers, he kicked at the lions. One slapped at him, hit his foot, and the youth fell to the floor of the pit, 16 feet below the rim of the wall. The lions then mauled him, and it appeared that he bled to death after an artery in his neck was slashed.

One of the lions, Caesar, a 16-year-old male, was killed last night by two bullets from a foreign-made rifle. Sis, an 11-year-old female, was shot in the spine. She died this morning.

The police said they had few clues to the shootings.

Jack Marks, the zoo director, said the zoo would prosecute anyone charged with the shootings. "You'd have to be sick to shoot an animal that has done nothing wrong by its own standards," Mr. Marks said. "No right-thinking person would go into the zoo in the middle of the night and shoot an animal in captivity."

Do you want me to tell you who I really am? You may think I am a college student of the second half of the twentieth century, but in fact I am a visitor from the far future, born in a year which by your system of reckoning would be called A.D. 2806. I can try to describe my native era to you, but there is little likelihood you would comprehend what I say. For instance does it mean anything to you when I tell you that I have two womb-mothers, one ovarian and one uterine, and that my spermfather in the somatic line was, strictly speaking, part dolphin and part ocelot? Or that I celebrated my fifth neurongate raising by taking part in an expedition to Proxy Nine, where I learned the eleven soul-diving drills and the seven contrary mantras? The trouble is that from your point of view we have moved beyond the technological into the incomprehensible. You could explain television to a man of the eleventh century in such a way that he would grasp the essential concept, if not the actual operative principles ("We have this box on which we are able to make pictures of faraway places appear, and we do this by taming the same power that makes lightning leap across the sky."), but how can I find even the basic words to help you visualize our simplest toys?

At any rate, it was eye-festival time, and for my project I chose to live in the year 1972. This required a good deal of preparation. Certain physical alterations were necessary—synthesizing body hair, for example—but the really difficult part was creating the cultural camouflage. I had to pick up speech patterns, historical background, a whole sense of *context*. (I also had to create a convincing autobiography. The time-field effect provides travelers like myself with an instant retroactive existence in the past, an established background of schooling and parentage and whatnot stretching over any desired period prior to point of arrival, but only if the appropriate programming is done.) I drew on the services of our leading historians and archaeologists, who supplied me with everything I needed, including an intensive training in late-twentieth-century youth culture. How glib I became! I can talk all your dialects: macrobiotics, ecology, hallucinogens, lib-sub-aleph, rock, astrology, yoga. Are you a *sanpaku* Capricorn? Are you plagued by sexism, bum trips, wobbly karma, malign planetary conjunctions? Ask me for advice. I know this stuff. I'm into everything that's current. I'm with the Revolution all the way.

Do you want to know something else? I think I may not be the only time-traveler who's here right now. I'm starting to form a theory that this entire generation may have come here from the future.

BELFAST, Northern Ireland, May 28 — Six people were killed early today in a big bomb explosion in Short Strand, a Roman Catholic section of Belfast.

Three of the dead, all men, were identified later as members of the Irish Republican Army. Security forces said they believed the bomb blew up accidentally while it was being taken to another part of the city.

One of the dead was identified as a well-known IRA explosives expert who had been high on the British Army's wanted list for some time. The three other victims, two men and a woman, could not be identified immediately.

Seventeen persons, including several children, were injured by the explosion, and 20 houses in the narrow street were so badly damaged that they will have to be demolished.

One day I woke up and could not breathe. All that day and through the days after, in the green parks and in the rooms of friends and even beside the sea, I could not breathe. The air was used up. Each ugly thing that I saw was ugly because of man—man-made or man-touched. And so I left my friends and lived alone.

EUGENE, Ore. (UPI) — A retired chef and his dog were buried together recently as per the master's wish.

Horace Lee Edwards, 71 years old, had lived alone with his dog for 22 years, since it was a pup. He expressed the wish that when he died, the dog be buried with him.

Members of Mr. Edwards' family put the dog to death after Mr. Edwards' illness. It was placed at its master's feet in his coffin.

I accept chaos. I am not sure whether it accepts me.

A memo to the Actualizer.

Dear Machine:

We need more assassins. The system itself is fundamentally violent, and we have tried to transform it through love. That didn't work. We gave them flowers, and they gave us bullets. All right. We've reached such a miserable point that the only way we can fight their violence is with violence of our own. The time has come to rip off the rippers-off. Therefore, old machine, your assignment for today is to turn out a corps of capable assassins, a cadre of convincing-looking artificial human beings who will serve the needs of the Movement. Killer androids, that's what we want.

These are the specs:

Age — between nineteen and twenty-five years old.

Height — from five-feet-five to five-feet-nine.

Weight — on the low side, or else very heavy.

Race — white, more or less.

Religion — Former Christian, now agnostic or atheist. Ex-Fundamentalist will do nicely.

Psychological Profile — intense, weird, a loner, a loser. A bad sexual history: impotence, premature ejaculation, inability to find willing partners. A bad relationship with siblings (if any) and parents. Subject should be a hobbyist (stamp or coin collecting, trapshooting, cross-country running, etc.), but not an intellectual. A touch of paranoia is desirable. Also free-floating ambitions impossible to fulfill.

Political Convictions — any. Preferably highly flexible. Willing to call himself a libertarian anarchist on Tuesday and a dedicated Marxist on Thursday, if he thinks it'll get him somewhere to make the switch. Willing to shoot with equal enthusiasm at presidential candidates, incumbent senators, baseball players, rock stars, traffic cops, or any other components of the mysterious *they* who hog the glory and keep him from attaining his true place in the universe.

Okay. You can supply the trimmings yourself, machine. Any color eyes so long as the eyes are a little bit on the glassy hyperthyroid side. Any color hair, although it will help if the hair is prematurely thinning and if our man blames his lack of success with women in part on that. Any marital history (single, divorced, widowed, married), provided that whatever liaison may have existed was unsatisfactory. The rest is up to you. Get with the job and use your creativity. Start stamping them out in quantity:

Oswald Sirhan Bremer Ray Czolgosz Guiteau
Oswald Sirhan Bremer Ray Czolgosz Guiteau
Oswald Sirhan Bremer Ray Czolgosz Guiteau
Oswald Sirhan Bremer Ray Czolgosz Guiteau
Oswald Sirhan Bremer Ray Czolgosz Guiteau
Oswald Sirhan Bremer Ray Czolgosz Guiteau
Oswald Sirhan Bremer Ray Czolgosz Guiteau
Oswald Sirhan Bremer Ray Czolgosz Guiteau

Give us the men. We'll find uses for them. And when they've done their filthy thing, we'll throw them back into the karmic hopper to be recycled, and God help us all.

Every day, thousands of ships routinely stain the sea with oily wastes. When an oil tanker has discharged its cargo, it must add weight of some other kind to remain stable; this is usually done by filling some of the ship's storage tanks with seawater. Before it can take on a new load of oil, the tanker must flush this watery ballast from its tanks; and as the water is pumped out, it takes with it the oily scum that had remained in the tanks when the last cargo was unloaded. Until 1964, each such flushing of an average forty-thousand-ton tanker sent eighty-three tons of oil into the sea. Improved flushing procedures have cut the usual oil discharge to about three tons. But there are so many tankers afloat—more than four thousand of them —that they nevertheless release several million tons of oil a year in this fashion. The forty-four thousand passenger, cargo, military, and pleasure ships now in service add an equal amount of pollution by flushing oily wastes from their bilges. All told, man may be putting as much as ten million tons of oil a year into the sea, according to one scientific estimate. When the explorer Thor Heyerdahl made a 3200-mile voyage from North Africa to the West Indies in a boat of papyrus reeds in the summer of 1970, he saw "a continuous stretch of at least 1400 miles of open Atlantic polluted by floating lumps of solidified, asphaltlike oil." French oceanographer Jacques-Yves Cousteau estimates that forty percent of the world's sea life has disappeared in the present century. The beaches near Boston Harbor have an average oil accumulation of 21.8 pounds of oil per mile, a figure that climbs to 1750 pounds per mile on one stretch on Cape Cod. The Scientific Center of Monaco reports, "On the Mediterranean seaboard, practically all the beaches are soiled by the petroleum refineries, and the sea bottom, which serves as a food reserve for marine fauna, is rendered barren by the same factors."

It's a coolish spring day and here I am in Washington, D.C. That's the Capitol down there, and there's the White House. I can't see the Washington Monument, because they haven't finished it yet; and of course there isn't any Lincoln Memorial, because Honest Abe is alive and well on Pennsylvania Avenue. Today is Friday, April 14, 1865. And here I am. Far out!

—We hold the power to effect change. Very well, what shall we change? The whole ugly racial thing?

—That's cool. But how do we go about it?

—Well, what about uprooting the entire institution of slavery by going back to the sixteenth century and blocking it at the outset?

—No, too many ramifications: we'd have to alter the dynamics of the entire imperialist-colonial thrust, and that's just too big a job even for a bunch of gods. Omnipotent we may be, but not indefatigable. If we blocked that impulse there, it would only crop up somewhere else along the time-line; no force that powerful can be stifled altogether.

—What we need is a pinpoint way of reversing the racial mess. Let us find a single event that lies at a crucial nexus in the history of black/white relations in the United States and unhappen it. Any suggestions?

—Sure, Thomas. The Lincoln assassination.

—Far out! Run it through the machine, see what the consequences would be.

So we do the simulations and twenty times out of twenty they come out with a recommend that we de-assassinate Lincoln. Groovy. Any baboon with a rifle can do an assassination, but only we can do a de-assassination. *Alors:* Lincoln goes on to complete his second term. The weak, ineffectual Andrew Johnson remains vice-president, and the Radical Republican faction in Congress doesn't succeed in enacting its "humble-the-proud traitors," screw-the-South policies. Under Lincoln's even-handed guidance, the South will be rebuilt sanely and welcomed back into the Union; there won't be any vindictive reconstruction era, and there won't be the equally vindictive Jim Crow reaction against the Carpetbaggers, which led to all the lynchings and restrictive laws; and maybe we can blot out a century of racial bitterness. Maybe.

That's Ford's Theater over there. *Our American Cousin* is playing tonight. Right now, John Wilkes Booth is holed up in some downtown hotel, I suppose, oiling his gun, rehearsing his speech. "Sic semper tyrannis!" is what he'll shout, and he'll blow away poor old Abe.

—One ticket for tonight's performance, please.

Look at the elegant ladies and gentlemen descending from their carriages. They know the president will be at the theater, and they're wearing their finest finery. And yes! That's the White House buggy! Is that imperious-looking lady Mary Todd Lincoln? It has to be. And there's the president, stepping right off the five-dollar bill. Graying beard, stooped shoulders, weary eyes, tired, wrinkled face. Poor old Abe. Am I doing you much of a favor by saving you tonight? Don't you want to lay your burden down? But history needs you, man. All dem li'l black boys and girls, dey need you. The president waves. I wave back. Greetings from the twentieth century, Mr. Lincoln! I'm here to rob you of your martyrdom!

Curtain going up. Abe smiles in his box. I can't follow the play. Words, just words. Time crawls, tick-tock, tick-tock, tick-tock. Ten o'clock at last. The moment's coming close. There, do you see him? There: the wild-eyed man with the big gun. Wow, that gun's the size of a cannon! And he's creeping up on the president. Why doesn't anybody notice? Is the play so goddamned interesting that nobody notices—

"Hey! Hey, you, John Wilkes Booth! Look over here, man! Look at me!"

Everybody turns as I shout. Booth turns too, and I rise and extend my arm and fire, not even needing to aim, just turning the weapon into an extension of my pointing hand as the Zen exercises have shown me how to do. The sound of the shot expands, filling the theater with a terrible reverberating boom, and Booth topples, blood fountaining from his chest. Now, finally, the president's bodyguards break from their freeze and come scrambling forward. I'm sorry, John. Nothing personal. History was in need of some changing, is all. Goodbye, 1865. Goodbye, President Abe. You've got an extension of your lease, thanks to me. The rest is up to you.

Our freedom . . . our liberation . . . can only come through a transformation of social structure and relationships. . . . No one group can be free while another is still held in bonds. We want to build a world where people can choose their futures, where they can love without dependency games, where they do not starve. We want to create a world where men and women can relate to each other and to children as sharing, loving equals. We must eliminate the twin oppressors . . . hierarchical and exploitative capitalism and its myths that keep us so securely in bonds . . . sexism, racism, and other evils created by those who rule to keep the rest of us apart.

—Do you, Alexander, take this man to be your lawful wedded mate?

—I do.

—Do you, George, take this man to be your lawful wedded mate?

—I do.

—Then, George and Alexander, by the power vested in me by the State of New York as ordained minister of the First Congregational Gay Communion of Upper Manhattan, I do hereby pronounce you man and man, wedded before God and in the eyes of mankind, and may you love happily ever after.

It's all done with the aid of a lot of science-fiction gadgetry. I won't apologize for that part of it. Apologies just aren't necessary. If you need gadgetry to get yourself off, you use gadgetry; the superficials simply don't enter into any real consideration of how you get where you want to be from where you're at. The aim is to eradicate the well-known evils of our society, and if we have to get there by means of time machines, thought-amplification headbands, anti-uptightness rays, molecular interpenetrator beams, superheterodyning levitator rods, and all the rest of that gaudy comic-book paraphernalia, so be it. It's the results that count.

Like I mean, take the day I blew the president's mind. You think I could have done that without all this gadgetry? Listen, simply getting into the White House is a trip and a half. You can't get hold of a reliable map of the interior of the White House, the part that the tourists aren't allowed to see; the maps that exist are phonies, and actually they keep rearranging the rooms so that espionage agents and assassins won't be able to find their way around. What is a bedroom one month is an office the next and a switchboard room the month after that. Some rooms can be folded up and removed altogether. It's a whole wild cloak-and-dagger number. So we set up our ultrasonic intercavitation scanner in Lafayette Park and got ourselves a trustworthy holographic representation of the inside of the building. That data enabled me to get my bearings once I was in there. But I also needed to be able to find the president in a hurry. Our method was to slap a beep transponder on him, which we did by catching the White House's head salad chef, zonking him on narcoleptic strobes, and programming him to hide the gimmick inside a tomato. The president ate the tomato at dinnertime and from that moment on we could trace him easily. Also the pattern of interference waves coming from the transponder told us whether anyone was with him.

So okay. I waited until he was alone one night, off in the Mauve Room rummaging through his file of autographed photos of football stars, and I levitated to a point 90 feet directly above that room, used our neutrino-flux desensitizer to knock out the White House security shield, and plummeted down via interpenetrator beam. I landed right in front of him. Give him credit: he didn't start to yell. He backed away and started to go for some kind of alarm button, but I said, "Cool it, Mr. President, you aren't going to get hurt. I just want to talk. Can you spare five minutes for a little rap?" And I beamed him with the conceptutron to relax him and make him receptive. "Okay, Chief?"

"You may speak, son," he replied. "I'm always eager to hear the voice of the public, and I'm particularly concerned with being responsive to the needs and problems of our younger generation. Our gallant young people who—"

"Groovy, Dick. Okay: now dig this. The country's falling apart, right? The ecology is deteriorating, the cities are decaying, the blacks are up in arms, the right-wingers are stocking up on napalm, the kids are getting maimed in one crazy foreign war after another, the prisons are creating criminals instead of rehabilitating them, the Victorian sexual codes are turning millions of potentially beautiful human beings into sickniks, the drug laws don't make any sense, the women are still hung up on the mother-chauffeur-cook-chambermaid trip, the men are still into the booze-guns-broads trip, the population is still growing and filling up the clean open spaces, the economic structure is set up to be self-destructive since capital and labor are in cahoots to screw the consumer, and so on. I'm sure you know the problems, since you're the president and you read a lot of newspapers. Okay. How did we get into this bummer? By accident? No. Through bad karma? I don't really think so. Through inescapable deterministic forces? Uh-uh. We got into it through dumbness, greed, and inertia. We're so greedy we don't even realize that it's ourselves we're robbing. But it can be fixed, Dick, *it can all be fixed!* We just have to wake up! And you're the man who can do it. Don't you want to go down in history as the man who helped this great country get itself together? You and thirty influential Congressmen and five members of the Supreme Court can do it. All you have to do is start reshaping the national consciousness through some executive directives backed up with Congressional action. Get on the tube, man, and tell all your silent majoritarians to shape up. Proclaim the reign of love. No more war, hear? It's over tomorrow. No more economic growth: we just settle for what we have, and we start cleaning up the rivers and lakes and forests. No more babies to be used as status symbols and pacifiers for idle housewives: from now on people will do babies only for the sake of bringing groovy new human beings into the world, two or three to a couple. As of tomorrow we abolish all laws against stuff that people do without hurting other people. And so on. We proclaim a new Bill of Rights granting every individual the right to a full and productive life according to his own style. Will you do that?"

"Well—"

"Let me make one thing perfectly clear," I said. "You're *going* to do it. You're going to decree an end to all the garbage that's been going down in this country. You know how I know you're going to do it? Because I've got this shiny little metal tube in my hand, and it emits vibrations that are real strong stuff, vibrations that are going to get your head together when I press the button. Ready or not, here I go. One, two, three . . . *zap.*"

"Right on, baby," the president said.

The rest is history.

Oh. Oh. Oh. Oh, God. If it could only be that easy. One, two, three, zap. But it doesn't work like that. I don't have any magic wand. What makes you think I did? How was I able to trick you into a suspension of disbelief? You, reader, sitting there on your rear end, what do you think I really am? A miracle man? Some kind of superbeing from Galaxy Ten? I'll tell you what I really am, me, Thomas C———. I'm a bunch of symbols on a piece of paper. I'm just something abstract trapped within a mere fiction. A hero in a story. Helpless, disembodied, unreal. UNREAL! Whereas you out there—you have eyes, lungs, feet, arms, a brain, a mouth, all that good stuff. You can function. You can move. You can act. Work for the Revolution! Strive for change! You're operating in the real world; you can do it if anybody can! Struggle toward— umph—glub—hey, get your filthy hands off me—power to the people! down with the fascist pigs—hey—help— HELP!

YAHRZEIT
by
Barry N. Malzberg

February 1982

Yesterday the tenth anniversary of Babe Leopold's death. Strange to think of him gone that long, Nate under the ground and out of the world but he must have been a frail, shambling little figure in those last years and it is useless to sentimentalize the man that he was; long gone before the death. Quivering little autobiographies he wrote in prison; participant in rehabilitation programs. Subject for malaria experiments, seeking atonement. Atonement! Well, it did not have to be this way.

Fifty-eight years or so, almost sixty past the crime as well. What it must have been like to have been eighteen and rich in Chicago in that old time, plucking a small boy from the schoolyard like a chicken and carrying him off to destiny with a companion and chisel at the wheel of a new rented sedan. Splendid times, great deeds! But of course he would have had to have been caught and repented. Babe was ahead of his time. Pitiful object; put this from the head.

Nevertheless, I felt compelled to do something in memory of the anniversary, Babe having been one of my enthusiasms of years back and one of the basic prophets as well. Selected, therefore, a chisel from the excellent batch of weaponry I kept behind this very desk and went out into the streets. A small boy would have been best but the law is not up to that yet; will not understand for at least a few more years that it is better to catch problems at the source, not outcome. A geriatric then. It is always a geriatric. I am getting so bored with them! But this would be with a chisel and in memory of the Babe; maybe I could make something special out of it. I cornered the one I wanted in a bare glade in the park, having tracked him for fifteen minutes for the isolation. Seventy-five or so with liver patches all over him; a high, quivering aspect to the nostrils in motion, which reminded me vaguely of my father, now unfortunately deceased. Newspapers under the arm, a brown paper bag dangling from his fingers. Ready, ready, ready to die; ten years past his time and needing release. I backed him against a tree, raising the chisel.

"No," he said, when he finally confronted me and understood the situation. I never like to take them from behind; part of the pleasure is in seeing and sharing their knowledge of death. Some shriek, some lean to embrace, others are apathetic, but ultimately with the geriatrics it is always the same: at last an acceptance. This is why I am getting bored with them. "Please," he whimpered, "I don't want to."

"I'm sorry," I said, raising the chisel. I always say that I am sorry; in some basic sense I am. It is dull to kill one geriatric after the next, even if one must take pleasure where one can and even if it is ultimately for the sake of the government. "It's got to be done."

"Please," he said again, "you don't want to do it. Not to me. I never bothered anyone. Listen, I'm a sick man: a heart condition. The doctors told me just last week that I'm going to die soon anyway." His eyes blinked. "If I'm going to die soon, it's just such a waste," he said, and I could see him try to work cunning into the proposal. "There are lots of healthy jerrys around. Get one of them and it would be a service. A year from now, six months I won't even be here, son. Son. You remind me of him, do you know that? I got to write him a letter soon; I owe him one."

"Sorry," I said again, "you know that illness is no excuse." Most of them lie anyway, whether from fear, confusion, or genuine senility I could not care. *For you, Babe,* I whispered, raising the chisel, *and for you too while I'm at it, Dick, you poor, born-too-early, out-of-your-time, sons of bitches.* I got him clean with the first shot in the forehead, cracking his skull open like the windshield of a rental car, then added another one in the guts for the double tribute. *You too, Dick.* The bag fell first and the geriatric on top of it. I hate to call them *jerrys* even though this is their own name for themselves; it deprives them of dignity.

I left him in the glade.

Later, as necessary, I phoned into the local center to report the elimination. "You'll find a chisel next to the body," I added somewhat obscurely, "it's a kind of tribute to someone."

"Surely sir," the blank voice of the secretary said, "and thank you very much for the service."

"Don't think of it."

"If you'll give me your name and coding number now, we'll see that it's properly entered to your credit."

"That's all right," I said, winking at the phone and already putting it down, "I don't want the credit. It isn't necessary. I did it in memory of a friend of mine."

A FEW MINUTES
by
Laurence M. Janifer

You sit down in the largest chair in the room,
There's no reason why the luxury of the place surprises
you, is there? it being your own living-room in your own
house, after all. Carol designed it especially for you and
your visitors, now that there are so many of them; you
ought to be used to being a famous man by now. Rich,
famous, virtually a National Resource . . . pride would be
a very easy trap to fall into, and perhaps that tiny shock of
surprise keeps you out of the trap.

You smile, a little; and Charley knows that smile nearly
as well as you do. "What's wrong?"

So you look across the room at Charley, lounging
against the fireplace-that-actually-works, and you realize,
perhaps for the very first time, that he's a man. Charles
Schumann, thirty years old, six-feet–one-inch tall, married, two children—he's been a man for quite a time, but
you'd never entirely seen that, seeing instead your son. "I
was just thinking—well, nothing much. The Committee's
going to be here in a few minutes."

"I know. And you were wondering whether there would
be a street named after you or a whole damned city."

Close enough; your smile broadens. "Well—it is important. One world. Or something very like it."

"One world," Charley says. Almost an actor's voice. A
solidly athletic body. And saved from the fate of a matinee
idol by an early interest in particle physics—your influence, perhaps, though you've always tried to keep from

directing the boy, and if he'd wanted to be an actor, actually . . .

"Sooner or later, it had to happen. No balance between nations stays stable forever."

"Of course not," Charley says. "Nation A emits a beta particle, becoming Nation A₁, and attracting Nation B, whose eigenstate—"

"Point made," you cut in. "Nothing's stable. Nothing at all, in the long run. But—the stability of nations could have been measured in years, if we'd been lucky, months if we hadn't. Between 1945 and 1993, God alone knows what prevented a major atomic war. A series of miracles, maybe."

"And then," Charley says, "came the big miracle. The Schumann miracle."

Pride? But you wish the words made you more uncomfortable than they do. "It was there. The application was there. If I hadn't found it, someone else—"

"Someone else," Charley says, and stretches. In the new gray cloaking, with that build and with the faintly withdrawn, faintly amused expression that settles on his face at rest, he must be fighting off the girls. A good deal more bother, that way, than his father had ever run into; but Charley and Jacqueline knew how lucky they were. "And by the time someone else did find it, and realized what he had, and translated it into hardware, and spent four months trying to convince the right people that he wasn't one more refugee from the funny farm—"

"All right." Praise at any length, thankfully, really does make you uncomfortable. "All right: but it was mostly luck."

"Oh, now, come on—"

"Luck," you say flatly. "And . . . well, I will say: luck, and knowing what to do with the luck when it came. But the muon decay chain—there wasn't any special reason for me to get interested in that, just then. Or to take the particular direction I did take."

"The hand of God," Charley says without embarrassment: Charley, for some fool reason, really does talk like that. Believes it, too; as if being alive and human weren't enough, so a complicated mythology had to be tacked onto it. "You might call it the hand of God—or, of course, you might call it luck."

"Whatever," you say. "It's the same thing."

"Exactly," Charley says, and grins. Well, you've learned not to argue with him, not on *that* subject.

And you reach for another subject. Not too far away. "You know, Charley, I don't have the faintest idea what to say to them."

The grin carves your son's face. "You've told it often enough. Prizes, honorary degrees . . . you can go through it one more time without any trouble."

"I suppose." But the idea of a permanent historical record, something for the sight-and-sound archive President Taine had finally pushed through the new World Council—why, the idea of the World Council itself was enough to make you blink. This one, this time, had to be right. This was the definitive version: even for Dr. Schumann, the story could only be recorded once. Equipment of archive quality was fantastically expensive—and fantastically in demand. The passion for history . . . "Well, we're making a new world, I suppose that's it."

"Sure," Charley says. "But don't tell them that: they know that."

"I wasn't—"

"Relax, aged parent." Almost, you looked round to see if Carol were laughing, the way she nearly always did at that phrase. But Carol was in Mauritania, doing a job no white person could have done: arranging African pledges for the Council. So that it wouldn't be a featureless, hopeless League of Nations or a nervous, equally useless UN; this time, the Council was going to have the power. Everyone knew that, and knew why, and accepted it; but a good many African states had the pride of novelty to deal with. They hadn't been independent countries so very long, and it took a woman whose ancestors were very visibly African to smooth the passage for them, from independence (and continuing, horrible danger) to the Council (and security for a slightly lessened nationhood, at least). "Just a joke. A small joke, meant to lighten tension, you know."

"Well, what *do* they want, then?"

"Your story, aged parent. Not theirs."

And with no smile at all: "Not all of it."

Charley nods. "I don't think they'd want all of it. That's for—personal archives. So far, anyhow. It'll take time . . ."

Not all of it, no. Not the early years, when—despite government directives, despite the written law—a physicist with a Negro wife was, somehow, a security risk; when you changed jobs to find a new set of neighbors who wouldn't look at you that way; even if Carol insisted it didn't matter, it by-God mattered to you. And besides, you knew how she felt. And then there were the jokes, the conversations cut short when you approached them . . .

Maybe no white man could ever know what it was like being black; but you'd found one way to come close. You'd married Carol, and it hadn't freed her, not at all: it had bound you instead.

But there had been the work, and the work was good. And then there had been Charley, who simply could not be afforded. Charley cost too much money, and that was all there was to it. And who knew, anyhow, what new troubles a child of that marriage might have. . . .

And Carol only nine weeks along. It would be inexpensive, it would even be easy. . . .

The arguments were, doubtless, very good. But somehow, in spite of them, there was Charley; and Charley made home a place to rest in (and no matter all that infant wailing and screaming!) and a place to relax in (and never mind the midnight bottle, the three A.M. bottle, the diaper pail . . .). Charley had kept them going for—my God, for fifteen years! It had taken that long, from the first sight of an oddity in a page of transformations . . .

Until, with the theory half-understood and no more than that, translated into a sort of tangled hardware, into one irreplaceable machine, it had been Charley who had saved the machine and the notes as well. When the fire had started (spontaneous combustion? lightning? no one ever knew), you'd headed for Carol's room; and when you woke up, you were in a hospital bed. Carol had jumped, landed safely in the damned rosebushes, and managed to get you out with the help of a neighbor and some dilatory firemen.

Nobody had been left to rescue the work, but Charley.

And then . . .

"After the fire," you say. "I can start there. Convincing the government—everybody knew a time machine was impossible, and how was a Congressman who couldn't do high-school algebra to get it into his head that we didn't *have* a time machine there."

"We?"

"You dragged it out."

"And you'd have rebuilt it," Charley says. "It'd have taken time, but you'd have rebuilt it."

"Time . . ." You light a cigarette and Charley frowns down at you: *that* fight's been going on for twenty-eight years. "Who knows if we'd have had time?"

"You could find out," Charley says, watching you smoke. But the stuff hasn't killed you yet, and it's your lungs. "Same way you found out I wasn't going to have any sisters, no matter what anybody did."

Another puff. "We'd have—liked that, I think," you say. "We didn't plan on only one child. When we were ready—and maybe, like you, even before we were ready. Since the sample turned out so well, after all."

"Sample?" Charley says. "You know, I'm not sure I like that." The grin blinks on and off in the big dark face. "But—what can't be helped . . ."

"I wonder, sometimes . . . but there was no way. Not even adoption." And your eyes begin to shut; Charley's voice snaps you back to the present.

"So it wasn't a time machine. It was a probability machine. And you finally got Senator Wellman to understand."

"After explaining it to him for five weeks—and being thought a fool all that time. He'd never have put up with me if I—if we—"

"If Carol hadn't swung some voting weight with the black community hereabouts," Charley said. "Might as well be honest about it—though not, I think, for the record."

"Not yet," you say. "In a few years, perhaps . . . five, ten years . . . things are settling down, you know."

"I know," Charley says. "I would."

And they are, they really are. One world . . . and a world with something called the race problem stuck away in the history texts, no part of the present at all . . .

"The machine could show the results of a given choice. But the choice had to be important."

Charley says: "Any choice is important." And that's been a long fight, too. But whatever you think and whatever your son thinks, the hardware works the way it works.

"The big ones," you say. "The nodal points. The ones that change—a nation. A society. A world."

"All right," Charley says, "We won't argue now—even if my having sisters or not was a nodal point. But if it could be made more responsive . . ." He shrugs. "I know. It can't. The uncertainty principle's part of the world, too." And then, slowly: "The only world there is."

"I'll tell them that," you say, "because they still don't understand it. All the stories . . . people liked to imagine that all the probability choices really existed, and that you could move from one to another. . . ."

"Wish fulfillment," Charley says, distantly. "Dream-stuff."

"Which is the one way it *couldn't* work," you say. "Energy levels—"

"And whatever you do," Charley breaks in, "don't give them that. We're still not teaching particle physics in the average high school."

"No. But they ought to understand by now—the machine can show you the result of a given choice. Show you which is the right road to take. It can even dig back into the past, some, and show you what the result of some choice you *didn't* make would have been; but you didn't make it, then. And you can't, now. You get the results of what you actually did choose. The others—don't exist any more."

"Never did."

"Exactly," you say. "Except as possibilities real

enough, maybe, to experience through a machine. But once the choice is past . . . that's all they are. All they ever can be."

"A good thing. Worlds where the atomic war happened . . . where . . ." Charley spreads his hands.

"Dream-stuff, as you said." Over Charley's right shoulder the wall clock goes on humming. "Hey, now—they really will be here. Any second."

"Want your makeup kit?"

"Now look, you—you damned brat—"

"Cool it, agèd parent," Charley said. "I only—"

The warning-chime sounds. "There they are."

"I'll open the door," Charley says. "You just sit there and look famous. After all, it's a big moment in—".

The headset is heavier than it seemed, though you've only been wearing it a few minutes. The machine draws more power than it should, too; an automatic glance at the bread-board dials tells you that. Though you aren't thinking about the dials.

A test run. A decision-point . . . fifteen years ago . . .

So you'd have had more peace, finished the machine a little bit more quickly, pushed it through to actual use by now, instead of a first, solo test . . .

(More power? Then that's where the fire—that's how the fire started! This time, you'll be able to . . .)

Carol is sleeping upstairs, while you sit, fifteen years younger, in the basement at the jerry-built machine, the machine which, in the real world (the only world), Senator Wellman hasn't even heard of yet. And the cause of the fire isn't going to matter, not at all. You're going to find out about that in less than a minute. You haven't been away long; in a way, you came back just in time. When the power gave out. When . . .

Thirty seconds or so, now. And you just might figure out, in those thirty seconds, who's telling you all this. Perhaps it's your own subconscious, trying to warn you, to blame you, to explain to you, one last time. . . .

It can't be me, you know. It can't be me, agèd parent: I'm dream-stuff now. All I ever can be.

I was quite real, once. But getting rid of me was cheap. And you couldn't afford . . .

And you don't believe in the supernatural. In the complicated mythology.

It's your last chance not to believe, agèd parent. I want no more than you to hear the sirens start. But *this is not a test:* the sirens have started.

It's all over. The choice was made.

You're—quite a decent guy, you know. In spite of . . .

Well. Forget all that. But . . .

I love you. If . . .

THE FRESHMAN ANGLE

by
Edgar Pangborn

Elmo obDavid Hunnington was suffering trouble under three heads; like a sensible boy he wrote them down on scratch paper:

> I. Assistant Professor Clance Mahew requires of me a discussion of the 20th century (Primitive Calendar usage) within the historical perspective, in 2000 words.
>> A. Is this the demand of a rational pedagogue?
>>> 1. Should an assistant professor of his ilk be defined as a pedagogue at all and not rather as a dictum-grinding laquey (sp?) of the establishment?

II. Do I really intend to become a historian?
  A. Family would like it but don't insist.
  B. How many bloody times have I changed my mind about this since, say, 5710? (Featherhead!)

III. Having spent forty dolas ($40) on that silk tunic (honest admission of sin), insufficient funds remain to purchase <u>Heretics Edition of Chaucer</u> for Nora's 18th birthday 3 wks off. Slob.
  A. Aid fr Andrei?
    1. No; he's already spent a wad on that pen for her.
  B. Begging:
    1. Rejected because no training in public relations.
  C. Offering fair white body in public streets:
    1. Rejected as unlikely to succeed. Also cf. III, B, 1.
  D. Establishment of Hunnington Foundation for Aid to Indigent Freshmen, spelling <u>eleemosynary</u> correctly:
    1. Unsound because requires more than 3 wks.
  E. Write home?
    1. . . . .
  F. Qu fr <u>Gibbon Decline and Fall of the Roman Empire</u> cribbed fr Snokes's <u>Cultural Panorama,</u> 7th Edition: <u>History . . . is indeed little more than the register of the crimes, follies, and misfortunes of mankind.</u>

Having studied the outline, Elmo searched for his desk scissors, which Nora had borrowed again; with his jackknife, he cut the page between I,A,1 and II. The first section he pasted on a fresh sheet, and he wrote across the top in capitals: NOTES ON THE FIFTIETH (TWENTIETH) CENTURY. He deleted the word *ilk,* inserting an ornate caret and placing over it the word *kidney*. The rest of the outline he scrumpled up and chewed morosely. He was spitting it out into the wastebasket when third-year student Andrei obMeredith Zenas strolled in, lean and grave, flung his architecture books into the armchair, and sat on the tiger-rug by the fireplace in the lotus position. "Curious habit."

"Had a Gibbon quote on it," said Elmo.

"Still odd. Gibbon—Gibbon—"

"Historian, 1734–1794 Primitive Calendar."

"I know, I was just nattering. That how you get all the A's? By chewing assignments? What profit if spit out?"

"Benign sir, never criticize others' possible protein deficiencies," said Elmo, watching his friend, counselor, and roommate lift his thin shape until he was standing on his head, arms folded. "That is very beautiful. How long can?"

"Twenty minutes the most I ever."

The other roommate Nora abMargaret Dane stamped in, her brains freshly rumpled by Post-Diluvian Literature II-B, and tossed Andrei's books out of the armchair and herself into it. A second-year student (sophomore to use an ancient term lately revived), she was already known as a poet of some force. "How long has he?"

"Minute or two. Said twenty the most he ever. In silent mood."

"And you, Elmo? You look like disaster stewed and strained."

"Oppressed in spirit. Look upon this muck!" Elmo flipped her the page with the pasted-on heading.

Nora viewed it soberly, sinking the shafts of her black-rimmed spectacles into her thick black curls. "Was spelled l-a-c-k-e-y in the fiftieth. And I would omit part about Mahew. Tact, man."

"First draft, Buttonbrain. For own guidance and instruction, as any cretin would know. Know anything about the fiftieth, love?"

"Age of the Wasters. Deluge Century. Red Plague."

"Common misconceptions, little sophomore. The Red Plague came in the first decade of the twenty-first, only properly speaking, there never was any twenty-first. Primitive Calendar went out in the Collapse with the rest of the waste paper."

"And for ten wormy old years eight centuries ago, you, a creeping freshman, would make an upper-class scholar a liar, my Elmo?"

"Further, not a deluge, sweetheart, except locally. It was a rise in water level over at least fifty years, beginning late in the fiftieth and continuing through the Collapse when nobody was capable of keeping records. It says here —see Snokes."

"Age of Wasters, anyhow. Start of mue-period. See Snokes."

Elmo's pain broke forth: "And I got to do it in historical perspective in *two goddamn thousand words!*"

"Allow me to analyze your tone of voice. Ah, yes— diagnosis simple." Nora slipped off her chlamys and dropped it on Andrei's notebooks. "Well, must shower. Post-Dil Lit would make anybody stink, even me. Why, dear crawling child, this is merely a thing done to freshmen. They search for the faint gleams of intellect that may appear even in the remote gray wastes of a skull like yours."

"Explains my headaches."

"Poor soul!" she said, and kissed his forehead, and pulled handfuls of his shoulder-length yellow hair, right and left, like ringing a bell. "A kind of initiation. Mahew's a nice joe, by the way. See, they want to know whether you think two thousand words too long or too short. Scholarly ambition versus freshman slobostasy."

"A conspiracy to make me think? Oh, I see the whole plot now."

"Yes, you've been warned." She paused with clawed fingers beside Andrei's quiet, lifted feet. Andrei said: "Don't."

"Wasn't going to," said Nora, and departed for the washroom.

Elmo hollered after her: "Anyhow there wasn't any old Post-Dil Lit until the *Collections* of Jermyn Graz, *obit* 5465."

Nora's reply through spattering water was an angry

howl: "Bloody furnace out again—*cooowwlld-d-d!* Low on firewood, some creep goofed his work-day, no doubt some ill-begotten freshman, birthed by a tinker's drab behind a hedge—hey, pentameter!"

"Meant to warn you," Andrei called, upside down.

"Fine time now! And by the way, there was so, Elmo. Barr Wain, fifty-fourth century if I'm a day old—I mean his stupid *Siege of Shattum*—mucky antique mooings but a poem nevertheless, my hearties, even if half of it was a steal from the very Old-Time *Song of Roland,* which goes back to thirty-ninth century no less, and a fat mystery how Wain ever got hold if it. And there were the *Narratives* of David deMoha—fifty-fourth century sure-enough." Nora came forth full of thorny learning, her admirable body lobster-pink from icy spring-water and toweling. "DeMoha was one of the the Nuin Heretics, if you don't know— those guys that tried to bring back some of the Old-Time knowledge. And he did sail around the world, did he not!"

"Good for him," said Elmo absently. "Look, it says here in Snokes: 'The terminal quarter of the fiftieth century was characterized by an awareness of rapidly approaching man-made disaster accompanied by a paralysis of will and a failure to develop a rational ethics in spite of all the teachings of history and of native intelligence. We can only wonder what might be the status of our culture now if the dazed billions of that century could have learned restraint and reason in time to avoid the Collapse. It was not to be. Decadence into antique magic, spookery, miscellaneous pieties, was only one of many retreats. Human beings shuddered away from the technological and psychological monsters they themselves had created and set free, and stumbled over the cliffs, led by the blind.' "

"Slaps it right to 'em, don't he?" said Andrei.

"And I must deal with *that* in two thousand words. In historical perspective, he do say through his thicket of beard."

"Why, if it's a fact," said Nora, combing her black curls, "you go collate it. That's what I'm always doing with facts."

Andrei's heels thumped. He rolled Nora's chlamys into

a pillow, selected a notebook, and lay there studying like one dead.

"Going to the Freshman Spring Orgy?"

"Suppose," said Elmo. "Maybe I'll ask a boy. The freshman bints are mainly pigs."

"Good precedent," Nora said. "Zeus and Shakespeare were queer. But I have observed three or four freshman quail who are not at all bad, by liberal standards."

Elmo growled around the pencil-end he was gnawing: "Dare say sooner orge with you."

"Why, anytime, steamy stripling. Anytime I say so."

"And I feel inclined, high-toned hoyden."

Andrei muttered: "How serene if you ungainly aboriginal types would scamper off to bed, or stop quarreling, or both."

Elmo lowered his feet from the desk and crouched over Snokes's *Cultural Panorama,* bane of freshmen, bible of historians. Tilted back in his chair, he had seen through the eastern window at his left the green-gold and pink and diminishing blue of early evening sky; now he could watch the mild Hudson Sea, and the small white beach a quarter-mile away, where in a few weeks the heavy south winds of March would bring the girls and boys bathing and romping. And because the evening was sweetly lucid he could see, far and faint, a blue irregularity of the horizon marking the eastern shore of this narrow part of the Hudson Sea—after all, only a great channel across the time-beaten earth between the Atlantic and Lorenta Seas, cutting off the wonderful island of Nuin from the mainland. Nuin is a venerable place to all of us, capital, place of beginnings, cultural and spiritual center of a somewhat thoughtful world.

The Hunnington family managed a trading company jointly with three other continua of Nupal and a small (five-mother) continuum—or commune, since they preferred the old classical term—near Mount Orlook in Ulsta. The families had many other interests, but the trading company kept them modestly prosperous, able to contribute a good surplus to the larger community's expenses.

Elmo's biofather David obSamel Hunnington dealt with
the company's paperwork; Elmo felt closer to one of his
commune-fathers, Alan obJonas Hunnington, whose share
of the trading-house work included that goodly loafing
called traveling, with spurts of lyrical horse-trading when
in port. Four years ago, in 5709, when Elmo obDavid was
thirteen and convalescent from a moderate attack of red-
pox fever, Alan had taken him on the great triangle cruise
aboard the company's fast, three-masted frigate *Amanda:*
from Nuber in Katskil, with white pine from the far north,
and sugar from the south, and canned goods, to Plymouth;
from Plymouth to Table Mountain (known in Old Time
as Cape Town, and crumbled traces of Old-Time ruins
were still there for Elmo's curious gaze) with English wool
and electrical fixtures and other fine manufactures; and return to Nuber with ivory, cameras, mahogany, chocolate.
A year well spent, as Alan obJonas had expected: Elmo
came back shining-healthy, no longer able to sing lead
soprano in the Nupal choir, and carrying a fresh cargo of
memories.

He remembered a rainy wind-dance of palms along the
Cornwall shore on the approach to New Dover. He remembered a rambling conversation with a startlingly old
violin-maker at Table Mountain. Such a conversation
could have taken place at Ceylon, Manila, Valpo, anywhere in the modern world, but it did happen at Table
Mountain, how many thousand miles from home?—
beyond the Tropic of Capricorn anyway. Elmo was as
happy remembering it as he had been while smelling the
roses in the artist's garden and feeling the cool onshore
winds, because the old man had treated him like a contemporary, with unexacting love.

He remembered with other overtones of pleasure the
fortnightly meetings in the open sea between big, racy
Amanda and the Government Copter that brought mail
and occasionally lowered or took up a passenger. *Amanda*'s radio would always have word of the approach hours
in advance. You could wait and watch, speculating with
Alan, who generally had a bet with the skipper about

some aspect of the rendezvous. And Copter would come waddling out of the horizon, far enough off schedule to have teased you for a while, and bumble into largeness, a comic lovely dream. Then she would show a logical structure of whirling blades and streamlined cabin, sliding in fantastically precise above the ship and hovering with that illusion of not moving at all, or only as a dream moves.

And if the sea is what sailors humorously call calm, the ladder dribbles down and is made fast, and there are the mail packages, and maybe a passenger slightly green in the cheeks. There's the ribald exchange of sailors' news and comment and impractical advice while Elmo's ears flap merrily in the verbal breeze.

Something of a polluter, the Copter, for her alcohol engine must be heavily powered to keep her safe in all weathers, and beastly expensive because so many of the materials needed for her building were hoggishly squandered in the long-ago—imagine being lavish with tin, or tungsten, or iron itself! Well, to every century its own evil —there'll be another one along in the next. But since Government allows only a hundred Copters to operate in the entire world service, the expense is bearable and the corruption slight.

Elmo secured a grip on his hair with his left hand. He dipped his ebony-handled steel pen (present from commune-mother Sylvia) in the Chinese jade inkwell (present from Andrei). He admired the architectural study for a theatre pinned to the wall above Andrei's desk: pure lines, no fuss; such a building would grow out of the earth as if the sky were another friend. Nora's desk, off to his right on the other side of the window, was fantastically neat as usual—amazing for a poet, until you remembered that she wrote most of her poetry with a stub pencil, in bed, in a beat-out notebook she was always losing. Evening light, a reflection of beginning sunset, was giving the big room unearthly color, flooding the cream-white walls with hints of yellow and rose; and the air was all a sweet stillness. The clock on the far wall of the study by the bedroom archway read a few minutes before six—almost time for the vesper bell to ring in the tower of University Hall. An hour after that the alto chimes downstairs will go *tang-tong-tang* for supper, and we shag ass down there for roast pork and mashed potatoes and punkin pie. Meanwhile, this should be a little time for working, and thinking. But other historians before Elmo have noted that the fiftieth century can affect one like a clawed hand poking out of a grave.

The small fire had burned low. Andrei put away his notebook and rolled over twice along the tigerskin to reach the woodbox without bothering to stand. He arranged fresh sticks; the new fire lived in motion, in the hearth and along the rises and hollows of Andrei's flesh as he lay contemplating oceans, shores, continents of his own thought. His upper lip was full, wanting the taste of living, his chin firm, his eyes unfathomably dark. Nora was lounging naked in the armchair watching the evening, the towel at her shoulders in casual lines of grace, and she was quiet as the light.

In a patch of bushes between Jermyn Hall and the beach, a white-throat sparrow sang his five celestial notes —again—and a third time. He burst from the leaves and darted across the evening; as if answering his signal, the vesper bell sounded from the tower. Presently the beacon on Grange Hill would shine, indicating that anyone of the University who needed stronger light than lamp or candle might properly use the power from waterfall and windmills until midnight. Nora smiled, liking this time of day. Andrei, unpredictable, sent Elmo an open, unguarded look of affection, brooding and bemused, all barriers down. Elmo's spine shivered: it was suddenly known to him how much he loved these two, and how rare a thing is the recognition of a present happiness.

One year more than half gone, of the five that the University of Sortees considered desirable for the degree of Bachelor of Arts. Four to go, only three for Nora, two for Andrei. He supposed he would stay here for the doctorate, if he held to his plan of becoming a historian. *(What is history, that you should catch it in a net of words?)* Four years is a wealth of time; Elmo was precociously aware that treasures of time are soon spent. The vesper bell rang on and on within him till Nora's voice dismissed it, speaking out of her own revery:

"A thought, Elmo: so far as time-lapse is concerned, the fiftieth century is to the present as the forty-second was to the fiftieth."

"Mm, yes. So what did the best minds of the fiftieth—were there any?—think about the century of the Crusades? Thanks, passion-flower. Crusades—Frederick Barbarossa banging away at the Popes, trying to swallow Italy, urping up undigested chunks of it, uhha . . . Well, both were centuries of imbecile warfare, but weren't alone in that. Forty-fourth was another such, with the Black Death an ulcerated hole in the middle of it. And then at the end of the forty-second, what they called the twelfth century after Christ, no Collapse. In fact, things looked up a bit, didn't they, for a couple of centuries?"

"Big bonny cathedrals," said Andrei, "some of which went whomp. Monastic orders. Albigensian Crusade."

"Something to be said for monastic orders maybe."

"You be monk, I be superior."

"Up yours too, venerable third-year monster."

"Historical parallels," Nora suggested, "are rickety suspension bridges over a torrent of truth."

"Figures of speech," said Elmo, "are rainbow bridges to a region where Assistant Professor Mahew would prefer I didn't walk."

Andrei said: "And love is more than bird-wing in the sun."

"O Andrei!—may I steal that?"

"What will you give me for it, nubile madam?"

"How he does run on in pentameter! I must think . . ."

She was saying something more, but Elmo lost it. His pen had long gone dry in waiting. He dipped it again in the jade well that was Andrei's gift, in the oak-gall ink that was dark as Andrei's eyes, and wrote with exploratory slowness:

> The fiftieth century began with a minor disturbance known as the First World War (4914–4918); only about nine million dead.

Essentially a European political uproar, this conflict marked the first major development of the internal combustion engine as a weapon of destruction—airplanes, tanks, etc.—although the possibilities were imperfectly realized. Another field opened for investigation was chemical warfare, mainly with phosgene and mustard gas. Defoliants were not thought of until the civilization was much further advanced in decay.

He interrupted his work, and Nora's soft conversation with drowsing Andrei, to ask: "Is this Monday, anybody know?"

Andrei said: "I think we had some sort of day off yesterday."

"Did we? Jasus!" said Nora. "I've been thinking this was Tuesday, all day long."

"So maybe it is. If so, I am doubtless screwed, because this fornicating paper has to be in Mahew's obscene clutches by Thursday."

Andrei asked: "Nora, are your hippies still hanging on the same hook as the bedroom calendar?"

"You may assume it, for purposes of polemic."

"Then the matter is simple: you go and lift them off, then I go and look at the calendar, then I come back, then I tell you what I have seen."

"Would you really be that large, that sweet, O my Andrei?"

"Why, certainly." Andrei cuddled his left arm under his cheek, returning to repose.

Nora said: "I'm afraid, poor soul, it really is Tuesday."

"Never mind," said Elmo bitterly. "I can bear it." He wrote, with many revisions, another sentence:

> The third decade of the century was occupied with flappers and things were some messed up in China.

Tang—tong—tang! . . .

In the charge down to the dining room, they linked arms with the trio from the room next down the hall and arrived at the foot of the stairs in two orderly sections, three abreast, Elmo with Dina Samid and Andrei, then Nora and Marget Helversan with Aron Sten in the middle. This might have seemed hazardous for fat Aron, but actually his poise was the most exact, and his feet in white moccasins twinkled him downstairs with the precision of wheels under a cart. The company then formed a flying wedge and secured one of the tables in the glassed-in porch, partly by virtue of superior force, partly because of Andrei's and Aron's dignity as third-year students. Unlike Andrei, Aron was inclined to battle for his rights if he could do it sitting down. No fourth- or fifth-year students were involved; these rarefied beings occupied a sacrosanct table on the porch with the best view of the Nupal hills and were traditionally immune to hornswoggling or ballock-busting except by each other. When Aron obEdard Sten reached fourth year, he would doubtless accept splendor as his due and wear the red beret proper to majors and seniors. Andrei would forget the beret half the time and kiss a freshman as soon as snap his fingers. At present, Aron was uneasy in the third-year position between millstones and spoke mildly, inquiring why Elmo looked like a wilted parsnip.

Elmo stated the problem as covered in the heads of his outline, I through I,A,1. "Why," said Aron, "a simple matter of Snoke-feathers. Pluck them, child, at will. Bread's wondrous, Lucy—you make it?"

Lucy Helversan waiting on table was Marget's older commune-sister, now doing her labor fortnight. Elmo was reminded that his next full fortnight would be coming up soon—woodcutting, greenhouse, chicken farm, whatever —but not till after the Spring Orgy. He enjoyed the labor fortnights—beat studying, sometimes. Lucy nodded, pleased, and swung her bottom out of the way of Aron's pinch.

"But look," said Elmo, "suppose—something not Snoke-feathers—"

"Poor soul's fevered," said Aron, and touched Elmo's

forehead with little kind fingers. "As I feared. Frontal
lobes near point of combustion. Sad. Been nice knowing
him, though. Friendly, handsome."

Elmo said: "Oh, shit."

"What you felt there," said Nora, "is backlash of a re-
finer's fire. They have him under observation. They—I
refer to our faculty, than whom—have begun to suspect
him, even as we do, of possessing a brain. Now if even the
Than-Whomers sense it, I think we ought to face it."

"But surely," said Andrei, "not *charge* him with it, not
openly, not like this. A brain-user should be allowed to
keep his habit secret and to proceed to the doctorate un-
tainted by suspicion."

"But," said round-eyed Dina Samid, "everybody's got
brains, haven't they? What for do you pick on Elmo?"

Nora met Elmo's gaze across the ensuing silence and
helplessly admitted: "I love her too. Maternally, sort of.
Glands."

"I know," said Aron. "I feel it. Different glands, of
course. I ponder, I study her, I try to understand, but my
conclusion is that for those who love her as we do, Dina
can be taken only on faith."

"And what for," said Margaret abEllan Helversan, her
dark brows knitting, "do you pick on Dina? She does more
than the rest of you to hold off the dullness of our times."

Freshman Dina blushed, looking at her friend in adora-
tion and bland bewilderment.

"My point exactly," Aron burbled, but Marget scowled
at him and Nora shushed him, remarking: "Hold off, Ancient—the darlings are at it again. I live for moments
when Andrei gets cross."

"The times are not dull," said Andrei. "That's a projec-
tion of teener discontent."

"Teener I may be," said sophomore Marget "and what
are you, Andrei?—nineteen? But I think I know when I'm
bored."

"Ah, you run up against the elemental troubles that always plague intelligent beings—growing old some time,
occasional sickness, death a certainty, frustration of desire
outrunning performance, or merely of not getting some-

thing you want—all that oppresses you. Then you mistake frustration for boredom—real boredom is a sickness and quite a different thing, Marget—and you blame the times for something that's inherent in the human condition."

"You have to admit the times are smug," said Marget. "We're not going anywhere, not aiming at anything. You can't suggest any kind of reform or change—people just look at you and go *beh beh* like a pack of constipated goats."

Elmo began: "I think—"

"Herd, darling," said Aron, "not pack. As for reform, or change, or originality of any kind, that's always been the toughest proposition on earth. Even in bad times people hate the thought of changing anything, or reforming their ways."

"And in good—" said Elmo.

"Or of entertaining any kind of original idea. In the famous revolutions of Old Time, the only method of change they could think of was to blast everything flat and cobble up something on the ruins with the same flaws."

Elmo shouted: "Look out, everybody! I'm going to say something. I think the present age is a good one, and I think so because I've been reading history."

"That's my boy," said Andrei.

"Everything just lovely, huh?" said Marget.

"I didn't say that. But as for not going anywhere, not aiming at anything—look: we move in the time-stream because we must, but should we always be struggling to break off to some new place, some new or supposedly new way of doing things, when the present place might be the best one we can find? Under the given conditions? You want a return to atomic energy? After the radiation deaths of the Collapse and with all the devastated areas that won't be fit for habitation for another thousand years, if then? Marget, you do sound like a fiftieth century progress-hound. All right, now you can sit back and call me a reactionary. *Beh beh!*"

Marget said: "I do. If we don't go forward, we stagnate."

"Said the three-plus billion of the fiftieth, word for

word, while manufacturing more herbicides. It was a cliché even then, and it ended in the Collapse. They even noticed that if you rush forward in a hell of a hurry, it helps to look where you're going. They just assumed, because so many bright-speaking, well-meaning spirits told them so, that everything was good if it was labeled progress."

"Well," said Dina Samid, "I do think lots of things nowadays are very nice. I mean, like sex for instance."

"Sweetheart," said Nora, "they did have sex in the fiftieth."

"In fact," said Aron, "as I remember my own ordeals in freshman and sophomore history under dear Dr. Mahew, that man of substance, indeed fatter than I am, there was an oft-repeated claim that sex was invented at some time during the fiftieth century. The claim has not been well established."

"But," said Dina, "they must have had it before then, mustn't they, because I mean if they didn't—well, how—"

Andrei spoke with controlled passion: "Aron, you can't have it all to yourself: I love her too. Jasus, how I love her!"

"Why, Andrei!" said Dina. "You mean me? You never said."

"Finish your punkin pie," said Marget, "and ignore him."

"*Beh beh!*" said Elmo, but Marget didn't smile, much. "By the way, fellow creatures, I've thought of a way we can all make money."

"He's mad," said Aron.

"A brain trust. Look, I'm always having magnificent ideas, each one easily worth a dola. So we form a company, let's keep it down to just the six of us, and offer the general public a reliable supply of brilliant thoughts at one dola apiece. Millions in it, don't you see?"

"Why, I think that's wonderful," said Dina. "You mean people would pay you money for thinking?"

"Precisely. We could even appeal to suckers outside the academic community. See how the money would roll in?"

"How much do you actually need?" Aron asked.

"Ten bucks."

"Man's hopelessly mad," said Aron. "But Jesus said unto them, 'A prophet—' "

" '—is not without honor—' " said Marget.

Andrei said: " '—save in his own country—' "

" '—and in his own house,' " said Nora. "Matthew 13 : 57. And you have to be at choir practice in an hour, mad Elmo. Want to go over with Marget and me?"

"Must excuse." To his own ears, Elmo sounded mean and sulky. "I go to compose malignant backscuttling therophiliac term paper, Dr. Clance obFrancis Mahew presiding."

"Oh, balls, tenor section's barely audible as it is," Nora complained. "Last week I listened for the heaven-moment in that Dowland madrigal, and the tenors were damn-all out to lunch. Without your head-tones, my Elmo, the whole section will squizzle off 'like snow upon the desert's dusty face,' Fitzgerald, *Rubaiyat,* forty-ninth century, I crap you not: this is a compliment; I love you."

"Dearly beloved contralto," Elmo snarled, "you go sing my part for me. The suet-heads will never know the difference."

Nora said: *"God,* I wish you boys would quit blasting away at me in pentameter!"

Back at his desk, comfortably naked in the balmy air, Elmo began work by crossing out his last sentence, saddened by a conviction that Dr. Mahew would never consider flappers all that important; maybe he'd sneak them in last under Cultural Development. The first paragraph might do, if copied off in a fair hand. This he did, by the soft illumination of his student lamp. It was burning well tonight, with a nicely trimmed wick, the refined vegetable oil pleasantly pungent like incense. At his desk against the opposite wall, his back to the window, Andrei was using the electric light for cool and deliberate work on one of his architectural drawings. At home in that luminous world among the high-wrought absolutes of design, Andrei obMeredith Zenas never sweated or fidgeted. No scattering of energy: it all funneled into a concentration keen as the tip of his pencil. Yet he was not apart from the present world. The bright lamp beyond his head set forth his profile in gold-edged silhouette, magic to the eyes but sentient and human. He must have been aware of Elmo's gaze, for while his hands still moved precisely with pencil and protractor, he was asking: "Term paper making headway?"

"Something more than Snoke-feathers. Fair to mimbling. I got to watching your hands."

"I love you too." Andrei completed the line.

"More than bird-wing," said Elmo, and happier, he returned by slow stages to the fiftieth century, first transforming the dots over all his *i*'s into sassy little square boxes. Then he wrote:

In the third and fourth decades of the fiftieth
century breathing spells occurred in the world
war, which appears to have been seldom recognized as one continuous event. The breathing
spells, usually called "peace," were interrupted
by extensive butcheries, especially in regions
called China and Spain and Abyssinia, some of
these described as civil wars. (This term referred
at that time to organized warfare confined within
the boundaries of special territories known as
"nations," a concept that poses difficulty to the
modern mind, although we need go back little
more than a hundred years to find clear examples
of the same phenomenon.) In the nation known
to the fiftieth century as Germany, assassination
was put on a basis of mass production. For this
operation during the Rise of Hitler (term drawn
perhaps from analogy of the rise of a bubble of
marsh gas), the term "genocide" was coined some
decades after the event, when public opinion became quite concerned about it. These upheavals
(4919–4938) resemble the "hesitation cuts"
found in suicides who die by the knife: impelled
to self-destruction, but at first unable to make the
decisive slash.

Mahew wouldn't like that. Similes, flights of rhetoric— acceptable if Snokes or a like authority got there first, but hardly from a freshman. Elmo's thought strayed, as he had known it would the moment his pen had touched that wound. Wound?—oh, fair enough word for what happens when a mind too young for defenses is cut by such a sharp truth as the fact that a human being can want to die and make it happen.

It had occurred in a neighboring continuum when Elmo was seven. The children were supposed to be told merely that Anna abLaura Stuart had died, but somehow the rest of the truth trickled down. Elmo got it from one of his older commune-sisters; the ground shivered and the day went blank. His commune-mother Sylvia had been first to sense his shock and trouble, to learn the cause and to aid him. "Anna bore a mue, Elmo. Yes, many women do and it's always a grief, but see, Anna was a person who had wanted and wanted to bear a child. Then, that. Women sometimes do want it, well, too much for reason. I felt that way myself, Elmo, but then I was lucky, I had your com-brothers Leo and Jon, and then I had the sterilization the way most of us do after two, and didn't mind. Anna was— not that lucky, dear. She wasn't interested enough in other things, I suppose she just stopped caring about staying alive. It doesn't happen nowadays except once in many thousand lives, Elmo. It wouldn't happen as it did to Anna more than once in a million, I suppose, because the way we've learned how to live now: every woman in the family can be a mother to every kid, and so if she can't bear her own it's not too bad. But it did happen to Anna. Think of what she did as the result of a sickness. It's a sickness that love can usually prevent. But first love has to understand, and I guess no one understood Anna quite well enough."

It helped. The full story, hesitation cuts and all, be- longed to later years. Sylvia always helped, as much by mood and manner as by her careful words; yet the shadow overtook Elmo now and then for some while afterward, in spite of her, darkening him at unforeseeable times, the shadow of the truth that sometimes a human being can want to die. Or, perhaps worse, just not want to live. Involuntarily he sighed. Andrei inquired: "Trouble?"

"Wrote a simile. Got to delete. Sighed in sympathy for the pain Mahew would feel at spectacle of freshman writing a—no I didn't either, I just—" he looked out the window, feeling Andrei's regard.

Andrei said only: "Road to Parnassus is paved with the polished skulls of pretty similes that rightly died in infancy."

"Ai-yi, poor little fellas!"

"Misplaced sympathy. Virtuous ones survive—in Nora's poems for instance. By the way, why not leave the little bastard in, just for thrills? Mahew might go splat, but he wouldn't downgrade your paper for it, not unless he's changed since last year when I was a jagged sophomore thorn in his meat."

"Why, Zenas, thou hast spoken, and the child shall live."

"Back to work, Hunnington."

The war was resumed officially in 4939, and after some piddling about, was brought to full concert pitch within a year, involving most of the nations of the earth and culminating in the destruction of Hiroshima and Nagasaki, cities of the already defeated nation of Japan, by the first and quite successful use of atomic bombs. The success, in fact, seems to have proved embarrassing, for atomic weapons were not used again except for "testing" (i.e., trials to see how many of them could be jacked off without rendering the planet entirely uninhabitable) until near the close of the century. Minor (non-atomic) phases of the century's war were faithfully pursued, however, in Korea and other localities, especially in the once theoretically independent nation of Vietnam. This territory was set apart by the United States and a few lesser powers as a proving ground for military hardware and defoliants, although survivors among the inhabitants are said to have

protested this procedure as a less than friendly
act: and eventually public opinion, having still a
few obsolescent means of expression, brought
about the withdrawal of armed forces, and even
chemical experts, from the ruined waste, greatly
to the annoyance of the governing military minds,
for it was believed that some excellent bomb-
targets yet remained.

The war then advanced with minor rumblings
and distractions into the last decade of the century and concluded with what has been variously
called the Atomic War, the Accidental Incident,
and the Twenty-Minute War. Since few docu-
ments and no historical analyses survive, specu-
lation must here be called upon to bridge what
history presents to us as a sullen void.

"Hoy, Andrei, come looka how my fat prose goes gib-
boning along! Elephant in a parade."

"You've seen elephants, Far-wanderer?"

"Uhha, at Table Mountain. Circus. Like walking barns.
You keep imagining they have a sense of humor."

"Hope to see those faraway places one day." Andrei
came to lean over and cross his arms under Elmo's chin,
and to read.

"There are short cruises, Mentor," said Elmo. "Vana—
Trindad—even Valpo through the Straits of Panama. I'd
admire to see the Shade Gardens of Valpo. They say people on holiday can loaf around naked all day long in the
half-sun—make love—chess, music, swimming in the
pools. But it would be good anywhere with you."

"Ai?—let's think about such a cruise."

"We could take off in July and be back in September.
Vana anyhow, maybe not the Valpo trip."

"The two of us only?"

"I'd like that best, Eudaimon."

"Agreed. . . . Really stuck for ten bucks?"

"Oh—hell's buttons—spent most of my allowance on
that tunic. A stupid vanity, and now I'm short of what I
need to get that Chaucer for Nora's birthday."

"Tunic looks good on you, but yes, it wasn't smart."

"Hate to write home for it. Could tell 'em to take it out of next quarter's. Feel kid-stupid."

"Do that, though. Or get Nora something cheaper she'd like just as much. I'd enjoy lending it to you, but a Mentor ought not, except for real emergencies. There's a discussion of that in the *Book of Greek Love*. I agree with the authors of that symposium."

"Time I read that, isn't it?"

"No, not quite. Read a little more in the Ancients first —the *Phaedrus,* say—the *Sonnets* of Shakespeare—one or two writers of the so-called Liberation at the close of your sad old fiftieth century. They really were getting slightly liberated just before things went on the skids, one of the big historic ironies. Then you can get into my copy of the *Book of Greek Love,* maybe on that cruise, and add your marginal notes to mine. . . ."

"Andrei?"

"Present, friend."

"Maybe I love you too much? Happiness—that's a sofa-pillow noise, a nothing word. I haven't a word for what I wish I could say. Only six months I've known you, and now I can't imagine trying to get along without you."

"I won't leave you. All the same, it's for me to show you how you could get along, and enjoy living too, if anything ever took me away. The Greeks understood that, though not quite as well as the writers of the modern book."

"I know—I suppose I know. Is it too soon to start thinking about founding a new continuum?—with Nora I hope, if she still likes us that much when the time comes, and maybe some other girl? After you have the doctorate? I wouldn't care where. I like to think of you designing a house for it."

"It's not too soon. I have it always in the back of my mind. Do you like the plan of the ten-year interval between additions of new members?"

"Ten—we start in the twenties, that makes a five-mother continuum by the time we're in the sixties. Yes, that's all right, Andrei. My family's a nine-mother—five year intervals. Too large, really. When I was small, I used to feel there were too many people around, though I didn't mind it as soon as I was big enough to enjoy working on our farm. We had a herd of those little cattle. White-Polls, that originated somewhere in Main—nice little things, only about half again the size of goats. A five-mother— ten to thirteen adults, plus the old, yes, that's plenty. With about a hundred hectares, I don't care where. I heard Government is about to open more islands in the Lorenta for new families. Might be good."

"We'll think in those terms. Ah, the prose—yes, you do gibbon along. It's not bad."

"Mahew will snort."

"You mean that literary flight with the suicide parallel? I question that, too, Elmo—because suicide is after all an act of will, however morbid, and I don't think the people of the fiftieth century had a true will to die. They painted themselves into a corner and stood there whimpering. I believe they just blundered, made a thousand blunders, but without the—the foolish dignity of an act of self-destruction. . . . Something was bothering you a few minutes ago."

"I knew of someone who killed herself, way back when I was seven. Not in our continuum, but people we knew. Sometimes it rises up at me even now, I don't understand why. Casts a long shadow."

"Tell me of it some time soon."

"I will, Eudaimon."

"And so back to work, Hunnington." Andrei kissed the top of his head and returned to his own desk. His face was hidden for a while, in one of his times of stillness. Then his pencil was moving once again, and Elmo's pen took up its labors:

> Whether the exchange of a dozen or so fission and fusion bombs between the Eastern and Western Hemispheres was the result of an accident or in response to rumors of aggressive action of some sort may never be known. In the historical perspective, it is clear that the mere possession

of these ghastly toys, in a deadly balance of tension between the two halves of an idiotically divided world, was enough to render it certain that sooner or later the things would be discharged. The fiftieth century appears to have felt no more respect for the laws of probabilities than a monkey with a box of matches.

The toys were indeed exploded. Moscow and Washington ceased to exist. The bomb intended for a direct hit on New York was a miss, devastating the central portion of what was known as Long Island, now mostly under water. In the incredible city were many survivors, and enough of its physical structure remained, awaiting the mercies of decay and inundation and the long labor of the tides, so that today the Black Rocks offer some interest to visitors from distant regions.

About a dozen other major cities are known to have been annihilated, including Leningrad, Detroit, Paris, Liverpool, and Peiping. It is estimated, though this can only be a searching guess (Snokes, Cultural Panorama, Ch. VII, §4), that from approximately four billion, the world's population was cut to about nine hundred million within a few weeks after the Twenty-Minute War (4996), more than two-thirds of the deaths being due to radiation sickness, violence, and starvation. A high proportion of these survivors were of course crippled or sterile or soon to die from other causes. Thus the originators of atomic weaponry, if any of them survived, might well have claimed that the experience was an outstanding success.

They may even be held somewhat responsible (Ingmon, Artifacts and Records of the 51st Century at Old St. Louis, Nupal Press, 5682, pp. 21–26) for many of the deaths attributed to the Red Plague fifteen or twenty years later. The garbled and superstition-ridden accounts of this calamity often suggest either a delayed action of radiation sickness or the effect of some viral or bacterial agency working on organisms too weakened to resist. The description of bright red petechiae, bone decay, mental disintegration, and rotting flesh are suggestive.

There were, it is true, other population-reducing factors at work. According to Willan's History of Agriculture, Ch. III, by about 4990 so much of the agricultural land of the globe had been so impoverished and corrupted by the ludicrous processes of poison-farming that all harvests were sharply diminishing and their quality worsening at a rate that alarmed even the experts. Probably the urban swarms would have expired in mass famines if the Twenty-Minute War had not done its work. And a further toll was taken, day after day and year after year, by respiratory diseases caused by the widening smog (known chokingly to fiftieth century wits—there were some!—as "Detroit mist"), which did not clear away until the fifty-second century. This abomination could have been prevented at any time during the middle of the fiftieth century by the development of rationally designed power sources in place of the internal combustion engine; but the latter was more readily exploitable, and the oil and automobile industries had swollen into monsters, which, like the Moloch of Carthage, must have their pleasures and be fed. Some lingering smog may have been noticed as late as the fifty-fourth century, for

Elmo stepped over to the bookcase beside Nora's desk, plucked a volume, and stood on one leg, reading, raising and lowering himself on the flexing arch of his foot, a mannerism adopted from Andrei, who said it was good for the ills of man or beast or freshman.

                    might not the curious line in Barr Wain's *Siege of Shattum,* "The healing luster of

a healing sky," refer to something more than dis-
persal of smoke from the air after the burning of
Shattum?

However, with all reasonable allowance for
such ancillary factors of destruction

"Andrei."

"Um?"

"I got in *ancillary,* Mahew's own darling *ancillary.*"

"Bless you, my child."

it would seem that the grand advance-
ment of atomic science in the fiftieth century—
in the abstract, one of the mightiest achievements of
human intelligence—was also the principal reason
why the world's population about a hundred
years later had sunk to approximately one hundred
million (Snokes, loc. cit., p. 321 seq.), a
weight of humanity which has not been greatly
exceeded since, and which is perhaps not too
severe for the slowly recovering planet to bear.

"Andrei, Eudaimon."

"Um-hum."

"I got in *loc. cit.* and *seq.*"

"Dear golden warrior."

Thus what might have been
achieved by reason and restraint was brought
about instead by blundering, folly, and the idiot
misuse of great discoveries, at the cost of
unmeasurable suffering, the depletion of irreplaceable resources, and a most needless lapse into
some seven hundred years of barbarism.

Nora wandered in singing her contralto part in a Dowland madrigal:

Tosse not my soule, I love twixt hope and fear—

Elmo came in where he belonged, only just in time:

> *—twixt hope and feare,*
> *Shew me some ground where I may firmly stand,*
> *Or surely fall—*

"O my Elmo, dear little yellow-haired gosling, the tenors stank! As I knew they would, especially in your lamented absence. Elmo, they *phthstank!* Even Jo Lamoy had a cold in the head, but came in hooting and useless from some grim sense of duty, poor darling. And by the way, Dr. Luma has changed his mind again about the other Dowland thing—*What If I Never Speede*—it's in the heaven-moment, or so I call it, the come-come-come part. First, he's having Marget take the little soprano notes solo —wow, she can do it! Second change, he wants her to dominate that passage the *first* time round, the rest of us an echo; then on the repeat reverse it, and she's the echo. What a beautiful old man it is! He confided to us he's finished another string quartet, the seventh in forty years. You missed a happy rehearsal, except for the moments when the tenors clonked, and Dr. Luna has grown as hardened to that as anyone ever can. And so you'll remember, my small baa-lamb, and not foghorn forth until the repeat?"

"If I seize her, Andrei, will you paddle?"

"I must give it thought. Ever notice how the women we love best are often the same ones who start shedding clothes the moment they enter a room?"

"It's the mark of a sunny, hopeful nature," said Elmo. "She never remembers where she dropped them, but she always thinks she will."

> *But if she will pitie my desire,*
> *and my love requite,*
> *Then ever shall shee live my deare delight.*
> *Come, come, come,*
> *while I have a heart to desire thee.*

"Can you catch her, Andrei? Too fast for me, and besides, I'm sitting down."

"I must give it thought."

> *Come, come, come,*
>   *for I will either love or admire thee*

She kissed both in passing and was gone in music to the bedroom. After a while Elmo lifted his drowsy head. "Andrei."

"Ahoy."

"Got 1308 words already, god damn, leaving room for 692 on cultural development and stuff."

"So culture takes a screwing, not for the first time. Toil on."

> In music and the visual arts, the fiftieth century was a time of sharp decline, filled with a sense of despair, a feeling—appropriate perhaps in an age when science was worshiped by the non-scientific instead of viewed in proportion—that all the traditional resources of art and music had been exhausted, and that therefore (odd reasoning) nothing remained to do but jettison the past and seek new thrills or perish. It seems to have occurred to very few that the subject matter of art is infinite. This reneging, this despair, itself no more than a confession of artistic sterility, was complicated by a haunting delusion that the concept of progress must somehow be applied to the arts, where it has always been irrelevant.
>
> Important music was written in the early part of the century. Mahler and Sibelius are enjoyed and venerated today with the masters of the preceding age. But from the later decades only the work of Britten and two or three others possessed the quality that won survival. The rest was panic art, or twittering.
>
> Understandably, almost no paintings remain from the period; indeed it seems that many

fiftieth century painters were (mercifully) in-
different to the survival of their materials. But
from printed reproductions that have been pre-
served, some opinion may be formed. It was
mainly an art of mental exhaustion, bankruptcy
of invention, and triviality of insight, of experi-
ment degenerated into experimentalism; and one
reads (Ingmon, loc. cit.) how rapidly fashions
shifted in the visual arts, how quickly each cult
that believed itself to be avant-garde ossified into
one more establishment. Still, it was not all pop
and Picasso-worship: serious work continued,
and even won occasional recognition before 4990
when the dark came down on everything. A few
marbles survive for us, done with awareness of
the ages. One also reads of fiftieth century iron-
ware sculpture being broken down (with due
precautions against witchcraft) to make spear-
and arrow-heads for fifty-second century hunters
and nomads. Perhaps no age has ever wholly
given itself over to trash and dull thinking.

Elmo moaned. "Three hundred forty-five words to go,
which must include literature and something to confuse
old Mahew into believing I have, ho-ho, historical perspective—but, balls of Zeus, Andrei, I will have, some
time. This paper's making me *want* to be a historian—I'd
thought I was losing that. I really want it—Jasus, what a
long road!"

"Long and twisty and I'm convinced you'll make it.
Well, you might point out that the decline and death of the
novel, lovingly announced about 2437 times in fiftieth
century criticism, has not yet taken place."

"Hoy, thanks. I can wriggle that in."

"And Elmo: goodly, portly, learned Dr. Mahew is not
about to count words. Also, if he did, he would be no-way
displeased by a word count of two thousand and one."

"I know. I'm a nitpicker, a goof, a slob."

Andrei came over to him. "None of those things, friend.
You're tired. Why not finish tomorrow?"

"Tomorrow, Math and Comp and Hist-Sci—besides, I want to get this monster out of the way. I'm booming. A fireball, a genius."

"Wouldn't surprise me. I'm going to bed—Nora's lonesome. Don't work too late, or we'll have to pry you up in the morning."

"No, I won't. Be with you soon. . . . Eudaimon—"

"Communicate, bright spirit."

"Leave me space on your side of the bed."

"Without fail, Companion."

The case of literature seemed a little more hopeful in the decades before the last war and collapse. Amid despair, weariness of spirit, military domination, political corruption carried to the point of nausea, disenchantment with a dream of progress, which had become little better than a pushing and shoving for fraudulent material comforts, and disillusion with revolutions, which did nothing but turn misery the other side up, a search for sustaining cultural and moral values still was pursued in many idioms, such as no previous age had ever felt compelled to carry on. Individuals of other ages had questioned and wondered and explored, struggled against outrageous odds to improve the human condition. But the search of the fiftieth century seems to have tried to reach down into the very heartlands of the human spirit.

Sometimes it appeared that the supposed lesser functions of literature, such as entertainment and appeals to the aesthetic life, were to be smothered by these heavy labors, but it never quite happened. The handful of writers whose work has survived knew, as Homer and Shakespeare knew, that human beings learn best when the learning is also entertainment for its own sake. This should explain why the death of the novel, so often celebrated with crocodile gulps by critics of the fiftieth century, has not yet occurred.

For some warm moments Elmo was distracted and pleased by the music of Nora chuckling at some words of Andrei's too soft to be distinguished. Then she was moaning in desire, and crying out, and after long sighing quiet, content. Elmo drowsed and daydreamed, rolling the ebony pen in his fingers to catch the light in beauty.

What is historical perspective? Looking across eight hundred years, may we wonder what the people of the fiftieth century thought when they gazed backward the same distance in time to the harsh century of the Crusades?—for they knew their history, those people of the fiftieth; they never had the excuse of not knowing the warning signals of history. They must have congratulated themselves, staring at that time—leprosy, the Inquisition, plague, serfdom, poverty, the most atrocious physical cruelties taken as a matter of course, a part of the day's entertainments. And the congratulation was justifiable: they had come a long way, in certain respects, from the stink of medieval cities, the heretic-burnings, the Siege of Jerusalem. Vicious cruelties they still practiced, in war and peace, but conscience often stirred. They no longer wallowed and rejoiced in savagery. Rather they tried to look away, or sweep the dirt under the rug; and when this could not be done, they attempted fumbling remedies. A small, poor step, but maybe not too contemptible a step for humanity, considering the shortness of eight hundred years.

If they had not foresight in spite of all their prophets, we need not blame them for not being superhuman.

And the boy was appalled by the length of the road, the grandeur of the task. *Nearly six thousand years of recorded history, and I am to explore it deeply enough to say something of value before the end of my life? Oh—*
Momentarily (knowing the upsurge of strength would

soon arrive), Elmo was unbearably tired and rested his eyes on the palms of his hands. The finely fitted oak floors of Jermyn Hall don't creak. He was not aware of Andrei's coming until he felt his friend's hand on his shoulder and heard a sliding of paper.

"Two thousand and seventy-seven words, give or take a dozen. No particular bloody good, Andrei, though he'll give me a blossoming A."

"Hush! I'm reading it. . . . It's bad, Elmo, only by contrast with what you'll be writing fifteen-twenty years from now. For what it is, I salute you. Good man, this Hunnington."

"*Satis est*. By the way, I'm writing home for ten bucks, with confession. She must have that Chaucer."

"Again salute, and how about a run down to the beach? Moon's up."

"Ahoy, ahoy! Nora coming?"

"No, sleeping like a babe in silk. This is for us. I'll give you a three-yard handicap."

"You'll do nothing of the kind. Starting here!" He was down the stairs and out on the open grass and running for the delight of it through moonlight in pure and tranquil air, running for youth and because no road was too long. He soon heard the moving stir of sea on sand where the tide was riding in, and his feet entered the sweet shock of the breakers when Andrei caught him in his arms.

"For a while I was afraid the fiftieth century had you."

"Oh no, Andrei! They couldn't spoil it. Not this earth. Good little earth."

"Good little star."

THE RESCUED GIRLS OF REFUGEE

by
Anne McCaffrey

The girls of Refugee are timid and obedient. The one leads to the other, and the other leads to the one. The old ones set them on this path in infancy and take good care to keep them there. This they have done ever since the Refugee World began.

The girl Bannay had been a slow time coming to the cave of the wisest Wise Woman, and once she was there, she knelt silent for many minutes.

Finally she said, "I am troubled."

"You, too, my child? In what way?"

"By a dream."

"Another dream?"

Bannay raised her clear eyes for an instant. "I have not been *troubled* by a dream before. But—" she dropped her gaze again "—Yes, dear and Wise Woman, by a dream. It came the night of the great thunders. A dream as clear as sunlight and I cannot shake it from my mind. Dreams *are* supposed to fade at dawn, aren't they?"

"Of course. Now, tell me of your dream. Leave nothing from the telling."

"You are so stern, dear Woman. Are you angry with me?"

"Child, child, the dream."

"It was very—vivid."

"Then easier remembered and quicker told."

Bannay still hesitated.

"If you are troubled by this dream, and I see you are, I

can give you neither solace nor counsel until I know its particulars."

"There are parts that might offend you. . . ."

"The dream, child!" The Wise Woman pulled her robe tighter around her.

Bannay began suddenly to speak: "It was full sun, the air fresh and warm and clear as if a drenching storm had cleansed the world of all impurities, rinsing field and foliage of all dust. I felt the flesh stretched thin upon my bones, and my bones were so light within me that I thought I could step on clouds and never fall. I walked along a path down a narrow valley, like those high upon the Great Plateau. But there were buildings on the steep slopes, obscured by bushes, the rooftops visible. And I knew they were real, though I have never seen a real building except in pictures. I had never been in that valley, either, yet it was uncommonly familiar to me. A sense of pleasurable excitement quickened my breath and I felt a tinge of chilly, dread expectancy. The two emotions, reluctance and delight, were sharply interwoven, like vine to tree; yet I do not know which supported the other. I was acutely aware of the phenomenon. I've never felt so . . . elated . . . before, even when I attained Womanhood and was given my name. . . . Suddenly the tall grasses on one side of the road parted and a person stepped forward, smiling."

Bannay covered her face with her hands and peeped through her fingers. "Wise Woman, it was—a—man!"

"*A man!*" the Wise Woman growled. "How could you identify a man?"

"The dream. The dream told me it was a man."

"Continue, if you please!"

"You *are* angry with me!"

"Continue!"

Bannay plaited her fingers in her skirt. "I was startled, and naturally I thought to run. But, confronted by a *man,* I was stunned. Before I could move, he fired a dart at me. I opened my mouth thinking to call for help, to warn the others, but my throat was filled with a coolness that stilled any sound. My limbs were frozen. Not cold, just immovable. I stared at him for an endless time; I was forced to look at his face. It was as if the details of his countenance were intended to be impressed indelibly on my mind."

The Wise Woman's face was almost invisible inside her hood. She said nothing.

"Believe me, Wise Woman, I am not trying to be offensive, but you don't often see dream faces so clearly."

"Continue!"

"He was taller than I; not shorter, as men are supposed to be. He was very tanned and his upper body bared so that I could see that he did indeed take care of himself—not shaggy and dirty, as we are told. He was well muscled and strong-looking and clean. His hair, high on his forehead, was white. His features, very bold; his eyes were blue and deeply set."

"Blue? Hah! Men have brown eyes and black hair, so it is written."

"I know that. And that is why his blue eyes were so noticeable," Bannay returned stubbornly. "His nose was aquiline, his lips full and wide, his chin strong and his jaw much bigger than mine. A forceful, intelligent face, but not menacing. And there was no threat in his manner. His attitude was thoughtful as he gazed at me. And then he smiled again, as if he wished me not to fear him. I saw him so clearly! Then I saw him not at all. When I became aware again it seemed as if only a moment had passed, but I was no longer in the valley; I was in a white room. And it was very abrupt. One moment, blackness! The next, I was in the white room."

Bannay stared into the dimness of the cave, remembering. "It seemed to be a very high-ceilinged room, or I was very small, for the top was very far away from me. I was aware that there was nothing harmful in this room, but something I must study and understand. That I was in this room to learn—and that was the sole reason for my being there. I was lifted up by gentle hands and then passed to other hands, as gentle but different. Firmer, stronger. I learned not to resist such hands but to cling to them for support and strength, for I was small. Then I was in another room, a pink room; for each of the many rooms I visited in that dream were painted different colors; as subtly different as the size, shape, and content of each room. Here I played with other children, some of whom were like me and some of whom were curiously unlike me. We played with toys, although I don't remember much about the toys themselves, only that I had entertaining hours playing with them. And then one of the unlike children began to struggle with me for the possession of that toy. I resisted and the other insisted. I don't know who won. Suddenly I was in the next chamber. It was green. And I knew myself to be older. In that room was one other person, an unlike person. We read together, although what we read I do not remember. The words were constructed differently. But the total experience was pleasant. The following experience was not pleasant, and I do not know what happened to me there. The room was red. A very deep red. An insistent red as if this uncongenial room was necessary before I could go on to something that would be better." Bannay fell silent for a moment, but took up the thread again before the Wise Woman could urge her on.

"The room whose color is most vivid in my mind is the most obscure as to its contents. The room was painted in a wondrous clear greeny-yellow or a yellowy-green, sparkling and fresh, lucid and . . . brilliant. Like the down of newly unfurling leaves as full sun approaches. This room was the most mysterious and enthralling. Whatever I learned there I longed for."

"What, then?"

"Wise Woman, I do not know! I would like to remember. But I cannot. Reluctantly I passed from it and on to visit other places, absorbing new tenets obediently, for all resistance to my lessons had dispersed. I fear, though, I must have been inattentive, for what the lessons taught is vague now. Vague; or perhaps not yet necessary for me to remember. Yes, that's the explanation. When the time comes, I'll remember."

The hooded figure made a sound that might have been a snort.

"The dream says when the time comes, I will remember," Bannay repeated mildly. "Then, instead of another room, I entered a long hallway, dark but not foreboding. I perceived I had finished my series of instructions. That I was ready to proceed. I knew I was to enter *this* door. I was to sit at the table with the old lady knitting and she would give me my final instruction. I opened the door and stood for a moment, stunned. The long narrow room was so full of people, all sitting at tables, all talking and eating. Among them were many full-grown men. There by the door was the table with the old lady. I discovered what *knitting* meant as I watched her working with needles and a bright thread. Yes, that was knitting! I hastily closed the door and slid into a chair beside her so that the males would not notice me. She looked up at me, her face lined and delicately blue-white. Now, Wise Woman, *her* eyes were brown!" Bannay paused triumphantly. The Wise Woman, however, said nothing.

"They were full of life and good humor. She seemed no one to fear, but someone to trust explicitly. She was, except for the brown eyes and a sense of being involved with life, much like Wise Women. Only older. She smiled and patted my hand, telling me what a good girl I had been and how well I had learned my lessons. Now I must take the next step. It would be the hardest one for me, but I must try. For if I could, I would have unknown riches and rewards of which I had been till now ignorant . . . that I had had to be reeducated to desire.

"Sitting in this room, she said, at one of the tables, was someone whose face I had been taught to recognize. One face only. I was to indicate to her which person I had been . . . yes, the word was *conditioned* . . . to recognize. From this recognition, she said, all else would follow.

"I was overcome with the terror of failure. And within me surged the overpowering longing to succeed. But how would I pick out one person . . . a special one . . . in all that crowd? What if I hadn't learned an essential lesson well enough? What was the penalty for failure?

"She smiled at me encouragingly.

"Timidly I raised my eyes to scan the room. It took all my courage to do so. It seemed to me that everyone would stop talking and turn to stare at me for my temerity. I glanced sweepingly at the lefthand corner of that long crowded room.

"One face immediately swam into focus. But—it was a *man's* face! Horrified, I looked quickly away, casting my eyes up and down the room. Faces there were, all kinds, all colors, all compositions. Yet no girl or woman struck me as requiring my attention. And no face stood out with such clarity to my eyes as that first one: a man with green eyes and wavy, red-brown hair.

"Confused and atremble, I turned anxiously to my mentor. She patted my hand, smiling her approval, and said, 'I can see that you have recognized someone. Look back at him.' It was all I could do to turn my head, but her gentle insistence encouraged me past my cowardice.

"I looked and he caught my glance this time. He smiled with a glad expression lightening his pensive face. To my terror he rose. He was like—and yet unlike anyone. Yet I knew his calm face, the plane of his cheek, the angle of his jaw, the curve of his gentle mouth, which I had never seen before. I looked away. He was instantly beside me and I knew that I must rise. He said no word to me, but his presence, now that he was close to me, was strangely reassuring. He bowed with great respect to the old lady and, with a firm hand on my elbow, indicated the way out.

"We left by a different door and emerged into a corridor. I remember he was talking, his voice a deeply pleasing rumble. He was taller than I; I remember thinking that, if I leaned back against him, my head would come to his chin. Of all his words, for he was quietly explaining something to me, I recall clearly only his name—Verden! —and his saying that I had been conditioned to recognize him and him alone. I had had to be taught to accept him. The fact that I had immediately identified him out of so many proved that I had been properly reoriented. It was important to him that I understand what had been done to me.

"We suddenly entered a room, a huge one, which had been partitioned into many other, smaller ones. Male people were busily dismantling the smaller sections. To my surprise, I recognized the partitions of the first room in which I had found myself . . . the curiously high, white room. Though he watched my reactions carefully, nervously, I could only smile. So an illusion had created the semblance of distance or height.

"The pink room came apart in the hands of the workmen as my escort reminded me of the lesson learned therein. I was still untroubled. That they had invaded my mind, regressed me to infancy, and impressed me like a chick—that was high-handed, true. But nothing less forceful would have served to overcome the unrelenting conditioning I had received since birth, he said. 'Fight fire with fire. We fought hypnopaedia with hypnopaedia.' Do you know what that means, Wise Woman? I don't, but it seemed so *right* when he said it."

Bannay chuckled, remembering the strange word. The Wise Woman's face could not be seen, and she said nothing. One clawed hand motioned for Bannay to continue.

"On the threshold of the yellow-green room, we paused. In the dream, I did not need his words to tell me what instructions I had received there. The knowledge was inherent in his presence, charged with the electricity of his nearness. Gratefully and with tremulous delight, I leaned against his strong length, to be upheld, as my knees refused to support me. His arms—so gentle, so fierce—were around my waist, his cheek against my forehead, his lips on mine. And I knew . . . *I knew* . . . what the dream had to teach me, and that now I must wake, and wait.

"But, dear and Wise Woman, I did not *wish* to wake! I *wanted* what the dream promised me from that room."

"It was a nightmare!"

"It was a dream, Wise Woman, but it did not seem a bad dream. Only a dream . . . how could it be otherwise? There are no men. There are no men among us here!" Her voice broke, and she looked at the Wise Woman, deeply troubled.

"Yes. Praise be, we are all daughters of women here!"

"That is all the consolation you have for me?"

"It is a stupid dream, Bannay, a completely unrealistic dream."

"Then . . . then it is permitted to dream it again?"

"What do you mean, child?"

"I want to dream it again. It was so real. So clear. So thrilling to a part of me that is always hungry."

"Enough! It was . . . the unsettled night . . . yes, that's the explanation. The thunder and storm caused the dreaming for all of you, child."

"The same dream for all of us?"

"Not all—a few," the Wise Woman said reluctantly.

"Why was it only a dream?"

"I have told you. We do not allow—we have never allowed—men on Refugee. We are safe here! There are no rooms, no brown-eyed women, no green-eyed men! I never heard of such a thing! What is that noise?"

"Wise Woman, what is wrong? Your face is so white. Here, let me help you to your couch."

"Run, girl, warn the others. Don't stand there, paralyzed. Run to the safety of the caves. Let the invaders know that their dream-conditioning failed. Hide yourself!"

"Why?" The girl was torn between the conditioning of a lifetime and the triggered knowledge flooding her conscious mind. "Verden!" cried Bannay, just as the Wise Woman answered her.

"WHY? *There are men in that ship up there!"*

"Thank you, Wise Woman, for the strength to disobey. Men . . . Verden . . ." said Bannay. She smiled like a woman and went to the mouth of the cave.

Left alone, the Wise Woman pulled her hood completely over her head and whimpered like a child.

Liberated girls came boldly streaming out of the caves, leaving those who had failed to dream—the fearful and the aged—behind them.

Bannay led them over the hill.

MATTHEW

by
Pamela Sargent

I was so busy that I almost forgot about it being close to Matthew's birthday. I was running around like a madman getting ready for the Enomoto birth, and then I realized it was April and I hadn't even gotten the kid a present and I was stuck with having to fight it out with Laura again.

I've got to admit Laura didn't get too upset about my visiting the little guy once a month since I would usually be gone only a couple of days; but every time his birthday came up, she'd raise hell because she knew it meant at least a week, and this time it was going to be even worse for two reasons.

One was, of course, the Enomoto birth.

The other was that I would be gone during Laura's fertile period, and she was going to kick up a storm over that. Laura is impressive when she's mad. She doesn't start by screaming; she just sort of stands and glares down at me, and then she starts talking very slowly and very precisely until I get to wishing I was in my hovercraft out over the Atlantic, and then she starts throwing anything lethal at me that she can get her hands on.

I could hear it all already.

She would start out by telling me how important it was that I be ready to broadcast the Enomoto birth. I knew how important it was, besides which the Enomotos were our very best friends and would be hurt if I didn't make it sound like the delivery of the century. And I would have to admit she was right. Hideo and Inger Enomoto were the only other couple living in Miami Beach, and we had been friends ever since Laura and I had gotten married and the Enomotos had come here from San Francisco. Hideo's about five-two with squinty little eyes and a big grin, and you wouldn't want him opposite you in a wrestling match. Inger's a huge blond girl who has the disconcerting habit of walking into walls, doors, and table edges, leaving a trail of broken glasses behind her.

Matthew's birthday was coming up, and Inger was seven months along, and God help me if she had a premature birth, because Laura would never let me forget it if I was lighting birthday candles instead of broadcasting the blessed event. She and Hideo weren't taking any chances. They were keeping old Inger in a wheelchair for the duration to make sure she didn't walk off the side of a ten-story building.

The other thing was that Laura was convinced I would not be able to resist Athena for a week-long period of time. "That bitch has got a kid already," she would say, "and you give her another one, I will wrap something around your cheating neck," at which point Laura would display a knife, stocking, a broken bottle, whichever seemed most appropriate.

I can't blame Laura. She's the most temperamental, fiery, jealous woman in the world, and she knows I love her for it. It keeps life interesting. We would have our dainty little spat, and after we'd clawed each other to pieces, we'd just fall into that oversized bed and have a hell of a good time apologizing. She'd leave me once a month and come back once a month, and I thought then that if I could only give her a kid, everything would be perfect, just fine . . . no.

Anyway, it was close to Matthew's birthday, and I was getting ready for the Enomoto birth and waiting for Laura to start trouble. I went home from the Americana, having decided we could broadcast the birth from outside among all those garish plants if the weather were nice, or from the lobby if it weren't, and I had also decided that we and the Enomotos could move there for the whole affair and put up any sightseers that might come by for the birth. I went home and Laura was on her ham radio, practicing her Chinese with Mei-ling. Our vidphone connections with Canton had been pretty poor. I tiptoed in, hoping she wouldn't notice me right away, and went over to the bar to dial myself a scotch and soda. I needed the fortification. I was dialing the third one when she signed off.

"It's getting close to Matthew's birthday," I blurted out. She ignored that. "You know, your Chinese is getting rusty," she said. "You ought to practice it more."

I couldn't figure out what the hell that remark had to do with anything. We had already agreed that I would do a bilingual broadcast in English and Russian, and Laura would handle the Chinese. But I didn't want to aggravate her, so I just said "Yeah" and dialed her a daiquiri.

"Mei-ling wants to practice her English next time, but you might think about at least sitting in when we're doing Chinese again. You're going to be illiterate if you keep this up."

"Illiterate is not the term, and you might be interested to know that Athena is teaching Matthew Greek," I replied. My remark didn't have much to do with anything either, but at least it got the subject back to Matthew.

"It figures," Laura said. "Nobody even speaks it any more. Wow."

I sat back and took a deep breath. "It's going to be Matthew's birthday, and I have to get a present and go north," I said swiftly. Then I curled into a sort of semifetal defense position and waited for the onslaught.

"That's what I *mean,* only an idiot would live way up there," Laura shouted, making one of those typically female inferential leaps from nowhere to somewhere in one large bound. "Hell, half the computer complexes are out of order there. I heard you can only dial for food, and then you have to *cook* it. It isn't even healthy because of the climate, you can get *pneumonia.*"

"Athena likes to rough it," I said. "Besides, she says it's good for Matthew. Builds resistance."

"Maine is no place to raise a kid," said Laura. "It's irresponsible. Hell, you can't even call the little bastard on the vidphone. I never even talked to your son, ever, not even on the radio. Do you think that's fair? He doesn't even come here to visit. How do you think I feel?"

I was getting edgy. This was a new line with Laura, and I didn't know how to handle it. "Look, Laura, she's his mother. I'm lucky she's nice enough to let me visit him."

"Nice enough!" Laura screamed. "She's a real sweetheart, isn't she!" Laura stood in front of me, trembling all over, and I forced myself to look into those freakish yellow eyes she has, which look so weird next to her dark skin.

"Laura, honey," I said, grasping her hands, "I didn't marry her because I wanted to marry you, I wish you'd try to remember that. But Matthew's my only kid. Try to understand."

And then Laura had to pull a surprise stunt on me. She fell right into my lap and began to weep. I was astounded. She fell into my arms and started to cry just when I was expecting at least a skull fracture. I was wondering why the hell she couldn't feed me the right lines. I was struck dumb. Mute and stupid.

"Damn it, David," Laura sobbed, "do you think I don't want to have a kid for you? I've been trying six years, and now you have to go up there when I'm ovulating." I had to admit that there was some justice in what Laura was saying.

I'd better start over. I keep evading the whole point of all this because I can't stand thinking about it, and I remember it too goddamn well, and I'm going to have to get it out. It was getting on toward Matthew's birthday, and he was going to be six years old, and I was running my ass off trying to get ready for the Enomoto birth. Matthew was a funny little kid, and I didn't know what to get him, so I wandered around the old deserted stores in Miami Beach and finally decided to get him one of those games that teaches you symbolic logic and an old textbook on multidimensional calculus that I was pretty sure Athena hadn't gotten him yet. On the way home, I began to wonder if that might seem a little stingy, so I scrounged around on the beach and picked up some interesting sea shells for his collection. Laura had rustled up a couple of ancient classics, *The House at Pooh Corner,* as I recall, and *Charlotte's Web,* because she really didn't understand what kind of kid Matthew was.

I got away from Laura with a minimal amount of nonsense and told her I'd try to cut the visit short in view of the Enomotos. I set my hovercraft for New York and took off, the computer complex wasn't working too well to the north of Boston, so I figured I'd guide it manually from there.

I began thinking about Athena when I got close to New York, partly because that was where I had met her. I had come to the city when I was about eighteen because I was interested in communications, and that's where one of the biggest old televising complexes is. I figured it might be more interesting than just sitting around the way a lot of people do, and I thought if I learned how to use the equipment, I could do an occasional broadcast when I was in the mood. Besides, it's more constructive than flying around to parties or talking to friends on the vidphone all day. I was working with an old guy named Raymond De Jong who did a couple of game shows, and when I met Athena, I had been there a year and had already done a couple of telecasts of births and deliveries.

De Jong sent me to Athena because he thought a decent communications man should have a good background, instead of just being a technician. "When you're making a commentary on some event," he had said, "it helps if you can throw in a little historical or philosophical bullshit, just to make it interesting." Athena was about thirty then and an expert in ancient Greek civilization. Her father had been incredibly proud of being Greek and had taught her the ancient language when she was a kid. Her mother was known all over the world, having had three healthy children. Athena was living in New York with her sister Aphrodite, who was eighteen and acne-scarred, with the worst buck teeth I have ever seen. Old Aphrodite made a play for me a few days after I met them and gave me a nasty cut with those lethal teeth of hers.

Athena, on the other hand, was a tall wench with red-gold hair and the greatest looking legs you can imagine. She televised lectures on the ancient world to any who were interested, and she lived the part. She was always walking around in those Grecian-style robes she made for herself, and she spent most of her free time prowling around the old 42nd Street Library and the Columbia ruins, poring over old texts. She had never gotten married, which was thought to be a bit subversive because with her heredity, the odds were good that she could have at least a couple of kids, maybe even three or four.

I might as well admit it. I sat through a hell of a lot of history sessions with Athena with no other motive than to hustle her into the sack. I even put up with Aphrodite just because she was her sister.

Athena's a hell of a woman. She was rational, steady, affectionate, and a hell of a good friend to have, but by the time I was screwing her regularly, I had already met Laura, who looks like an African princess and could send my blood pounding in my temples with just one look from those weird yellow eyes.

And then Athena told me she was pregnant. She already knew I wanted to marry Laura and in that reasonable way of hers told me I'd better announce the marriage right away before she announced the pregnancy. She knew damn well that if I wasn't already married when she did, half the world was going to be breathing down my neck to marry Athena, and the public pressure just might be too much for me. As it was, there were enough people who thought I should broadcast a divorce. Athena also knew, from what I had told her, that Laura wasn't the kind of woman who would settle for less than a public commitment. So Laura and I said our vows to each other with De Jong and Athena as witness, and then I sent Laura back to my old place in Miami while I was waiting for my kid to be born.

As I said, Athena's a hell of a person. I broadcast the delivery myself, announced my own son's birth, and there he was, Matthew Contemanopoulos Feinberg, eight pounds, seven ounces, yelling his head off at the whole damn earth.

He was born without hands.

That bothered Athena. She was a little sadder and quieter after that, and as soon as she was well enough, she packed up her things and moved up to Maine and stopped broadcasting her lectures. I kept visiting them of course. We made Matthew's birthday the big event of the year, and we both worried about him together because he was such a strange little guy.

About a month after the delivery, her brother Plato paid me a friendly little visit and bounced me off the walls. I really can't blame him. Athena deserves more than what she's got, especially now.

I keep wandering off, but I'll try to get back to the point. It was Matthew's birthday, and I was going to Maine with his presents. Athena lived in a big house not far from the ocean shore, and it was fairly primitive going. No vidphone, a small color TV instead of a Tri-D wall, a small vidtape complex, a kitchen you could only dial groceries from, and then you had to cook them yourself. Even that wasn't too reliable. You could dial for ground beef and wind up with two pounds of coffee.

Athena met me at the front door, and she looked even thinner and sadder than I remembered. I thought I'd give her my present right away to cheer her up. It was an old vidtape I'd managed to splice together of a speech by a pre-Plague politician named Spiragnew, who I didn't know a thing about except that he was Greek, so I thought she'd get a charge out of it. We went inside, and she dialed me a scotch and soda from her bar, and then we sat down and stared at each other for a while.

She didn't need to tell me she was worried about Matthew.

"Uh, well," I said finally.

"David, I don't know what to do," she said. "He's been really quiet lately, and depressed, and he doesn't even talk to me very much anymore. He used to be so interested in his math, and he was getting along marvelously with his Greek, and now he doesn't even bother with it. He's so moody, David."

"Look, it's probably just a stage," I said. I didn't want to say what I really thought. I wasn't a very good father, and a boy needs that. Visiting him wasn't much of a substitute and I knew it.

"That isn't all," Athena said. She got up and dialed a martini for herself and sat down again. "He's been dialing the computer information bank. For statistics. And records of births. And statistics on population and every other thing that has to do with all of it."

I began to feel a little apprehensive at that. "Well, you know Matthew," I said jovially, trying to grin. "He's probably plotting one of those graphs of his."

"He hasn't," Athena said. "And I heard him last night on the radio, practicing his Russian with that friend of his in Leningrad, you know, Yuri. And they were discussing the whole thing."

"Look, Athena," I said, trying to be casual, "I don't know that he's doing anything really strange. Everybody's interested in births. Hell, births are the most popular thing we broadcast."

Athena sighed. "That's not what he's doing. He found out. That we're all going to be extinct. The whole race. He and Yuri were saying it. That we're dying out."

I didn't say anything for a while. That's the kind of thing you don't think about much, and to say it out loud like that, I just couldn't believe it.

"Look, that's ridiculous," I said at last. "If Matthew's going to get morbid about this, it's not going to do anybody any good. I'll talk to him, but I don't want you worrying."

"I'll try," she said. She got up and went into the kitchen to prepare for Matthew's birthday party.

Matthew had been wandering along the coast, and he came in about an hour later and shook hands with me solemnly, using his prosthetic, and then went up to his room. He was still there when Athena called him to supper.

We always made a big deal about the party. Athena had cooked Matthew his favorite, this Greek veal dish with peppers, and she had dialed a bottle of champagne, which we let Matthew have a small glass of, and then she brought in the homemade cake with six candles that Matthew dutifully blew out.

I tried to keep the conversation light. I talked about my preparations for the Enomoto delivery and described just how we were going to bounce the Tri-D signal off one of the old satellites, and how there was a group of visitors coming in from California for the event. Matthew didn't say much, and he didn't eat much, and when the meal was over and he had his presents, he went off and began to read one of Laura's books. Athena looked at me sadly and began to take dishes off the table. I helped her put them into the dispose-all and then went back into the living room.

Matthew was reading *Charlotte's Web*. He looked up as I came into the room.

"How's the book?" I asked, not expecting much of a reply. Matthew looked up at me with the gray eyes he had inherited from Athena. That isn't really accurate. He had inherited the color from Athena, but Athena's eyes, even when she was tired, always looked inquisitive, or sad, or happy. Matthew's eyes always looked dead, expressionless.

"It's not bad," he replied. "The author doesn't try to make nature more palatable to the child, and he doesn't talk down to him. An adult might gain something from reading it." Then he put the book down.

"I suppose," he went on, in his tired voice, "that Athena told you she's upset about my behavior."

"Yeah," I said, "but I told her not to worry. I think I ought to hear your side before I start getting jumpy too."

"There really isn't anything for me to say," he continued. "I've been investigating a problem. Some of the conclusions I reached are upsetting. I've been discussing it with Yuri."

I was, at this point, beginning to get a bad case of the creeps, and frankly I wasn't sure why. Matthew had always been funny, and he sounded about the same as he always had.

I should be a little clearer about this. It became obvious to Athena and myself pretty early in Matthew's life that he was very bright. He was reading avidly when he was two and was exploring higher mathematics at an age when I had found algebra a pain in the ass. By the time he was five, he was taking his friend Yuri on in games of chess over the radio and beating him regularly, although Yuri was nineteen and supposedly the top chessmaster in the world.

Athena would worry about him, but I didn't, at least not so much. I was kind of proud of the little guy. I'd spend so much time bragging about him to Hideo that I'm surprised Hideo wouldn't run from the room every time I mentioned the kid. I'd tell Athena not to get upset, and she would just look at me and say, "Yes, I know. Matthew's a genius. Mentally. But he's still a little boy emotionally, and one of these days I'm afraid he'll run across something that his mind can handle and his emotions can't, and, David, I don't know what it will do to him then."

Athena had a point. But as long as Matthew was playing around with math, and we didn't talk to him about the situation or let him know, I didn't see much point in getting upset.

This was different, though, I have to admit, and I sat there in the living room with Matthew and started having one hell of a case of the creeps.

"Well, just what have you been discussing with Yuri?" I asked, and I must have sounded pretty harsh when I said it because I was trying to control myself.

He didn't answer me outright. Instead, he started getting oblique as hell about the whole thing.

"Do you know where most of the people in the world are living now?" he asked me.

"No."

"In this country, along the western coast and the temperate areas of the eastern coast. In Europe, along the Mediterranean coast. In Russia and China, near the old urban centers. A few in Japan and England."

"So what?" I blurted out.

"Don't you wonder why?" Matthew asked.

I thought about it for a few seconds. "Hell, no, I don't wonder why. Probably because of the climate."

"That wouldn't explain Russia and England," Matthew said.

"Probably because that's where the computer complexes are still working with the most efficiency. What are we playing, Matthew, twenty questions? Look, I'm your father, and I don't want a lot of folderol. Now just what have you been up to?"

Matthew looked at me coldly. "Doesn't that strike you as odd, David? I mean just moving and staying where the computers are still operating well."

"Hell, no, if you ask me, it makes a lot more sense than moving to where they don't work." I was beginning to wonder if Matthew had the brains I had credited him with having.

Matthew sighed and gave me the same look he would probably have given a cretin. "It doesn't make more sense than trying to repair the ones that aren't functioning."

"Matthew, I thought you were smart. Nobody knows enough to do that, and besides, there's plenty of places to live where they do work, so it doesn't matter. Now, will you get to the point?"

Athena came into the living room then, turned on the small TV and sat down. "I'm just going to watch the news from Russia, some Ukrainian couple is supposed to have a kid this week, and it'll be their second, so I wouldn't want to miss it."

"I think I'll go to my room," Matthew said. I followed him out and up the stairs of the old house to his room.

The room was a mess. That bothered me because Matthew was an orderly kid and always kept everything in place. Frankly, I was getting agitated. There were long data sheets from the computer scattered all over the floor and books just piled in sloppy heaps all around. Twenty people wouldn't use the computer that much in a year. I cleared a place on the bed and sat down.

"All right, young man, let's stop fooling around. I want some straight answers. What the hell have you been up to?"

I wish now I could forget the whole conversation. I wish

to hell somebody had blanked those computers, I mean, everybody knows it all anyway; and I wish somebody had at least kept Matthew from going near them. But nobody did. I sure didn't. I wasn't around enough.

Matthew sat down next to his desk. He looked tired. "All right, David. Yuri and I have been exploring the population decline." The kid just blurted it out like that. It was obscene, pointless. My stomach turned over.

"How much history do you know?" he asked.

"Enough," I replied.

"Then you know what the pre-Plague population was at the beginning of the twenty-first century."

"Between five and six billion," I said. My throat was really dry and I began to wish I had dialed myself a drink before I came upstairs. "Look, Matthew, I don't think much about this business, and if you don't mind my saying so, I don't think it's healthy. Now you had better come to the point, because I want to know exactly what you've been getting into."

"After the first Plague," Matthew said in a toneless voice, "it was down to five hundred million. After the survivors recovered from the devastation, it seems they began to realize that it wasn't as bad as it might have seemed. There was a high level of technology and enough people to keep things going. The computers were handling most things anyway, and the Plague had hit hardest in underdeveloped areas. Unfortunately, the viruses were still dormant. Twenty years later, the second Plague hit and left about thirty million survivors. It was after this that a vaccine was discovered and the population immunized. Unfortunately, it was also discovered in due time that most of the population was sterile." Matthew paused. "How many people are alive now, David? You know, don't you?"

I was shaking. "Hell, I don't know. A hundred thousand. A lot."

"An overestimation," Matthew said. "About seventy-five thousand."

I was really getting upset. "Now, you listen to me, Matthew. You shouldn't dwell on this bullshit. We're doing all right. It's not the sort of thing people think about."

He ignored me. "Yuri got a list of Plague symptoms from his computer data center. He got curious. We started looking into it. We found out things. We think someone, or some group, synthesized the virus and deliberately released it without actually realizing how virulent it was."

I exploded. "Matthew, that's insane. Don't even say it."

Matthew picked up a pile of data sheets. "Think about it, David. A world with six billion people, most of them starving. A rising birth rate. Depletion of resources. Most of the wealth centered in a few countries. What do you do? I viewed some old vidtapes. The possibility of genocide was openly discussed as a solution."

I was shaking. I thought someone had erased those damn things before.

"The Plague broke out first in India and Africa, then South America. We think whoever might have released the virus wanted it confined to those regions. But it spread."

"Matthew, this is all a lot of morbid ancient history, and there's no sense going into it now. There isn't any more Plague. We've got a good setup. People can do pretty much what they want."

"Except have children," Matthew said.

"Just what are you driving at, Matthew?" I shouted. It was no wonder Athena was upset with the kid.

He just looked at me with those dead eyes. "We're dying out, David. I don't know why, but we are. No one wants to think about it. Talking about it isn't allowed. Everybody gets excited when a baby's born, but nobody's doing anything about the problem. Maybe we still carry residual effects from the Plague. But nobody's doing anything because the whole topic is forbidden. If you think about it, you're insane, or upsetting things. You're just supposed to do what you like, dial your drinks or drugs, and enjoy yourself. And you don't even tell the kids. You can't even train us anymore so we could do something about it. Do you think we're all stupid? Don't you think we should know? You don't even really use the computers, not really, not for anything important." Matthew stared at his prosthetic hands. "And look at the kids you do have. Freaks. I'm one. Yuri's another. I'll bet we're not the only ones."

I was trying to control myself. "Matthew, I think I've heard just about enough from you. Now I want you to throw all this damn data into the dispose-all, and then I want you in bed. And I don't want you thinking about this anymore. Do I make myself clear?"

"Sure, David."

"All right." I left the room and went back downstairs. Athena had turned off the TV and was reading.

"They didn't have the baby yet," she said, putting down the book and looking up. "Oh, my God, David, you're upset too."

"You bet I am." I dialed another drink, a double. I wanted to be anesthetized. "There's only one thing to do. I'm going to get hold of Ramon Martinez in San Diego—he knows medicine, and he does a lot of reading on nervous disorders—and then you and I are going to take Matthew out there as soon as possible. If we have to put him on special drugs, we will. And in the meantime, he is not to go near that computer or have any little chats with Yuri."

"Oh, no, David," she said. "It's not that bad, it can't be."

"Athena, you've got to face facts. I had a pretty hair-raising discussion with our son, and he's a little too young to be holding psychotic ideas that would unbalance anybody, let alone a kid." Athena started crying and I took her by the shoulders. "Now come on, honey, you've got to face up to it. Nobody should let a kid think about it."

"All right, David," she said tonelessly.

"I'll call Martinez tomorrow and fix it up." I heard footsteps and turned around. It was Matthew, with about twelve tons of data sheets. He walked quietly into the kitchen and put them into the dispose-all and then came out.

"I'll tuck you in, Matthew," said Athena, and then she

walked over and put her arm around the little fellow's shoulders, and they walked upstairs.

And that was the last time I saw him that way, my only son, probably the only kid I'll ever have. He must have wandered out of the house early in the morning, and when he didn't come back, we went to look for him. We walked to an old school playground where Athena said he would go sometimes. He wasn't there among the rusty swings and the broken see-saw; he wasn't on the bench where Athena said he usually sat staring at the empty swings.

But he had been there earlier. Athena found his cap by the old bench. We circled back toward the coast, that rocky, savage-looking shore, and as we came to the edge of one of the high rocky cliffs, we heard what he must have heard.

Voices. High, childlike voices on the wind, laughing voices down near the shore.

Athena looked at me, startled by the sound. She began to hurry toward the edge of the cliff, but I grabbed her arm tightly. I didn't want her near the edge.

It was only the wind, of course. I knew that as soon as the voices faded and the wind died down. We heard only the waves smashing against the rocky shore. We climbed down to the small sandy part of the beach along some rocks near the cliff.

Athena saw him first, a small broken body on the rocks under the cliff, and she began to scream and tear at her hair until I grabbed her hands, trying to restrain her. We knew, even before I went over and picked up his body, even before I carried my son back to her, that he was gone.

We buried him ourselves, near the bench in the school-yard, and then old man Contemanopoulos came to take his daughter Athena back to New York, away from the old house and the rocky shore. She took none of Matthew's things with her. She never went back, as far as I know. Neither have I.

He must have heard the voices too, that's what I told Laura, he must have heard them and then lost his balance when he ran to see if there were children on the beach. At least, that's what I think; maybe it's more comforting than any alternative would be, the possibility that he might have hurtled off that cliff deliberately. Matthew was too intelligent to believe there actually were children on the beach, but what might he have felt when he heard the voices of the wind?

"He shouldn't have found out so young," I said to Laura when I could finally talk about it. "He would have felt differently when he was older, he could have lived with what we have, at least."

"Maybe not," she said. "Maybe it would have been even harder for him then."

Hideo and Inger have been sympathetic about the whole thing, but they're only human, and now they brag to me about their daughter Reiko Birgitta and show her off while I try to smile and hide my feelings.

We went to the beach yesterday, the five of us. Reiko's starting to crawl now, and we watched her gurgle at the sand and shriek at the gulls. Reiko, one of the last ones, probably, even though she doesn't know it yet and won't find out if Hideo can help it.

There's no point in thinking about the future now, nor the past, which compiled humanity's dreams and goals; and so I sat and watched the glint of the sun on Inger's light hair, Laura's dark feet pressing into the white sand, and Hideo kneeling by Reiko as she explored the shore, little fists grasping the sand, then letting it slip through the small fingers.

THE DEFENSELESS DEAD
by
Larry Niven

The dead lay side by side beneath the glass. Long ago, in a roomier world, these older ones had been entombed each in his own double-walled casket. Now they lay shoulder to shoulder, more or less in chronological order, looking up, their features faintly distorted by thirty centimeters of liquid nitrogen sandwiched between two thick sheets of glass.

We were deep underground. I could feel it. I could hear it in the endlessly whispering echoes of our footsteps.

Elsewhere in the Vault some sleepers wore clothing, formal costumery of a dozen periods. In two long tanks on another floor, the sleepers had been prettied up with low-temperature cosmetics, and sometimes with a kind of flesh-colored putty to fill and cover major wounds. A weird practice. It hadn't lasted beyond the middle of the last century. After all, these sleepers planned to return to life someday. The damage should show at a glance.

With these, it did.

They were all from the tail end of the twentieth century. They looked like hell. Some were clearly beyond saving, accident cases whose wills had consigned them to the Freezer Banks regardless. Each sleeper was marked by a plaque describing everything that was wrong with his mind and body, in script so fine and so archaic as to be almost unreadable.

Battered or torn or wasted by disease, they all wore the same look of patient resignation. Their hair was disintegrating, very slowly. It had fallen in a thick gray crescent about each head.

"People used to call them *corpsicles*, frozen dead. Or *Homo snapiens*. You can imagine what would happen if you dropped one."

Mr. Restarick did not smile. These people were in his charge, and he took his task seriously. His eyes seemed to look through rather than at me, and his clothes were ten to fifty years out of style. He seemed to be gradually losing himself here in the past. He said, "We've over six thousand of them here. Do you think we'll ever bring them back to life?" I was an ARM; I might know.

"Do you?"

"Sometimes I wonder." He dropped his gaze. "Not Harrison Cohn. Look at him, torn open like that. And *her,* with half her face shot off; she'd be a vegetable if you brought her back." Restarick spoke in pity. He felt no horror, no disgust, no squeamish qualms. My own stomach was crawling. "The later ones don't look this bad. Up until 1989 the doctors couldn't freeze anyone who wasn't clinically dead."

"That doesn't make *sense*. Why not?"

"They'd have been up for murder. When what they were doing was *saving* lives." He shrugged angrily. "Sometimes they'd stop a patient's heart and then restart it, to satisfy the legalities."

Sure, that made a lot of sense. I didn't dare laugh out loud. I pointed. "How about him?"

He was a rangy man of about forty-five, healthy-looking, with no visible marks of death, violent or otherwise. The long lean face still wore a look of command, though the deep-set eyes were almost closed. His lips were slightly parted, showing teeth straighted by braces in the ancient fashion.

Mr. Restarick glanced at the plaque. "Leviticus Hale, 1991. Oh, yes. Hale was a paranoid. He must have been the first they ever froze for *that*. They guessed right, too. If we brought him back now, we could cure him."

"If."

"It's been done."

"Sure. One out of three ain't bad. He'd probably take the chance himself. But then, he's crazy." I looked around at rows of long double-walled liquid nitrogen tanks. The place was huge and full of echoes, and this was only the top floor. The Vault of Eternity was ten stories deep in earthquake-free bedrock. "Six thousand, you said. But the Vault was built for ten thousand, wasn't it?"

He nodded. "We're a third empty."

"Get many customer these days?"

He laughed at me "You're kidding. Nobody gets himself frozen these days. He might wake up a piece at a time!"

"That's what I wondered."

"Ten years ago we were thinking of digging new vaults. All those crazy kids, perfectly healthy, getting themselves frozen so they could wake up in a brave new world. I had to watch while the ambulances came and carted them away for spare parts! We're a good third empty now since the Freezer Law passed!"

That business with the kids had been odd, all right. A fad or a religion or a madness, except that it had gone on for much too long.

The Freezeout Kids. Most of them were textbook cases of *anomie*, kids in their late teens who felt trapped in an imperfect world. History taught them (those that listened) that earlier times had been much worse. Perhaps they thought that the world was moving toward perfection.

Some had gambled. Not many in any given year; but it had been going on ever since the first experimental Freezer Vault revivals, a generation before I was born. It was better than suicide. They were young, they were healthy, they stood a better chance of revival than any of the frozen, damaged dead. They were poorly adapted to their society. Why not risk it?

Two years ago they had been answered. The General Assembly and the world vote had passed the Freezer Bill into law.

There were those in frozen sleep who had not had the foresight to set up a trust fund, or who had selected the wrong trustee or invested in the wrong stocks. If medicine or a miracle had revived them now, they would have been on the dole, with no money and no trace of useful education and, in about half the cases, no evident ability to survive in *any* society.

Were they in frozen sleep or frozen death? In law, there had always been that point of indecision. The Freezer Law cleared it up to some extent. It declared any person in frozen sleep, who could not support himself should society choose to reawaken him, to be dead in law.

And a third of the world's frozen dead, twelve hundred thousand of them, had gone into the organ banks.

"You were in charge then?"

The old man nodded. "I've been on the day shift at the Vault for almost forty years. I watched the ambulances fly away with three thousand of my people. I think of them as my people," he said a bit defensively.

"The law can't seem to decide if they're alive or dead. Think of them any way you like."

"People who trusted me. What did those Freezeout Kids do that was worth killing them for?"

I thought: they wanted to sleep it out while others broke their back turning the world into Paradise. But it's no capital crime.

"They had nobody to defend them. Nobody but me." He trailed off. After a bit, and with visible effort, he pulled himself back to the present. "Well, never mind. What can I do for the United Nations police, Mr. Hamilton?"

"Oh, I'm not here as an ARM agent. I'm just here to, to—" Hell, I didn't know myself. It was a news broadcast that had jarred me into coming here. I said, "They're planning to introduce another Freezer Bill."

"What?"

"A Second Freezer Bill. Naming a different group. The communal organ banks must be empty again," I said bitterly.

Mr. Restarick started to shake. "Oh, no. No. They can't do that again. They, they can't."

I gripped his arm, to reassure him or to hold him. He looked about to faint. "Maybe they can't. The first Freezer

Law was supposed to stop organlegging, but it didn't. Maybe the citizens will vote this one down."

I left as soon as I could.

The Second Freezer Bill made slow, steady progress without much opposition. I caught some of it in the boob cube. A perturbingly large number of citizens were petitioning the Security Council for confiscation of what they described as "the frozen corpses of a large number of people who were insane when they died. Parts of these corpses could possibly be recovered for badly needed organ replacements. . . ."

They never mentioned that said corpses might someday be recovered whole and living. They often mentioned that said corpses could not be safely recovered *now;* and they could prove it with experts; and they had a thousand experts waiting their turns to testify.

They never mentioned biochemical cures for insanity. They spoke of the lack of a worldwide need for mental patients and for insanity-carrying genes.

They hammered constantly on the need for organ transplant material.

I just about gave up watching news broadcasts. I was an ARM, a member of the United Nations police force, and I wasn't supposed to get involved in politics. It was none of my business.

It didn't become my business until I ran across a familiar name, eleven months later.

Taffy was people-watching. That demure look didn't fool me. A secretive glee looked out of her soft brown eyes, and they shifted left every time she raised her dessert spoon.

I didn't try to follow her eyes for fear of blowing her cover. Come, I will conceal nothing from you: I don't *care* who's eating at the next table in a public restaurant. Instead, I lit a cigarette, shifted it to my imaginary hand (the weight tugging gently at my mind) and settled back to enjoy my surroundings.

High Cliffs is an enormous pyramidal city-in-a-building

in northern California. Midgard is on the first shopping level, way back near the service core. There's no view, but the restaurant makes up for it with a spectacular set of environment walls.

From inside, Midgard seems to be halfway up the trunk of an enormous tree, big enough to stretch from Hell to Heaven. Perpetual war is waged in the vast distances, on various limbs of the tree, between warriors of oddly distorted size and shape. World-sized beasts show occasionally: a wolf attacks the moon, a sleeping serpent coils round the restaurant itself, the eye of a curious brown squirrel suddenly blocks one row of windows. . . .

"Isn't that Holden Chambers?"

"Who?" The name sounded vaguely familiar.

"Four tables over, sitting alone."

I looked. He was tall and skinny, and much younger than most of Midgard's clientele. Long blond hair, weak chin—he was really the type who ought to grow a beard. I was sure I'd never seen him before.

Taffy frowned. "I wonder why he's eating alone. Do you suppose someone broke a date?"

The name clicked. "Holden Chambers. Kidnapping case. Someone kidnapped him and his sister, years ago. One of Bera's cases."

Taffy put down her dessert spoon and looked at me curiously. "I didn't know the ARM took kidnapping cases."

"We don't. Kidnapping would be a regional problem. Bera thought—" I stopped, because Chambers looked around suddenly, right at me. He seemed surprised and annoyed.

I hadn't realised how rudely I was staring. I looked away, embarrassed. "Bera thought an organlegging gang might be involved. Some of the gang turned to kidnapping about that time, after the Freezer Law slid their markets out from under them. Is Chambers still looking at me?" I felt his eyes on the back of my neck.

"Yah."

"I wonder why."

"*Do* you indeed." Taffy knew, the way she was grinning. She gave me another two seconds of suspense, then said, "You're doing the cigarette trick."

"Oh. Right." I transferred the cigarette to a hand of flesh and blood. It's silly to forget how startling that can be: a cigarette or a pencil or a jigger of bourbon floating in midair. I've used it myself for shock effect.

Taffy said, "He's been in the boob cube a lot lately. He's the number-eight corpsicle heir, world wide. Didn't you know?"

"Corpsicle heir?"

"You know what *corpsicle* means? When the Freezer Vaults first opened——"

"I know. I didn't know they'd started using the word again."

"Well, never mind *that*. The *point* is that if the Second Freezer Bill passes, about three hundred thousand corpsicles will be declared formally dead. Some of those frozen dead men have money. The money will go to their next of kin."

"*Oh.* And Chambers has an ancestor in a vault somewhere, does he?"

"Somewhere in Michigan. He's got an odd, Biblical name."

"Not Leviticus Hale?"

She stared. "Now, just how the bleep did you know that?"

"Just a stab in the dark." I didn't know what had made me say it. Leviticus Hale, dead, had a memorable face and a memorable name.

Strange, though, that I'd never thought of money as a motive for voting for the Second Freezer Bill. The first Freezer Law had applied only to the destitute, the Freezeout Kids.

Here are people who could not possibly adjust to any time in which they might be revived. They couldn't even adjust to their own times. Most of them weren't even sick, *they didn't have* that *much excuse for foisting themselves on a nebulous future. Often they paid each other's way into the Freezer Vaults. If revived they would be paupers,*

*unemployable, uneducated by any possible present or fu-
ture standards; permanent malcontents.*

*Young, healthy, useless to themselves and society. And
the organ banks are always empty. . . .*

The arguments for the Second Freezer Bill were not
that much different. The corpisicles named in Group II
had money, but they were insane. Today there were chemical cures for most forms of insanity. But the memory of
having been insane, the habitual thought patterns formed
by paranoia or schizophrenia, these would remain, these
would require psychotherapy. And how to cure them in
men and women whose patterns of experience were up to
a hundred and forty years out of date to start with?

And the organ banks are always empty. . . . Sure, I
could see it. The citizens wanted to live forever. One day
they'd work their way down to me, Gil Hamilton.

"You can't win," I said.

Taffy said, "How so?"

"If you're destitute, they won't revive you because you
can't support yourself. If you're rich, your heirs want the
money. It's hard to defend yourself when you're dead."

"Everyone who loved them is dead too." She looked
too seriously into her coffee cup. "I didn't really pay much
attention when they passed the Freezer Law. At the hospital we don't even know where the spare parts come from:
criminals, corpsicles, captured organlegging stock, it all
looks the same. Lately I find myself wondering."

Taffy had once finished a lung transplant with hands
and sterile steel, after the hospital machines had quit at an
embarrassing moment. A squeamish woman couldn't have
done that. But the transplants themselves were bothering
her lately. Since she met me. A surgeon and an organ-
legger-hunting ARM, we made a strange pairing.

When I looked again, a quartet of nudists had taken
over Chambers' table. Healthy, athletic, smooth-shaven,
they jarred oddly with the World-Ash beyond the windows. Olympus would have fit them better.

We split the tab, paid, and left.

* * *

The first shopping level of High Cliffs had an odd indoor-outdoor feel to it. We came out into a broad walk lined with shops and trees and theaters and sidewalk cafes, under a flat concrete sky forty feet up and glowing with light. Far away, a mountainous black horizon showed in a narrow band between concrete sky and firmament.

The crowds had gone, but in some of the sidewalk cafes, a few citizens still watched the world go by. We walked toward the black band of horizon, holding hands, taking our time. There was no way to hurry Taffy when she was passing shop windows. All I could do was stop when she did, wearing or not wearing an indulgent smile. My sporan swung at my waist, heavy with a weight I had ceased to notice long ago.

Taffy tugged my arm, turning sharply to look into a furniture store. Maybe it was the Womb Room arrangement she wanted me to see: a desk and easy chair and boob cube and videotape and hi-fi setup, all combined in flowing curves of artificial woods. But what I noticed was a dazzling pulse of green light on the glass and a puff of green flame spurting from the back of the chair.

Very strange. Surrealistic, I thought. Then the impressions sorted out, and I pushed Taffy hard in the small of her back and flung myself rolling in the other direction. Green light flashed briefly, very near.

Some puzzled citizens stopped to watch what I was doing.

I ripped my sporan apart with both hands. The seam gave and everything spilled out, rolling coins and credit cards and ARM ident and cigarettes and the regulation off-duty weapon that I had only used twice in my life, though I had to fumble past it every time I paid a dinner check. It was Derringer-sized: a butt and trigger and two compressed air cartridges firing clusters of anaesthetic crystal slivers.

The window reflection had been a break. Usually you can't tell *where* the pulse from a hunting laser might have come from.

Green light flashed near my elbow. The pavement cracked loudly and peppered me with particles. I fought an urge to fling myself backward. The afterimage was on my retina, a green line thin as a razor's edge, pointing him out.

There in a narrow cross street: a shadow man, posed kneeling, waiting for his gun to pulse again. I sent a cloud of mercy-needles toward him. He slapped at his face, turned to run, and fell skidding.

I stayed where I was. There might be more.

Taffy was curled on the pavement with her head buried in her arms. There was no blood around her. When I saw her legs shift, I knew she wasn't dead. I still didn't know if she'd been hit.

Nobody else tried to shoot at us.

The man with the gun lay where he was for almost a minute. Then he started twitching.

He was in convulsions when I got to him. Mercy-needles aren't supposed to do that. I got his tongue out of his throat so he couldn't choke, but I wasn't carrying medicines that could help. When the High Cliffs police arrived, he was dead.

Inspector Swan was a picture-poster cop, tri-racial and handsome as hell in an orange uniform that seemed tailored to him, so well did he fit it. He had the gun open in front of him and was probing at the electronic guts of it with a pair of tweezers. He said, "You don't have any idea why he was shooting at you?"

"That's right."

"You're an ARM. What do you work on these days?"

"Organlegging, mostly. Tracking down gangs that have gone into hiding." I was massaging Taffy's neck and shoulders, trying to calm her down. She was still shivering. The muscles under my hands were very tight.

Swan frowned. "Such an easy answer. But he couldn't be part of an organlegging gang, could he? Not with that gun."

"True." I ran my thumbs around the curve of Taffy's shoulder blades. She reached around and squeezed my hand.

The gun. I hadn't really expected Swan to see the implications. It was an unmodified hunting laser, right off the rack.

Officially, nobody in the world makes guns to kill people. Under the conventions, not even armies use them; and the United Nations police use mercy-weapons, with the intent that the criminals concerned should be unharmed for trial—and, later, for the organ banks. The only killing weapons made are for killing animals. They are supposed to be, well, sportsmanlike.

A continuous-firing X-ray laser would be easy enough to make. It would chop down anything living, no matter how fast it fled, no matter what it hid behind. The beast wouldn't even know it was being shot at until you waved the beam through its body: an invisible sword blade a mile long.

But that's butchery. The prey should have a chance; it should at least know it's being shot at. A standard hunting laser fires a pulse of visible light and won't fire again for about a second. It's no better than a rifle, except that you don't have to allow for windage, the range is close enough to infinite, you can't run out of bullets, it doesn't mess up the meat, and there's no recoil. That's what makes it sportsmanlike.

Against me it had been just sportsmanlike enough. He was dead. I wasn't.

"Not that it's so censored easy to modify a hunting laser," said Swan. "It takes some basic electronics. I could do it myself—"

"So could I. Why not? We've both had police training."

"The point is, I don't *know* anyone who couldn't *find* someone to modify a hunting laser, give it a faster pulse or even a continuous beam. Your friend must have been afraid to bring anyone else into it. He must have had a very personal grudge against you. You're sure you don't recognise him?"

"I never saw him before. Not with *that* face."

"And he's dead," said Swan.

"That doesn't really prove anything. Some people have allergic reactions to police anaesthetics."

"You used a standard ARM weapon?"

"Yah. I didn't even fire both barrels. I *couldn't* have put a *lot* of needles in him. But there are allergic reactions."

"Especially if you take something to bring them on." Swan put the gun down and stood up. "Now, I'm just a city cop, and I don't know that much about ARM business. But I've heard that organleggers sometimes take something so they won't just go to sleep when an ARM anaesthetic hits them."

"Yah. Organleggers don't like becoming spare parts themselves. I do have a theory, Inspector."

"Try me."

"He's a retired organlegger. A lot of them retired when the Freezer Bill passed. Their markets were gone, and they'd made their pile, some of them. They split up and became honest citizens. A respected citizen may keep a hunting laser on his wall, but it isn't modified. He could modify it if he had to, with a day's notice."

"Then said respected citizen spotted an old enemy."

"Going into a restaurant, maybe. And he just had time to go home for his gun, while we ate dinner."

"Sounds reasonable. How do we check it?"

"If you'll do a rejection spectrum on his brain tissue and send everything you get to ARM Headquarters, we'll do the rest. An organlegger can change his face and fingerprints as he censored pleases, but he can't change his tolerance to transplants. Chances are he's on record."

"And you'll let me know."

"Right."

Swan checked in via the radio on his scooter. I beeped my clicker at a cruising taxi, waited for it to settle, then helped Taffy into it. Her movements were slow and jerky. Her hands were cold, her face still pale with shock.

Swan called from his scooter. "Hamilton!"

I stopped halfway into the taxi. "Yah?"

"He's a local," Swam boomed. His voice carried like an actor's. "Mortimer Lincoln, ninety-fourth floor. Been living here since—" He checked again with his radio. "April, 2123 I'd guess that's about six months after they passed the Freezer Law."

"Thanks." I typed an address on the cab's destination board. The cab hummed and rose.

I watched High Cliffs recede, a pyramid as big as a mountain, glowing with light. The city guarded by Inspector Swan was all in one building. It would make his job easier, I thought. Society would be a bit more organized.

Taffy spoke for the first time in a good while. "Nobody's ever shot at me before."

"It's all over now. I think he was shooting at me anyway."

"I suppose." Suddenly she was shaking. I took her in my arms and held her. She talked into my shirt collar. "I didn't know what was happening. That green light, I thought it was *pretty*. I didn't know what happened until you knocked me down, and then that green line flashed at you and I heard the sidewalk go *ping,* and I didn't know what to *do!* I—"

"You did fine."

"I wanted to *help!* I didn't know, maybe you were dead, and there wasn't anything I could do. If you hadn't had a gun—Do you always carry a gun?"

"Always."

"I never knew." Without moving, she seemed to pull away from me a little.

At one time the Amalgamated Regional Militia had been a federation of Civil Defense bodies in a number of nations. Later it had become the police force of the United Nations itself. They had kept the name. Probably they liked the acronym.

ARM Headquarters in Los Angeles was a relatively new building. By early morning light, it looked almost like a flowering plant: all balconies and open bridges around a central stalk. It did not look institutional, at least from outside. Inside? Well, mine was an inside office, comfortable enough, but not very big, and with no windows.

Jackson Bera had already run the dead man to earth. "No question about it," he told me. "His rejection spectrum checks perfectly. Anthony Tiller, known organlegger, suspected member of the Anubis gang. First came on the scene around 2120; he probably had another name and face before that. Disappeared April or May 2123."

"That fits." I thought about it. "No, dammit, it doesn't. He must have been out of his mind. He was home free. Safe and comfortable. Why would he blow it all to kill a man who never harmed a hair of his head?"

"You don't *really* expect an organlegger to behave like a well-adjusted member of society."

I answered Bera's grin. "I guess not. . . . Hey. You said *Anubis,* didn't you? The Anubis gang, not the Loren gang."

"That's what it says on the hard copy. Shall I query for probability?"

"Please." Bera programs a computer better than I do. I talked while he tapped at the keyboard in my desk. "Whoever the bleep he was, Anubis controlled the illicit medical facilities over a big section of the Midwest. Loren had a piece of the North American west coast, smaller area, bigger population. The difference is that I killed Loren myself, by squeezing the life out of his heart with my imaginary hand, which is a very personal thing, as you will realize, Jackson. Whereas I never touched Anubis or any of his gang, nor even interfered with his profits, to the best of my knowledge."

"I did," said Bera. "Maybe he thought I was you." Which is hilarious, because Bera is dark brown and a foot taller than me if you include the hair that puffs out around his head like a black powder explosion. "You missed something. Anubis was an intriguing character. He changed faces and ears and fingerprints whenever he got the urge. We're pretty sure he was male, but even that isn't worth a *big* bet. He's changed his height at least once. Full leg transplant."

"Loren couldn't do that. Loren was a pretty sick boy. He probably went into organlegging because he needed the transplant supply."

"Not Anubis. Anubis must have had a sky-high rejection threshold."

"Jackson, *you're proud of Anubis.*"

Bera was shocked to his core. "The hell! He's a dirty murdering organlegger! If I'd *caught* him, I'd be proud of

Anubis—" He stopped, because my desk screen was getting information.

The computer in the basement of the ARM building gave Anthony Tiller no chance at all of being part of the Loren gang, and a probability in the nineties that he had run with the Jackal God. One point was that Anubis and the rest had all dropped out of sight around the end of April, 2123, when Anthony Tiller-Mortimer Lincoln changed his face and moved into High Cliffs.

"It could still have been revenge," Bera suggested. "Loren and Anubis knew each other. We know that much. They set up the boundary between their territories at least twelve years ago, by negotiation. Loren took over Anubis' territory when Anubis retired. And you killed Loren."

I scoffed. "And Tiller the Killer gave up his cover to get me, two years after the gang broke up?"

"Maybe it wasn't revenge. Maybe Anubis wants to make a comeback."

"Or maybe this Tiller just flipped. Withdrawal symptoms. He hadn't killed anyone for almost two years, poor baby. I wish he'd picked a better time."

"Why?"

"Taffy was with me. She's still twitching."

"You didn't tell me that! She wasn't hit, was she?"

"No, just scared."

Bera relaxed. His hand caressed the interface where his hair faded into air, feather-lightly, in the nervous way another man might scratch his hand. "I'd hate to see you two split up."

"Oh, it's not . . ." anything like that serious, I'd have told him, but he knew better. "Yah. We didn't get much sleep last night. It isn't just being shot at, you know."

"I know."

"Taffy's a surgeon. She thinks of transplant stocks as raw material. Tools. She'd be crippled without an organ bank. She doesn't think of the stuff as human . . . or she never used to, till she met me."

"I've never heard either of you talk about it."

"We don't, even to each other, but it's there. Most transplants are condemned criminals, captured by heroes such as you and me. Some of the stuff is respectable citizens captured by organleggers, broken up into illicit organ banks and eventually recaptured by said heroes. They don't tell Taffy which is which. She works with pieces of people. I don't think she can live with me and not live with that."

"Getting shot at by an ex-organlegger couldn't have helped much. We'd better see to it that it doesn't happen again."

"Jackson, he was just a nut."

"He used to be with Anubis."

"I never had anything to do with Anubis." Which reminded me. "You did, though, didn't you? Do you remember anything about the Holden Chambers kidnapping."

Bera looked at me peculiarly. "Holden and Charlotte Chambers, yah. You've got a good memory. There's a fair chance Anubis was involved."

"Tell me about it."

"There was a rash of kidnappings about that time, all over the world. You know how organlegging works. The legitimate hospitals are always short of transplants. Some sick citizens are too much in a hurry to wait their turns. The gangs kidnap a healthy citizen, break him up into spare parts, throw away the brain, use the rest for illegal operations. That's the way it was until the Freezer Law cut the market out from under them."

"I remember."

"Some gangs turned to kidnapping for ransom. Why not? It's just what they were set up for. If the family couldn't pay off, the victim could always become a donor. It made people much more likely to pay off.

"The only strange thing about the Chambers kidnap was that Holden and Charlotte Chambers both disappeared about the same time, around six at night." Bera had been tapping at the computer controls. He looked at the screen and said, "Make that six twenty. March 21, 2123. But they were miles apart, Charlotte at a restaurant with a date, Holden at Washburn University attending a night class. Now why would a kidnap gang think they needed them both?"

"Any ideas?"

"They might have thought that the Chambers trustees were more likely to pay off on both of them. We'll never know now. We never got any of the kidnappers. We were lucky to get the kids back."

"What made you think it was Anubis?"

"It was Anubis territory. The Chamber kidnap was only the last of half a dozen in that area. Smooth operations, no excitement, no hitches, victims returned intact after the ransom was paid." He glared. "No, I'm *not* proud of Anubis. It's just that he tended not to make mistakes, and he was used to making people disappear."

"Uh huh."

"They made themselves disappear, the whole gang, around the time of that last kidnap. We assume they were building up a stake."

"How much did they get?"

"On the Chambers kids? A hundred thousand."

"They'd have made ten times that selling them as transplants. They must have been hard up."

"You know it. Nobody was buying. What does all this have to do with your being shot at?"

"A wild idea. Could Anubis be interested in the Chambers kids *again?*"

Bera gave me a funny look. "No way. What for? They bled them white the first time. A hundred thousand UN marks isn't play money."

After Bera left I sat there not believing it.

Anubis had vanished. Loren had acted immediately to take over Anubis' territory. Where had they gone, Anubis and the others?

Into Loren's organ banks?

Bera couldn't see Anubis being suckered like that. Maybe he had too high an opinion of Anubis. But Anthony Tiller had hunted with Anubis, and now Tiller had surfaced again. . . .

I didn't like the idea that any random ex-organlegger

might decide to kill me the instant he saw me. Finally I did something about it. I asked the computer for data on the Chambers kidnapping.

I scanned it fast. There wasn't much Bera hadn't told me. I wondered, though, why he hadn't mentioned Charlotte's condition.

When ARM police found the Chambers kids drugged on a hotel parking roof, they had both been in good physical condition. Holden had been a little scared, a little relieved, just beginning to get mad. But Charlotte had been in catatonic withdrawal. At last notice, she was still in catatonic withdrawal. She had never spoken with coherence about the kidnapping, nor about anything else.

Something had been done to her. Something terrible. Maybe Bera had taught himself not to think about it.

Otherwise the kidnappers had behaved almost with rectitude. The ransom had been paid, the victims had been returned. They had been on that roof, drugged, for less than twenty minutes. They showed no bruises, no signs of maltreatment . . . another sign that their kidnappers were organleggers. Organleggers aren't sadists. They don't have that much respect for the stuff.

I noted that the ransom had been paid by an attorney. The Chambers were orphans. If they'd both been killed, the executor of their estate would have been out of a job. From that viewpoint it made sense to capture them both . . . but not all *that* much sense.

There couldn't be a motive for kidnapping them again. They didn't have the money. Except—

It hit me joltingly. *The Second Freezer Bill.*

Holden Chambers' number was in the basement computer. I was dialing it when second thoughts interrupted. Instead I called downstairs and set a team to locating possible bugs in Chambers' home or phone. They weren't to interfere with the bugs or to alert possible listeners. Routine stuff.

Once before, the Chambers kids had disappeared. If we weren't lucky, they might disappear again. Sometimes the

ARM business was like digging a pit in quicksand. If you dug hard enough, you could maintain a noticeable depression, but as soon as you stopped . . .

The Freezer Law of 2122 had given the ARM a field day. Some of the gangs had simply retired. Some had tried to keep going and wound up selling an operation to an ARM plant. Some had tried to reach other markets; but there weren't any, not even for Loren, who had tried to expand into the asteroid belt and found they wouldn't have him either.

And some had tried kidnapping; but inexperience kept tripping them up. The name of a victim points straight at a kidnapper's only possible market. Too often the ARMs had been waiting.

We'd cleaned them out. Organlegging should have been an extinct profession this past year. The vanished jackals I spent my days hunting should have posed no present threat to society.

Except that the legitimate transplants released by the Freezer Law were running out. And a peculiar thing was happening. People had started to disappear from stalled vehicles, singles apartment houses, crowded city slide-walks.

Earth wanted the organleggers back. No, that wasn't fair. But enough citizens wanted to extend their own lives, at any cost . . .

If Anubis was alive, he might well be thinking of going back into business.

The point was that he would need backing. Loren had taken over his medical facilities when Anubis retired. Eventually we'd located those and destroyed them. Anubis would have to start over.

Let the Second Freezer Bill pass, and Leviticus Hale would be spare parts. Charlotte and Holden Chambers would be heirs to . . . how much?

I got that via a call to the local NBA news department. In one hundred and thirty-four years, Leviticus Hale's original three hundred and twenty thousand US dollars had become seventy-five million UN marks.

I spent the rest of the morning on routine. They call it *legwork,* though it's mostly done by phone and computer keyboard. The word covers some unbelievable long shots.

We were investigating every member of every Citizen's Committee to Oppose the Second Freezer Bill in the world. The suggestion had come down from Old Man Garner. He thought we might find that a coalition of organleggers had pooled advertising money to keep the corpsicles off the market. The results that morning didn't look promising.

I half hoped it wouldn't work out. Suppose those committees *did* turn out to be backed by organleggers? It would make prime time news, anywhere in the world. The Second Freezer Bill would pass like *that.* But it had to be checked. There had been opposition to the first Freezer Bill, too, when the gangs had had more money. We'd have to check that too.

Money. We spent a good deal of computer time looking for unexplained money. The average criminal tends to think that once he's got the money, he's home free, the game is over.

We hadn't caught a sniff of Loren or Anubis that way.

Where had Anubis spent his money? Maybe he'd just hidden it away somewhere, or maybe Loren had killed him for it. And Tiller had shot at me because he didn't like my face. Legwork is gambling, time against results.

It developed that Holden Chambers' environs were free of eavesdropping devices. I called him about noon.

There appeared within my phone screen a red-faced, white-haired man of great dignity. He asked to whom I wished to speak. I told him and displayed my ARM ident. He nodded and put me on HOLD.

Moments later Holden Chambers smiled distractedly at me and said, "Sorry about that. I've been getting considerable static from the news lately. Zero acts as a kind of, ah, buffer."

He was wearing a minimum kilt, a knee-length towel meant to be snatched up and fastened around the waist when a man is sitting around naked and his phone rings.

He was lean and undermuscled, ascetic. The intellectual look was spoiled by a receding chin. Past his shoulder I could see a table, piled high: a tape viewer, a double handful of tape spools, a hand-sized voice recorder, two pens, and a stack of paper. I say, "Sorry to interrupt your studying."

"That's all right. It's tough getting back to it after Year's-End. Maybe you remember." He studied my face, thoughtfully. "Haven't I seen you— *Oh*. The floating cigarette."

"That's right."

"How did you do that?"

"I've got an imaginary arm." And it's a great conversational device, an ice-breaker of wondrous potency. I was a marvel, a talking sea serpent, the way the kid was looking at me. "I lost an arm once, mining rocks in the Belt. A sliver of asteroid rock sheared it off clean to the shoulder."

He looked awed.

"I got it replaced, of course." And found out later that the replacement had come out of a captured and illicit organ bank. Some innocent bystander had once been attached to my right arm; but I didn't tell many people that. "But for a year I was a one-armed man. Well, here was a whole section of my brain developed to control a right arm, and no right arm. I started developing psychic powers: psychokinesis and extra sensory perception. I started using them like an imaginary arm. Psychokinesis is easy enough to develop when you live in a low-gravity environment." I paused just less than long enough for him to form a question. "Somebody tried to kill me outside Midgard last night. That's why I called."

I hadn't expected him to burst into a fit of the giggles. "Sorry," he got out. "It sounds like you lead an active life!"

"Yah. It didn't seem that funny at the time. I don't suppose you noticed anything unusual last night?"

"Just the usual shootings and muggings, and there was one guy with a cigarette floating in front of his face." He sobered before my clearly deficient sense of humor.

"Look, I *am* sorry, but one minute you're talking about a meteor shearing your arm off, and the next it's bullets whizzing past your ear."

"Sure, I see your point."

"I left before you did. I know censored well I did. What happened?"

"Somebody shot at us with a hunting laser. He was probably just a nut. He was also part of the gang that kidnapped—" I saw his stricken look. "Yah, them. There's probably no connection, but we wondered if you might have noticed anything. Like a familiar face."

He shook his head. "They change faces, don't they?"

"Usually. How did you leave?"

"Taxi. I live in Bakersfield, about twenty minutes from High Cliffs. Where did all this happen? I caught my taxi on the third shopping level."

"That kills it. We were on the first."

"I'm not really sorry. He might have shot at me too."

I'd been trying to decide whether to tell him that the kidnap gang might be interested in him again. Whether to scare the lights out of him on another long shot, or leave him off guard for a possible kidnap attempt. He seemed stable enough, but you never know.

I temporized. "Mister Chambers, we'd like you to try to identify the man who tried to kill me last night. He probably did change his face—"

"Yah." He was uneasy. Many citizens would be, if asked to look a dead man in the face. "But I suppose you've got to try it. I'll stop in tomorrow afternoon, after class."

So. Tomorrow we'd see what he was made of.

He asked, "What about that imaginary arm? I've never heard of a psi talking that way about his talent."

"I wasn't being cute," I told him. "It's an arm, as far as I'm concerned. My limited imagination. I can feel things out with my fingertips, but not if they're further away than an arm can reach. I can lift things at the same distance. A jigger of bourbon is about the biggest thing I can lift. Most psis can't do nearly that well."

"But they can reach further. Why not try a hypnotist?"

"And lose the whole arm? I don't want to risk that."

He looked disappointed in me. "What can you do with an imaginary arm that you can't do with a real one?"

"I can pick up hot things without burning myself."

"*Yah!*" He hadn't thought of that.

"And I can reach through walls. In the Belt, I could reach through my suit and do precision work in vacuum. I can reach *two* ways through a phone screen. Fiddle with the works, or—here, I'll show you."

It doesn't always work. But I was getting a good picture. Chambers showed life-sized, in color and stereo, through four square feet of screen. It looked like I could reach right into it. So I did. I reached into the screen with my imaginary hand, picked a pencil off the table in front of him and twirled it like a baton.

He threw himself backward out of his chair. He landed rolling. I saw his face, pale grey with terror, before he rolled away and out of view. A few seconds later the screen went blank. He must have turned the knob from off-screen.

If I'd touched his face, I could have understood it. But all I'd done was lift a pencil. What the hell?

My fault, I guessed. Some people see psi powers as supernatural, eerie, threatening. I shouldn't have been showing off like that. But Holden hadn't looked the type. Brash, a bit nervous, but fascinated rather than repulsed by the possibilities of an invisible, immaterial hand.

Then, terror.

I didn't try to call him back. I dithered about putting a guard on him, decided not to. A guard might be noticed. But I ordered a tracer implanted in him. Anubis could pick Chambers up at any time. He needn't wait for the General Assembly to declare Leviticus Hale dead.

A tracer needle was a useful thing. It would be fired at Chambers from ambush. He'd probably never notice the sting, the hole would be only a pinprick, and it would tell us just where he was from then on.

I thought Charlotte Chambers could use a tracer too, so I picked up a palm-size pressure implanter downstairs. I also traded the discharged barrel on my sidearm for a fresh one. The feel of the gun in my hand sent vivid green lines sizzling past my mind's eye.

Lastly I ordered a standard information package, C priority, on what Chambers had been doing for the last two years. It would probably arrive in a day or so.

The face of Kansas was black and orange-white with great dark gaps in it, a town nestled in each gap. The weather domes of various townships had shifted kilotons of snow outward, to deepen the drifts across the flat countryside. In the light of an early winter sunset, the snowbound landscape was orange-white, stripped with the broad black shadows of a few cities-within-buildings like High Cliffs. It all seemed eerie and abstract, sliding west beneath the folded wings of our plane.

We slowed hard in midair. The wings unfolded, and we settled over downtown Topeka.

This was going to look odd on my expense account. All this way to see a girl who hadn't spoken sense in three years. Probably it would be disallowed . . . yet she was as much a part of the case as her brother. Anyone planning to recapture Holden Chambers for reransom would want Charlotte too.

Menninger Institute was a pretty place. Besides the twelve stories of glass and mock-brick that formed the main building, there were at least a dozen outbuildings of varied ages and designs that ran from boxlike rectangles to free-form organics poured in foam plastic. They were all wide apart, separated by green lawns and trees and flower beds. A place of peace, a place with elbow room. Pairs and larger groups passed me on the curving walks: an aide and a patient, or an aide and several less-disturbed patients. The aides were obvious at a glance.

"When a patient is well enough to go outside for a walk, then he needs the greenery and the room," Doctor Hartman told me. "It's part of his therapy. Going outside is a giant step."

"Do you get many agorophobes?"

"No, that's not what I was talking about. It's the lock that counts. To anyone else that lock is a prison, but to many patients it comes to represent security. Someone else to make the decisions, to keep the world outside."

Doctor Hartman was short and round and blond. A comfortable person, easygoing, patient, sure of himself. Just the man to trust with your destiny, assuming you were tired of running it yourself.

I asked, "Do you get many cures?"

"Certainly. As a matter of fact, we generally won't take patients unless we feel we can cure them."

"That must do wonders for the record."

He was not offended. "It does even more for the patients. Knowing that we know they can be cured makes them feel the same way. And the incurably insane . . . can be damned depressing." Momentarily he seemed to sag under an enormous weight. Then he was himself again. "They can affect the other patients. Fortunately there aren't many incurables, these days."

"Was Charlotte Chambers one of the curables?"

"We thought so. After all, it was only shock. There was no previous history of personality disturbances. Her blood psychochemicals were near enough normal. We tried everything in the records. Stroking. Fiddling with her chemistry. Psychotherapy didn't get very far. Either she's deaf, or she doesn't listen—and she won't talk. Sometimes I think she hears everything we say . . . but she doesn't respond."

We had reached a powerful-looking locked door. Doctor Hartman searched through a key ring, touched a key to the lock. "We call it the violent ward, but it's more properly the severely disturbed ward. I wish to hell we *could* get some violence out of some of them. Like Charlotte. They won't even *look* at reality, much less try to fight it. Here we are."

Her door opened outward into the corridor. My nasty professional mind tagged the fact: if you tried to hang yourself from the door, anyone could see you from either end of the corridor. It would be very public.

In these upper rooms the windows were frosted. I suppose there's good reason why some patients shouldn't be reminded that they are twelve stories up. The room was small but well lighted and brightly painted, with a bed and a padded chair and a tridee screen set flush with the wall. There wasn't a sharp corner anywhere in the room.

Charlotte was in the chair, looking straight ahead of her, her hands folded in her lap. Her hair was short and not particularly neat. Her yellow dress was of some wrinkleproof fabric. She looked resigned, I thought, resigned to some ultimately awful thing. She did not notice us as we came in.

I whispered, "Why is she still here, if you can't cure her?"

Doctor Hartman spoke in a normal tone. "At first we thought it was catatonic withdrawal. That we could have cured. This isn't the first time someone has suggested moving her. She's still here because I want to know what's *wrong* with her. She's been like this ever since they brought her in."

She still hadn't noticed us. The doctor talked as if she couldn't hear us. "Do the ARMs have any idea what was done to her? If we knew that, we might be better able to treat her."

I shook my head. "I was going to ask you. What *could* they have done to her?"

He shook his head.

"Try another angle, then. What couldn't they have done to her? There were no bruises, broken bones, anything like that—"

"No internal injuries either. No surgery was performed on her. There was the evidence of drugging. I understand they were organleggers?"

"It looks likely." She could have been pretty, I thought. It wasn't the lack of cosmetics, or even the gaunt look. It was the empty eyes, isolated above high cheekbones, looking at nothing. "Could she be blind?"

"No. The optic nerves function perfectly."

She reminded me of a wirehead. You can't get a wirehead's attention either, when house current is trickling down a fine wire from the top of his skull into the pleasure center of his brain. But no, the pure egocentric joy of a wirehead hardly matched Charlotte's egocentric misery.

"Tell me," said Doctor Hartman. "How badly could an organlegger frighten a young girl?"

"We don't get many citizens back from organleggers. I . . . honestly can't think of any upper limit. They could have taken her on a tour of the medical facilities. They could have made her watch while they broke up a prospect for stuff." I didn't like what my imagination was doing. There are things you don't think about, because the point is to protect the prospects, keep the Lorens and the Anubises from reaching them at all. But you can't help thinking about them anyway, so you push them back, push them back. These things must have been in my head for a long time. "They had the facilities to partly break her up and put her back together again and leave her conscious the whole time. You wouldn't have found scars. The only scars they can't cure with modern medicine are in the bone itself. They could have done any kind of temporary transplant—and they must have been bored, Doctor. Business was slow. But—"

"Stop." He was grey around the edges. His voice was weak and hoarse.

"But organleggers aren't sadists, generally. They don't have that much respect for the stuff. They wouldn't play that kind of game unless they had something special against her."

"My God, you play rough games. How can you sleep nights, knowing what you know?"

"None of your business, Doctor. In your opinion, is it likely that she was frightened into this state?"

"Not all at once. We could have brought her out of it if it had happened all at once. I suppose she may have been frightened repeatedly. How long did they have her?"

"Nine days."

Hartman looked worse yet. Definitely he was not ARM material.

I dug in my sporan for the pressure implanter. "I'd like your permission to put a tracer needle in her. I won't hurt her."

"There's no need to whisper, Mr. Hamilton—"

"Was I?" Yes, dammit, I'd been holding my voice low,

as if I were afraid to disturb her. In a normal voice I said, "The tracer could help us locate her in case she disappears."

"Disappears? Why should she do that? You can see for yourself—"

"That's the worst of it. The same gang of organleggers that got her the first time may be trying to kidnap her again. Just how good is your . . . security. . . ." I trailed off. Charlotte Chambers had turned around and was looking at me.

Hartman's hand closed hard on my upper arm. He was warning me. Calmly, reassuringly, he said, "Don't worry, Charlotte. I'm Doctor Hartman. You're in good hands. We'll take care of you."

Charlotte was half out of her chair, twisted around to search my face. I tried to look harmless. Naturally I knew better than to try to guess what she was thinking. Why should her eyes be big with hope? Frantic, desperate hope. When I'd just uttered a terrible threat.

Whatever she was looking for, she didn't find it in my face. What looked like hope gradually died out of her eyes, and she sank back in her chair, looking straight ahead of her, without interest. Doctor Hartman gestured, and I took the hint and left.

Twenty minutes later he joined me in the visitor's waiting room. "Hamilton, that's the first time she's ever shown that much awareness. What could possibly have sparked it?"

I shook my head. "I wanted to ask, just how good is your security?"

"I'll warn the aides. We can refuse to permit her visitors unless accompanied by an ARM agent. Is that good enough?"

"It may be, but I want to plant a tracer in her. Just in case.

"All right."

"Doctor, what was that in her expression?"

"I thought it was hope. Hamilton, I will just bet it was your voice that did it. You may sound like someone she knows. Let me take a recording of your voice, and we'll see if we can find a psychiatrist who sounds like you."

When I put the tracer in her, she never so much as twitched.

All the way home her face haunted me. As if she'd waited two years in that chair, not bothering to move or think, until I came. Until finally I came.

My right side seems weightless. It throws me off stride as I back away, back away. My right arm ends at the shoulder. Where my left eye was is an empty socket. Something vague shuffles out of the dark, looks at me with its one left eye, reaches for me with its one right arm. I back away, back away, fending it off with my imaginary arm. It comes closer, I touch it, I reach into it. Horrible! The scars! Loren's pleural cavity is a patchwork of transplants. I want to snatch my hand away. Instead, I reach deeper, find his borrowed heart, and squeeze. And squeeze.

How can I sleep nights, knowing what I know? Well, Doctor, some nights I dream.

Taffy opened her eyes to find me sitting up in bed, staring at a dark wall. She said, "What?"

"Bad dream."

"Oh." She scratched me under the ear, for reassurance.

"How awake are you?"

She sighed. "Wide awake."

"Corpsicle. Where did you hear the word corpsicle? In the boob cube? From a friend?"

"I don't remember. Why?"

"Just a thought. Never mind. I'll ask Luke Garner."

I got up and made us some hot chocolate with bourbon flavoring. It knocked us out like a cluster of mercy needles.

Lucas Garner was a man who had won a gamble with fate. Medical technology had progressed as he grew older, so that his expected lifespan kept moving ahead of him. He was not yet the oldest living member of the Struldbrugs' Club, but he was getting on, getting on.

His spinal nerves had worn out long since, marooning him in a ground-effect travel chair. His face hung loose from his skull, in folds. But his arms were apishly strong, and his brain still worked. He was my boss.

"Corpsicle," he said. "Corpsicle. Right. They've been saying it on tridee. I didn't notice, but you're right. It's funny they should start using that word again."

"How did it get started?"

"Popsicle. A popsicle was frozen sherbet on a stick. You licked it off."

I winced at the mental picture that evoked. Leviticus Hale, covered with frost, a stake up his anus, a gigantic tongue—

"A *wooden* stick." Garner had a grin to scare babies. Grinning, he was almost a work of art: an antique, a hundred and eighty-odd years old, like a Hannes Bok illustration of Lovecraft. "That's how long ago it was. They didn't start freezing people until the nineteen sixties or seventies, but we were still putting wooden sticks in popsicles. Why would anyone use it now?"

"Who uses it? Newscasters? I don't watch the boob cube much."

"Newscasters, yah, and lawyers . . . How are you making out on the Committees to Oppose the Second Freezer Bill?"

It took me a moment to make the switch. "No positive results. The program's still running, and results are slow in some parts of the world, Africa, the Middle East. . . . They all seem to be solid citizens."

"Well, it's worth a try. We've been looking into the other side of it, too. If organleggers are trying to block the Second Freezer Bill, they might well try to intimidate or kill off anyone who *backs* the Second Freezer Bill. Follow me?"

"I suppose."

"So we have to know who to protect. It's strictly business, of course. The ARM isn't supposed to get involved in politics."

Garner reached sideways to tap one-handed at the computer keyboard in his desk. His bulky floating chair wouldn't fit under the keyboard. Tape slid from the slot, two feet of it. He handed it to me.

"Mostly lawyers," he said. "A number of sociologists and humanities professors. Religious leaders pushing their own brand of immortality; we've got religious factions on both sides of the question. These are the people who publicly back the Second Freezer Bill. I'd guess they're the ones who started using the word *corpsicle*."

"Thanks."

"Cute word, isn't it? A joke. If you said *frozen sleep* someone might take you seriously. Someone might even wonder if they were really dead. Which is the key question, isn't it? The corpsicles they want are the ones who were healthiest, the ones who have the best chance of being brought back to life someday. These are the people they want revived a piece at a time. By me that's lousy."

"Me too." I glanced down at the list. "I presume you haven't actually warned any of these people."

"No, you idiot. They'd go straight to a newscaster and tell him that all their opponents are organleggers."

I nodded. "Thanks for the help. If anything comes of this—"

"Sit down. Run your eyes down those names. See if you spot anything."

I didn't know most of them, of course, not even in the Americas. There were a few prominent defense lawyers, and at least one federal judge, and Raymond Sinclair the physicist, and a string of newscast stations, and—"Clark and Nash? An advertising firm?"

"A number of advertising firms in a number of countries. Most of these people are probably sincere enough, and they'll talk to *anyone,* but the coverage has to come from somewhere. It's coming from these firms. That word *corpsicle has* to be an advertising stunt. The publicity on the corpsicle heirs: they may have had a hand in that too. You know about the corpsicle heirs?"

"Not a lot."

"NBA Broadcasting has been running down the heirs to the richest members of Group II, the ones who were committed to the Freezer Vaults for reasons that don't harm their value as—stuff." Garner spat the word. It was organ-legger slang. "The paupers all went into the organ banks on the first Freezer Law, of course, so Group II boasts some considerable wealth. NBA found a few heirs who would never have turned up otherwise. I imagine a lot of them will be voting for the Second Freezer Bill—"

"Yah."

"Only the top dozen have been getting the publicity. But it's still a powerful argument, isn't it? If the corpsicles are in frozen sleep, that's one thing. If they're *dead,* then people are being denied their rightful inheritance."

I asked the obvious question. "Who's paying for the advertising?"

"Now, we wondered about that. The firms wouldn't say. We dug a little further."

"And?"

"They don't know either." Garner grinned like Satan. "They were hired by firms that aren't listed anywhere. A number of firms, whose representatives only appeared once. They paid their fees in lump sums."

"It sounds like—no. They're on the wrong side."

"Right. Why would an organlegger be *pushing* the Second Freezer Bill?"

I thought it over. "How about this? A number of old, sickly, wealthy men and women set up a fund to see to it that the public supply of spare parts isn't threatened. It's legal, at least; which dealing with an organlegger isn't. With enough of them it might even be cheaper."

"We thought of that. We're running a program on it. I've even been asking some subtle questions around the Struldbrugs' Club, just because I'm a member. It has to be subtle. Legal it may be, but they wouldn't want publicity."

"No."

"And then I got your report this morning. Anubis and the Chambers kid, huh? Wouldn't it be nice if it went a bit further than that?"

"I don't follow you."

At this moment Garner looked like something that was ready to pounce. "Wouldn't it be wonderful if a federation of organleggers was backing the Second Freezer Bill. The idea would be to kidnap *all* of the top corpsicle heirs *just before the bill passes*. Most people worth kidnapping can afford to protect themselves. Guards, house alarms, wrist alarms. A corpsicle heir can't do that yet."

Garner leaned forward in his chair, doing the work with his arms. "If we could prove this, and give it some publicity, wouldn't it shoot hell out of the Second Freezer Law?"

There was a memo on my desk when I got back. The data package on Holden Chambers was in the computer memory, waiting for me. I remembered that Holden himself would be here this afternoon, unless the arm trick had scared him off.

I punched for the package and read it through, trying to decide just how sane the kid was. Most of the information had come from the college medical center. They'd been worried about him too.

The kidnapping had interrupted his freshman year at Washburn. His grades had dropped sharply afterward, then sloped back to a marginal passing grade. In September he'd changed his major from architecture to biochemistry. He'd made the switch easily. His grades had been average or better during these last two years.

He lived alone, in one of those tiny apartments whose furnishings are all memory plastic, extruded as needed. Technology was cheaper than elbow room. The apartment house did have some communal facilities, sauna, pool, cleaning robots, party room, room-service kitchen, clothing dispensary. . . . I wondered why he didn't get a roommate. It would have saved him money, for one thing. But his sex life had always been somewhat passive, and he'd never been gregarious, according to the file. He'd just about pulled the hole in after him for some months after the kidnapping. As if he'd lost all faith in humanity.

If he'd been off the beam then, he seemed to have recovered. Even his sex life had improved. That information had not come from the college medical center, but from records from the communal kitchen (breakfast for two, late night room service), and some recent recorded phone messages. All quite public; there was no reason for me to be feeling like a peeping Tom. The publicity on the corpsicle heirs may have done him some good, started girls chasing him for a change. A few had spent the night, but he didn't seem to be seeing anyone steadily.

I had wondered how he could afford a servant. The answer made me feel stupid. The secretary named Zero turned out to be a computer construct, an answering service.

Chambers was not penniless. After the ransom was paid, the trust fund had contained about twenty thousand marks. Charlotte's care had eaten into that. The trustees were giving Holden enough to pay his tuition and still live comfortably. There would be some left when he graduated, but it would be earmarked for Charlotte.

I turned off the screen and thought about it. He'd had a jolt. He'd recovered. Some do, some don't. He'd been in perfect health, which has a lot to do with surviving emotional shock. If he was your friend today, you would avoid certain subjects in his presence.

And he'd thrown himself backward in blind terror when a pencil rose from his desk and started to pinwheel. How normal was that? I just didn't know. I was too used to my imaginary arm.

Anthony Tiller was in a cold box, face up. That face had been hideously contorted during his last minutes, but it showed none of that now. He was as expressionless as any dead man. The frozen sleepers at the Vault of Eternity had looked like that. Superficially, most of them had been in worse shape than he was.

Holden Chambers studied him with interest. "So that's what an organlegger looks like."

"An organlegger looks like anything he wants to."

He grimaced at that. He bent close to study the dead man's face. He circled the cold box with his hands clasped behind his back. He wanted to look nonchalant, but he was still walking wide of me. I didn't think the dead man bothered him.

He said the same thing I'd said two nights ago. "Nope. Not with that face."

"Well, it was worth a try. Let's go to my office. It's more comfortable."

He smiled. "Good."

He dawdled in the corridors. He looked into open offices, smiled at anyone who looked up, asked me mostly intelligent questions in a low voice. He was enjoying himself: a tourist in ARM Headquarters. But he trailed back when I tried to take the middle of the corridor, so that we wound up walking on opposite sides. Finally I asked him about it.

I thought he wasn't going to answer. Then, "It was that pencil trick."

"What about it?"

He sighed, as one who despairs of ever finding the right words. "I don't like to be touched. I mean, I get along with girls all right, but generally I don't like to be touched."

"I didn't—"

"But you *could* have. And without my *knowing*. I couldn't see it, I might not even feel it. It just bothered the censored hell out of me, you reaching out of a phone screen like that! A phone call isn't supposed to be that, that *personal*." He stopped suddenly, looking down the corridor. "Isn't that Lucas Garner?"

"Yah."

"Lucas Garner!" He was awed and delighted. "He runs it all, doesn't he? How old is he now?"

"In his hundred and eighties." I thought of introducing him, but Luke's chair slid off in a different direction.

My office is just big enough for me, my desk, two chairs, and an array of spigots in the wall. I poured him tea and me coffee. I said, "I went to visit your sister."

"Charlotte? How is she?"

"I doubt she's changed since the last time you saw her. She doesn't notice anything around her . . . except for one incident, when she turned around and stared at me."

"Why? What did you do? What did you say?" he demanded.

Well, here it came. "I was telling her doctor that the same gang that kidnapped her once might want her again."

Strange things happened around his mouth. Bewilderment, fear, disbelief. "What the bleep made you say that?"

"It's a possibility. You're both corpiscle heirs. Tiller the Killer could have been watching you when he spotted *me* watching you. He couldn't have that."

"No, I suppose not. . . ." He was trying to take it lightly, and he failed. "Do you seriously think they might want me—us—again?"

"It's a possibility," I repeated. "If Tiller was inside the restaurant, he could have spotted me by my floating cigarette. It's more distinctive than my face. Don't look so worried. We've got a tracer on you, we could track him anywhere he took you."

"In me?" He didn't like that much better—too personal?—but he didn't make an issue of it.

"Holden, I keep wondering what they could have done to your sister—"

He interrupted, coldly. "I stopped wondering that, long ago."

"—that they didn't do to you. It's more than curiosity. If the doctors knew what was done to her, if they knew what it is in her memory—"

"Dammit! Don't you think I want to help her? She's my sister!"

"All right." What was I playing psychiatrist for, anyway? Or was it detective I was playing? He didn't know anything. He was at the eye of several storms at once, and he must be getting sick and tired of it. I ought to send him home.

He spoke first. I could barely hear him. "You know what they did to me? A nerve block at the neck. A little widget taped to the back of my neck with surgical skin. I couldn't feel anything below the neck, and I couldn't move. They put that on me, dumped me on a bed and left me. For nine days. Every so often they'd turn me on again and let me drink and eat something and go to the bathroom."

"Did anyone tell you they'd break you up for stuff if they didn't get the ransom?"

He thought about it. "N-no. I could pretty well guess it. They never said anything to me at all. They treated me like I was dead. They examined me for, oh, it felt like hours, poking and prodding me with their hands and their instruments, rolling me around like dead meat. I couldn't feel any of it, but I could see it all. If they did that to Charlotte . . . maybe she thinks she's dead." His voice rose. "I've been through this again and again, with the ARMs, with Doctor Hartman, with the Washburn medical staff. Let's drop it, shall we?"

"Sure. I'm sorry. We don't learn tact in this business. We learn to ask questions. Any question."

And yet, and yet, the look on her face.

I asked him one more question as I was escorting him out. Almost offhandedly. "What do you think of the Second Freezer Bill?"

"I don't have a UN vote yet."

"That's not what I asked."

He faced me belligerently. "Look, there's a lot of money involved. A *lot* of money. It would pay for Charlotte the rest of her life. It would fix my face. But Hale, Leviticus Hale—" He pronounced the name accurately, and with no flicker of a smile. "He's a relative, isn't he? My great-to-the-third-grandfather. They could bring him back someday; it's possible. So what do I do? If I had a vote, I'd have to decide. But I'm not twenty-five yet, so I don't have to worry about it."

"Interviews."

"I don't give interviews. You just got the same answer everyone else gets. It's on tape, on file with Zero. Goodby, Mister Hamilton."

Other ARM departments had thinned our ranks during the lull following the Freezer Law. Over the next couple of weeks they began to trickle back. We needed operatives to implant tracers in unsuspecting victims and to monitor their welfare afterward. We needed an augmented staff to follow their tracer blips on the screens downstairs.

We were sore tempted to tell all of the corpsicle heirs what was happening, and have them check in with us at regular intervals. Say, every fifteen minutes. It would have made things much easier. It might also have influenced their votes, altered the quality of the interviews they gave out.

But we didn't want to alert our quarry, the still-hypothetical coalition of organleggers now monitoring the same corpsicle heirs we were interested in. And the backlash vote would be ferocious if we were wrong. And we weren't supposed to be interested in politics.

We operated without the knowledge of the corpsicle heirs. There were two thousand of them in all parts of the world, almost three hundred in the western United States, with an expected legacy of 50,000 UN marks or more—a limit we set for our own convenience, because it was about all we could handle.

One thing helped the manpower situation. We had reached another lull. Missing persons complaints had dropped to near zero, all over the world.

"We should have been expecting that," Bera commented. "For the last year or so most of their customers must have stopped going to organleggers. They're waiting to see if the Second Freezer Bill will go through. Now all the gangs are stuck with full organ banks and no customers. If they learned anything from last time, they'll pull in their horns and wait it out. Of course I'm only guessing—" But it looked likely enough. At any rate, we had the men we needed.

We monitored the top dozen corpsicle heirs twenty-four hours a day. The rest we checked at random intervals. The tracers could only tell us where they were, not who they were with or whether they wanted to be there. We had to keep checking to see if anyone had disappeared.

We sat back to await results.

The Security Council passed the Second Freezer Bill on February 3, 2125. Now it would go to the world vote in late March. The voting public numbered ten billion, of whom perhaps sixty percent would bother to phone in their votes.

I took to watching the boob cube again.

NBA Broadcasting continued its coverage of the corpsicle heirs and its editorials in favor of the Bill. Proponents took every opportunity to point out that many corpsicle heirs still remained to be discovered. (And YOU might be one.) Taffy and I watched a parade in New York in favor of the bill: banners and placards (SAVE THE LIVING, NOT THE DEAD . . . IT'S *YOUR* LIFE AT STAKE . . . CORPSICLES KEEP BEER COLD) and one censored big mob of chanting people. The transportation costs must have been formidable.

The various Committees to Oppose the Bill were also active. In the Americas, they pointed out that, although about forty percent of people in frozen sleep were in the Americas, the spare parts derived would go to the world at large. In Africa and Asia, it was discovered that the Americas had most of the corpsicle heirs. In Egypt, an analogy was made between the pyramids and the freezer vaults: both bids for immortality. It didn't go over well.

Polls indicated that the Chinese sectors would vote against the bill. NBA newscasters spoke of ancestor worship and reminded the public that six ex-chairmen resided in Chinese freezer vaults, alongside myriad lesser ex-officials. Immortality was a respected tradition in China.

The Committees to Oppose reminded the world's voting public that some of the wealthiest of the frozen dead had heirs in the Belt. Were Earth's resources to be spread indiscriminately among the asteroidal rocks? I started to hate both sides. Fortunately the UN cut that line off fast by threatening injunction. Earth needed Belt resources too heavily.

Our own results began to come in.

Mortimer Lincoln, alias Anthony Tiller, had not been at Midgard the night he tried to kill me. He'd eaten alone in his apartment, a meal sent from the communal kitchen. Which meant that he himself could not have been watching Chambers.

We found no sign of anyone lurking behind Holden

Chambers, or behind any of the other corpsicle heirs, pub-
licized or not, with one general exception. Newsmen. The
media were unabashedly and constantly interested in the
corpsicle heirs, priority based on the money they stood to
inherit. We faced a depressing hypothesis: the potential
kidnappers were spending all their time watching the boob
cube, letting the media do their tracking for them. But
perhaps the connection was closer.

We started investigating newscast stations.

In mid-February I pulled Holden Chambers in and had
him examined for an outlaw tracer. It was a move of des-
peration. Organleggers don't use such tools. They special-
ize in medicine. Our own tracer was still working, and it
was the only tracer in him. Chambers was icily angry. We
had interrupted his studying for a mid-term exam.

We managed to search three of the top dozen when they
had medical checkups. Nothing.

Our investigations of the newscast stations turned up
very little. Clark and Nash was running a good many one-
minute spots through NBA. Other advertising firms had
similar lines of possible influence over other stations,
broadcasting companies, and cassette newszines. But we
were looking for newsmen who had popped up from nowhere, with backgrounds forged or nonexistent. Ex-organ-
leggers in new jobs. We didn't find any.

I called Menningers one empty afternoon. Charlotte
Chambers was still catatonic. "I've got Lowndes of New
York working with me," Hartman told me. "He has precisely your voice, and good qualifications too. Charlotte
hasn't responded yet. We've been wondering: could it
have been the *way* you were talking?"

"You mean the accent? It's Kansas with an overlay of
west coast and Belter."

"No, Lowndes has that too. I mean organlegger slang."

"I use it. Bad habit."

"That could be it." He made a face. "But we can't act
on it. It might just scare her completely into herself."

"That's where she is now. I'd risk it."

"You're not a psychiatrist," he said.

I hung up and brooded. Negatives, all negatives.

I didn't hear the hissing sound until it was almost on me. I looked up then, and it was Luke Garner's ground-effect travel chair sliding accurately through the door. He watched me a moment, then said, "What are you looking so grim about?"

"Nothing. All the nothing we've been getting instead of results."

"Uh huh." He let the chair settle. "It's beginning to look like Tiller the Killer wasn't on assignment."

"That would blow the whole thing, wouldn't it? I did a lot of extrapolating from two beams of green light. One ex-organlegger tries to make holes in one ARM agent, and now we've committed tens of thousands of man-hours and seventy or eighty computer-hours on the strength of it. If they'd been planning to tie us up, they couldn't have done it better."

"You know, I think you'd take it as a personal insult if Tiller shot at you just because he didn't like you."

I had to laugh. "How personal can you get?"

"That's better. Now will you stop sweating this? It's just another long shot. You know what legwork is like. We bet a lot of man-effort on this one because the odds looked good. Look how many organleggers would have to be in on it if it were true! We'd have a chance to snaffle them all. But if it doesn't work out, why sweat it?"

"The Second Freezer Bill," I said, as if he didn't know.

"The will of the people be done."

"Censor the people! They're murdering those dead men!"

Garner's face twitched oddly. I said, "What's funny?"

He let the laugh out. It sounded like a chicken screaming for help. *"Censor. Bleep.* They didn't used to be swear words. They were euphemisms. You'd put them in a book or on teevee, when you wanted a word they wouldn't let you use."

I shrugged. "Words are funny. *Damn* used to be a technical term in theology, if you want to look at it that way."

"I know, but they *sound* funny. When you start saying *bleep* and *censored* it ruins your masculine image."

"Censor my masculine image. What do we do about the corpsicle heirs? Call off the surveillance?"

"No. There's too much in the pot already." Garner looked broodingly into one bare wall of my office. "Wouldn't it be nice if we could persuade ten billion people to use prosthetics instead of transplants?"

Guilt glowed in my right arm, my left eye. I said, "Prosthetics don't feel. I might have settled for a prosthetic arm—" dammit, I'd had the choice! "—but an eye? Luke, suppose it was possible to graft new legs on you. Would you take them?"

"Oh, dear, I do wish you hadn't asked me that," he said venomously.

"Sorry. I withdraw the question."

He brooded. It was a lousy thing to ask a man. He was still stuck with it; he couldn't spit it out.

I asked, "Did you have any special reason for dropping in?"

Luke shook himself. "Yah. I got the impression you were taking all this as a personal defeat. I stopped down to cheer you up."

We laughed at each other. "Listen," he said, "there are worse things than the organ bank problem. When I was young—your age, my child—it was almost impossible to get anyone convicted of a capital crime. Life sentences weren't for life. Psychology and psychiatry, such as they were, were concerned with curing criminals, returning them to society. The United States Supreme Court almost voted the death penalty unconstitutional."

"Sounds wonderful. How did it work out?"

"We had an impressive reign of terror. A lot of people got killed. Meanwhile transplant techniques were getting better and better. Eventually Vermont made the organ banks the official means of execution. That idea spread very damn fast."

"Yah." I remembered history courses.

"Now we don't even *have* prisons. The organ banks are always short. As soon as the UN votes the death penalty for a crime, most people stop committing it. Naturally."

"So we get the death penalty for having children without a license, or cheating on income tax, or running too many red traffic lights. Luke, I've seen what it *does* to people to keep voting more and more death penalties. They lose their respect for life."

"But the other situation was just as bad, Gil. Don't forget it."

"So now we've got the death penalty for being poor."

"The Freezer Law? I won't defend it. Except that that's the penalty for being poor and *dead.*"

"Should it be a capital crime?"

"No, but it's not too bright either. If a man expects to be brought back to life, he should be prepared to pay the medical fees. Now, hold it. I know a lot of the pauper groups had trust funds set up. They were wiped out by depressions, bad investments. Why the hell do you think banks take interest for a loan? They're being paid for the *risk.* The risk that the loan won't be paid back."

"Did you vote for the Freezer Law?"

"No, of course not."

"I must be spoiling for a fight. I'm glad you dropped by, Luke."

"Don't mention it."

"I keep thinking the ten billion voters will eventually work their way down to me. Go ahead, grin. Who'd want *your* liver?"

Garner cackled. "Somebody could murder me for my skeleton. Not to put inside him. For a museum."

We left it at that.

The news broke a couple of days later. Several North American hospitals had been reviving corpsicles.

How they had kept the secret was a mystery. Those corpsicles who had survived the treatment—twenty-two of them, out of thirty-five attempts—had been clinically alive for some ten months, conscious for shorter periods.

For the next week it was all the news there was. Taffy and I watched interviews with the dead men, with the doctors, with members of the Security Council. The move was not illegal. As publicity against the Second Freezer Bill, it may have been a mistake.

All of the revived corpsicles had been insane. Else why risk it?

Some of the casualties had died because their insanity was caused by brain damage. The rest were—cured, but only in a biochemical sense. Each had been insane long enough for their doctors to decide that there was no hope. Now they were stranded in a foreign land, their homes forever lost in the mists of time. Revivification had saved them from an ugly, humiliating death at the hands of most of the human race, a fate that smacked of cannibalism and ghouls. The paranoids were hardly surprised. The rest reacted like paranoids.

In the boob cube, they came across as a bunch of frightened mental patients.

One night we watched a string of interviews on the big screen in Taffy's bedroom wall. They weren't well handled. Too much "How do you feel about the wonders of the present?" when the poor boobs hadn't come out of their shells long enough to know or care. Many wouldn't believe anything they were told or shown. Others didn't care about anything but space exploration—a largely Belter activity which Earth's voting public tended to ignore. Too much of it was at the level of this last one: an interviewer explaining to a woman that a boob cube was not a *cube*, that the word referred only to the three-dimensional effect. The poor woman was badly rattled and not too bright in the first place.

Taffy was sitting cross-legged on the bed, combing out her long, dark hair so that it flowed over her shoulders in shining curves. "She's an early one," she said critically. "There may have been oxygen starvation of the brain during freezing."

"That's what *you* see. All the average citizen sees is the way she acts. She's obviously not ready to join society."

"Dammit, Gil, she's *alive*. Shouldn't that be miracle enough for anyone?"

"Maybe. Maybe the average voter liked her better the other way."

Taffy brushed at her hair with angry vigor. "They're *alive*."

"I wonder if they revived Leviticus Hale."

"Leviti— Oh. Not at Saint John's." Taffy worked there. She'd know.

"I haven't seen him in the cube. They should have revived him," I said. "With that patriarchal visage he'd make a *great* impression. He might even try the Messiah bit. 'Yea, brethren, I have returned from the dead to lead you—' None of the others have tried that yet."

"Good thing, too." Her strokes slowed. "A lot of them died in the thawing process, and afterward. From cell wall ruptures."

Ten minutes later I got up and used the phone. Taffy showed her amusement. "Is it that important?"

"Maybe not." I dialed the Vault of Eternity in New Jersey. I knew I'd be wondering until I did.

Mr. Restarick was on night watch. He seemed glad to see me. He'd have been glad to see anyone who would talk back. His clothes were the same mismatch of ancient styles, but they didn't look as anachronistic now as they had a year ago. The boob cube had been lousy with corpsicles wearing approximations of their own styles.

Yes, he remembered me. Yes, Leviticus Hale was still in place. The hospitals had taken two of his wards, and both had survived, he told me proudly. The administrators had wanted Hale too; they'd liked his looks and his publicity value, dating as he did from the last century but one. But they hadn't been able to get permission from the next of kin.

Taffy watched me watching a blank phone screen. "What's wrong?"

"The Chambers kid. Remember Holden Chambers, the corpsicle heir? He lied to me. He refused permission for the hospitals to revive Leviticus Hale. A *year* ago."

"Oh." She thought it over, then reacted with a charity typical of her. "It's a lot of money just for not signing a paper."

The cube was showing an old flick, a remake of a Shakespeare play. We turned it to landscape and went to sleep.

I back away, back away. The composite ghost comes

near, using somebody's arm and somebody's eye and Loren's pleural cavity containing somebody's heart and somebody's lung and somebody's other lung, and I can feel it all inside him with my fingertips. Horrible. I reach deeper. Somebody's heart wiggles in my hand like a caught fish.

Taffy found me in the kitchen making hot chocolate. For two. I know damn well she can't sleep when I'm restless. She said, "Why don't you tell me about it?"

"Because it's ugly."

"I think you'd better tell me." She came into my arms, rubbed her cheek against mine.

I said to her ear, "Get the poison out of my system? Sure, and into yours."

"All right." I could take it either way.

The chocolate was ready. I disengaged myself and poured it, added meager splashes of bourbon. She sipped reflectively. She said, "Is it always Loren?"

"Yah. Damn him."

"Never—this one you're after now?"

"Anubis? I never dealt with him. He was Bera's assignment. Anyway, he retired before I was properly trained. Gave his territory to Loren. The market in stuff was so bad that Loren had to double his territory just to keep going." I was talking too much. I was desperate to talk to someone, to get back my grip on reality. These damn nightmares.

"What did they do, flip a coin?"

"For what? Oh. No, there was never a question about who was going to retire. Loren was a sick man. It must have been why he went into the business. He needed the supply of transplants. And he couldn't get out because he needed constant shots. His rejection spectrum must have been a bad joke. Anubis was different."

She sipped at her chocolate. She shouldn't have to know this, but I couldn't stop talking. "Anubis changed body parts at whim. We'll never get him. He probably made himself over completely when he . . . retired."

Taffy touched my shoulder. "Let's go back to bed."

"All right." But my own voice ran on in my head. *His*

only problem was the money. How could he hide a fortune that size? And the new identity. A new personality with lots of conspicuous money . . . and, if he tried to live somewhere else, a foreign accent too. But there's less privacy here, and he's known. . . . I sipped the chocolate, watching the landscape in the boob cube. *What could he do to make a new identity convincing?* The landscape scene was night on some mountaintop, bare tumbled rock backed by churning clouds. Restful.

I thought of something he could do.

I got out of bed and called Bera.

Taffy watched me in amazement. "It's three in the morning," she pointed out.

"I know."

Lila Bera was sleepy and naked and ready to kill someone. Me. She said, "Gil, it better be good."

"It's good. Tell Jackson I can locate Anubis."

Bera popped up beside her, demanded, "Where?" His hair was miraculously intact, a puffy black dandelion ready to blow. He was squint-eyed and grimacing with sleep, and as naked as . . . as I was, come to that. This thing superseded good manners.

I told him where Anubis was.

I had his attention then. I talked fast, sketching in the intermediate steps. "Does it sound reasonable? I can't tell. It's three in the morning. I may not be thinking right."

Bera ran both hands through his hair, a swift, violent gesture that left his natural in shreds. "Why didn't I think of that? Why didn't *anyone* think of that?"

"The waste. When the stuff from one condemned ax murderer can save a dozen lives, it just doesn't occur to you—"

"Right right right. Skip that. What do we do?"

"Alert Headquarters. Then call Holden Chambers. I may be able to tell just by talking to him. Otherwise we'll have to go over."

"Yah." Bera grinned through the pain of interrupted sleep. "He's not going to like being called at three in the morning."

* * *

The white-haired man informed me that Holden Chambers was not to be disturbed. He was reaching for a (mythical) cutoff switch when I said, "ARM business, life and death," and displayed my ARM ident. He nodded and put me on HOLD.

Very convincing. But he'd gone through some of the same motions every time I'd called.

Chambers appeared, wearing a different minimum kilt. He backed up a few feet (wary of ghostly intrusions?) and sat down on the uneasy edge of a water bed. He rubbed his eyes and said, "Censor it, I was up past midnight studying. What now?"

"You're in danger. Immediate danger. Don't panic, but don't go back to bed either. We're coming over."

"You're kidding." He studied my face in the phone screen. "You're not, are you? Aaall right, I'll put some clothes on. What kind of danger?"

"I can't tell you that. Don't go anywhere."

I called Bera back.

He met me in the lobby. We used his taxi. An ARM ident in the credit slot turns any cab into a police car. Bera said, "Couldn't you tell?"

"No, he was too far back. I had to say *something*, so I warned him not to go anywhere."

"I wonder if that was a good idea."

"It doesn't matter. Anubis only has about fifteen minutes to act, and even then we could follow him."

There was no immediate answer to our ring. Maybe he was surprised to see us outside his door. Ordinarily you can't get into the parking-roof elevator unless a tenant lets you in; but an ARM ident unlocks most doors.

Bera's patience snapped. "I think he's gone. We'd better call—"

Chambers opened the door. "All right, what's it all about? Come—" He saw our guns.

Bera hit the door hard and branched right; I branched left. Those tiny apartments don't have many places to hide. The water bed was gone, replaced by an L-shaped couch and coffee table. There was nothing behind the couch. I covered the bathroom while Bera kicked the door open.

Nobody here but us. Chambers lost his astonished look, smiled and clapped for us. I bowed.

"You *must* have been serious," he said. "What kind of danger? Couldn't it have waited for morning?"

"Yah, but I couldn't have slept," I said, coming toward him. "I'm going to owe you a big fat apology if this doesn't work out."

He backed away.

"Hold still. This will only take a second." I advanced on him. Bera was behind him now. He hadn't hurried. His long legs give him deceptive speed.

Chambers backed away, backed away, backed into Bera and squeaked in surprise. He dithered, then made a break for the bathroom.

Bera reached out, wrapped one arm around Chambers' waist and pinned his arms with the other. Chambers struggled like a madman. I stepped wide around them, moved in sideways to avoid Chambers' thrashing legs, reached out to touch his face with my imaginary hand.

He froze. Then he screamed.

And if I was wrong, it was going to be embarrassing. But it all fitted: the very noticeable frozen body of Leviticus Hale, Anubis' very noticeable fortune and plethora of unsaleable transplant stocks, the cigarette trick, the man with the hunting laser, and Chambers' terror. "That's what you were afraid of," I told him. "You never dreamed I could reach through a phone screen and do *this*."

I reached into his head. I felt smooth muscle and grainy bone and sinus cavities like bubbles. He tossed his head, but my hand went with it. I ran imaginary fingertips along the smooth inner surface of his skull.

It was there. A ridge of scar, barely raised above the rest of the bone, too fine for X-rays. It ran in a closed curve from the base of his skull up through the temples to intersect his eye sockets.

"It's him," I said.

Bera screamed in his ear. "You pig!"

Anubis went limp.

"I can't find a joining at the brain stem. They must have transplanted the spinal cord too: the whole central nervous system." I found scars along the vertebrae. "That's what they did, all right."

Anubis spoke almost casually, as if he'd lost a chess game. "All right, that's a gotcha. I concede. Let's sit down."

"Sure." Bera threw him at the couch. He hit it, more or less. He adjusted himself, looking astonished at Bera's bad behavior. What was the man so excited about?

Bera told him. "You pig. *Coring* him like that, making a *vehicle* out of the poor bastard. We never thought of a brain transplant."

"It's a wonder I thought of it myself. The stuff from one donor is worth over a million marks in surgery charges. Why should anyone use a whole prospect for one transplant? But once I thought of it, it made all kinds of sense. The stuff wasn't selling anyway."

Funny: they both talked as if they'd known each other a long time. There aren't many people an organlegger will regard as *people,* but an ARM is one of them. We're organleggers too, in a sense.

Bera was holding a sonic on him. Anubis ignored it. He said, "The only problem was the money."

"Then you thought of the corpsicle heirs," I said.

"Yah. I went looking for a rich corpsicle with a young, healthy, direct-line heir. Leviticus Hale seemed made for the part. He was the first one I noticed."

"He's pretty noticeable, isn't he? A healthy middle-aged man sleeping there among all those battered accident cases. Only two heirs, both orphans, one kind of introverted, the other . . . What did you do to Charlotte?"

"Charlotte Chambers? We drove her mad. We had to. She was the only one who'd notice if Holden Chambers suddenly got too different."

"What did you *do* to her?"

"We made a wirehead out of her."

"The hell. Someone would have noticed the contact in her scalp."

"No, no, no. We used one of those helmets you find in the ecstasy shops. It stimulates a current in the pleasure center of the brain, by induction, so a customer can try it out before the peddler actually drops the wire into his brain. We kept her in the helmet for nine days, on full. When we stopped the current, she just wasn't interested in anything anymore."

"How did you know it would work?"

"Oh, we tried it out on a few prospects. It worked fine. It didn't hurt them after they were broken up."

"Okay." I went to the phone and dialed ARM Headquarters.

"It solved the money problem beautifully," he ran on. "I plowed most of it into advertising charges. And there's nothing suspicious about Leviticus Hale's money. When the Second Freezer Bill goes through—well, I guess not. Not now. Unless—"

"No," Bera said for both of us.

I told the man on duty where we were, and to stop monitoring the tracers, and to call in the operatives watching corpsicle heirs. Then I hung up.

"I spent six months studying Chambers' college courses. I didn't want to blow his career. Six months! Answer me one," said Anubis, curiously anxious. "Where did I go wrong? What gave me away?"

"You were beautiful," I told him wearily. "You never went out of character. You should have been an actor. Would have been safer, too. We didn't suspect anything until—" I looked at my watch. "Forty-five minutes ago."

"Censored dammit! You would say that. When I saw you looking at me in Midgard I thought that was it. That floating cigarette. You'd got Loren, now you were after me."

I couldn't help it. I roared. Anubis sat there, taking it. He was beginning to blush.

They were shouting something, something I couldn't make out. Something with a beat. *DAdadadaDAdadada . . .*

There was just room for me and Jackson Bera and

Luke Garner's travel chair on the tiny balcony outside Garner's office. Far below, the marchers flowed past the ARM building in half-orderly procession. Teams of them carried huge banners. LET THEM STAY DEAD, one suggested; and another in small print: why not revive them a bit at a time? FOR YOUR FATHER'S SAKE, a third said with deadly logic.

They were roped off from the spectators, roped off into a column down the middle of Wilshire. The spectators were even thicker. It looked like all of Los Angeles had turned out to watch. Some of them carried placards too. THEY WANT TO LIVE TOO, and ARE YOU A FREEZER VAULT HEIR?

"What is it they're shouting?" Bera wondered. "It's not the marchers, it's the spectators. They're drowning out the marchers."

DAdadadaDAdadadaDAdadada, it rippled up to us on stray wind currents.

"We could see it better inside, in the boob cube," Garner said without moving. What held us was a metaphysical force, the knowledge that one is *there,* a witness. Abruptly Garner asked, "How's Charlotte Chambers?"

"I don't know." I didn't want to talk about it.

"Didn't you call Menninger Institute this morning?"

"I mean I don't know how to take it. They've done a wirehead operation on her. They're giving her just enough current to keep her interested. It's *working,* I mean she's *talking* to people, but . . ."

"It's got to be better than being catatonic," Bera said.

"Does it? There's no way to turn off a wirehead. She'll have to go through life with a battery under her hat. When she comes back far enough into the real world, she'll find a way to boost the current and bug right out again."

"Think of her as walking wounded." Bera shrugged, shifting an invisible weight on his shoulders. "There *isn't* any good answer. She's been *hurt,* man!"

"There's more to it than that," said Luke Garner. "We need to know if she can be cured. There are more wireheads every day. It's a new vice. We need to learn how to control it. What the bleep is happening down there?"

The bystanders were surging against the ropes. Suddenly they were through in a dozen places, converging on the marchers. It was a swirling mob scene. They were still chanting, and suddenly I caught it.

ORganleggersORganleggersORganleggers . . .

"That's it!" Bera shouted in pleased surprise. "Anubis is getting too much publicity. It's good versus evil!"

The rioters started to collapse in curved ribbon patterns. Copters overhead were spraying them with sonic stun cannon.

Bera said, "They'll never pass the Second Freezer Bill now."

Never is a long time to Luke Garner. He said, "Not this time, anyway. We ought to start thinking about that. A lot of people have been applying for operations at the legitimate hospitals. There's quite a waiting list. When the Second Freezer Bill fails—"

I saw it. "They'll start going to organleggers. We can keep track of them. Tracers."

"That's what I had in mind."

AN INFINITY OF LOVING
by
David Gerrold

Once she surprised him in the shower by climbing in with him.

Once he surprised her with a spray can of shaving lather, and they made love, laughing in the foam.

Once they sat and looked at each other across the dinner table and forgot to eat.

Once she leaned over to him and kissed him gently on the eyelids.

Once they went swimming at three in the morning without bathing suits, and after they had dried each other off, they fell asleep in each other's arms.

Or, to put it another way, they were in love. Young and in love.

And in that, they were lucky, for consider the odds against it: consider, for instance, how slim the chances were that (a) this particular boy should meet (b) this particular girl in (c) this particular place and at (d) this particular time; and most important of all, (e), that each should be in a receptive state of mind, allowing them to respond favorably to each other.

Consider the alternate possibilities: suppose he had stopped at the post office first; he would have arrived at the laundromat ten minutes after she had already left. Or suppose he had remembered for once to bring change, or that the change machine was not out of order; he would have had no reason to speak to her.

And consider: if she had not had trouble with her car that morning, necessitating a hasty call to the Automobile Club emergency road service, she would have already been finished with most of her chores, including her laundry. Or, if she had not just cashed a check that afternoon, she would not have had the change he asked for. Or, if her period had come just a day later, she would not have been in any kind of a mood to respond to him.

Or consider what factors went into his choice of that particular laundromat, or her choice of that particular college to attend, or his choice of that particular city to live in. Or consider the factors that allowed them both to be born in circumstances that were neither chronologically nor geographically opposed to their meeting and falling in love.

Consider, most of all, the mere fact that he should so delight in her and be able to delight her in return—that special sense of attraction, which each held for the other, and that special sense of sharing, which enveloped them both.

Consider the fact that they *fitted*. Consider how lucky they were.

Of course, if it were not these two individuals meeting, then perhaps it would have been some other combination. There might have been some other girl that he could have loved as thoroughly; there might have been some other man that she could have loved so completely—but there wasn't. There was he and there was she and there was each other.

An individual is unique, existing only once and never again duplicated—a special flicker of personality that flashes briefly in the long darkness of nonexistence, glowing with its own particular radiance only for a bit before vanishing back into the nothingness. That *this* individual and *that* individual should both flicker into existence at just the right time and just the right place—well, that was a source of delight and amazement and continual surprise to both of them.

It was the fact that they were so right for each other, the fact that they fitted so well; they could not believe how lucky they were.

And lucky they were indeed. After all, consider how many people there are who never really will know what it is to love.

This love was a good love. It was honest, it was true—and best of all, there were no hooks in it. It existed not because it had to, but because it wanted to. For once, want and need were the same thing.

It was a beautiful love.

That they were young and attractive only enhanced its beauty, but if they had not been so favored, it still would have been beautiful.

Consider the great variety of possible human couplings that this could have been:

He old and she young.

She old and he young.

He black and she white.

She black and he white.

He born a female and she a male.

Or both born as males.

Or both as females.

Or one of them deformed. Or crippled, or retarded.

Consider the infinite number of combinations. Had it been any of these, it still wouldn't have lessened the beauty of what they shared. It would have only made it more difficult for others to comprehend.

But this was the ideal combination—easy to understand—easier still to be envious of.

He was handsome—a face not chiseled, but sculptured as in fine wood; clear skin, even features, short nose, brown hair and hints of lighter blond, and eyes so deeply blue that they were luminous.

Yes, he was slightly vain about his features—and his body too, which was adequate though not as immediately striking. He was trim, not skinny, but neither well muscled. He was strong and beautiful in his own altogether way.

He had confidence in himself, he had a voice like soft velvet, and he had a mind that concerned itself with its surroundings. He acted upon life almost as much as it acted upon him.

That he had been favored by fate was apparent. He had been favored more than anybody had any right to be. He knew it and he was pleased by it; he had become accustomed to things working the way he expected.

And that was his biggest fault.

She—ah, yes—she had hair so red it glowed like silk in the sunlight, eyes so green (blue-green really) they flared like jewels, deep and mysterious. Her skin was so wonderfully fair that she wore little or no make-up at all, and she seemed to glow from within.

She was afraid of the world—just a little bit—and its complexity. There were things out there that were hostile; they could hurt her if she was careless, so she admired him because of his self-confidence and his ability to do all those things she couldn't; her eyes showed it. And because she worshiped him so, she delighted in doing things for him that he couldn't; things that she could do, things that would let her fill in the gaps, and together the two of them could be as one.

To her, he was almost too good to be true; she watched him shamelessly, undressing and caressing him with her eyes.

And he, he realized this—and he couldn't believe it. That any girl/woman could so thoroughly immerse herself in his life was an overpowering joy; it was a confirmation that there was indeed something *lovable* in him. It was what he needed to be complete.

She was too good to lose—indeed too good to ever risk hurting. He went out of his way to do little things for her. And those little things made her love him even more.

One can't be loved until one is first lovable—and that each loved the other so much made them both more lovable. And that in turn made each more loving.

So they opened themselves to each other. He opened himself for the first time and so did she; they plunged headlong into sharing and confessed their secret fears, expunged their private hurts and traded their mutual fantasies.

Because he trusted her so fully, because she trusted him, because of what they shared together, they were creative in their lovemaking—and that very creativeness (which would have shocked them in any other partner) delighted/teased/pleased them to even greater heights. They were curious about each other's bodies, and they satisfied that curiosity; they wanted to delight each other, and they did that too. They moved and touched with a joyous laughing lust.

And finally, came that moment

She whispered, "I feel like I'm on the edge of death . . ." That ultimate ecstasy, when emotions become too great to be expressed, when words alone can't control the joy, can't communicate it—that point even beyond gasps and giggles when only tears can release the overpowering intensity of happiness.

"I don't believe it," she sobbed. "I'm so happy, I'm crying." She could hardly get the words out.

He couldn't answer her, because he was crying too. He held her tight, and they cried together, and they laughed at the silliness of it all, and their tears mingled on each other's cheeks.

The next time they cried it was for a different reason.

A left front tire had blown out while traveling at seventy miles an hour in the far left lane of the freeway. The car had lurched—swerved, skidded, bumpety-bump—screeched across three lanes, narrowly missing a pickup truck.

A maniacal cultist and his band of followers massacred seven people in a suburban home.

The police fired into a crowd of demonstrating students, killing three of them.

A famous rock star died of an accidental overdose of drugs, and a week later, a presidential candidate was assassinated.

Perhaps the two of them had been directly touched by some of these incidents, perhaps not—it didn't make much difference. The times were such that no one could long ignore the one recurring fact of human fragility—that *all* men are perpetually on the edge of death.

It touched him, how close he was to death, how close they both were. Suppose that pickup truck had been just a little faster. Suppose they had been visiting in Laurel Canyon. Suppose they had turned out for the demonstration—or even for the political rally. How close would the bullet have come?

So he cried at the unfairness of it all. Trapped in life, they were thus condemned to death. The dreadful inevitability of it chilled his flesh and made him unable to speak.

She asked him what was the matter and he said, "I can't explain, I can't say—"

"Is it something I've done, oh dearest, please let me share your tears."

He shook his head no, but she kept asking; so at last he whispered, "It's death—I'm afraid of it."

"Oh, no, no—" She tried to deny it. "Death isn't to be feared. It's to be accepted."

"I know, I know—but it's not just my own death I fear —it's the death of us. The death of our love."

And at that, she felt the chill, although she did not yet know why she should feel so.

"We're two people," he explained. "Two. Sooner or later, one of us will die and the other will be alone. And I can't bear that thought. I can't bear the thought of me without you—or the thought of you without me. I don't want to hurt you—ever." And he cried again, great heaving sobs.

She cried too, for she could not stand to see him in such sorrow.

Perhaps it was a foolish thing to cry over. Perhaps not. The terrible part about love is that it is always doomed. Always. Even if it should last a lifetime, it has to end with death.

At last she kissed away his tears and whispered, "But my love—that's what makes it so precious. Because it's so impermanent. Because it can only happen once."

He lay there and looked at her, but said nothing.

She said, "What we must be happy about is that we have each other now, that we have this happiness, and that nobody will ever be able to take it away from us. This love is ours."

"But it's not, it's not," he insisted. "It's only for a little while—and then time, that damnable thief, will steal it from us." The tears were streaked on his face. "It's not enough. Why couldn't it last forever? Why shouldn't it? Why should we have to grow old? Will I still love you after years of watching your beautiful body decay? Will you still love me when I'm withered and wasted? Will we learn to hate each other because the familiar actions will have become so boring that they're contemptuous? Will death be only a blessed release from a painful binding? Or will it be a parting that—that destroys us?" His voice caught suddenly. "We could die tomorrow—either one of us, or both," he realized. "An accident could rob us of our future, we could be cheated even of that. Oh, I love you, but we're doomed to sorrow!" And then the tears flowed again, because in the night, alone, with only the two of them in that big bed, with only each other, forever seemed like such an incredible vastness, a long long emptiness—

How lucky it was that the two of them should have found each other, when all the other possibilities were just as likely. How lucky that both of them should be so right for each other.

They both cried that night, in each other's arms.

They were young, and the young are always slightly foolish. It gives a flavor of whimsy and zest to their lovemaking, which the old can only remember and envy. There was an innocence and naiveté that only the young and the young at heart can experience.

But always after that night, that one eternal and aware night, always it seemed as if their lovemaking had an air of urgency about it—as if this might be the last time that they would hold each other, the last time that they would be able to look longingly into each other's eyes and be immersed in that beautiful intensity of emotion.

They were so very much in love.

There was an alternative to sorrow.

And in that they were lucky too. For this was the age when the secret had been unlocked, and the answer was there for the asking.

He brought up the subject first. She was hesitant, a bit scared—and very cautious. "Is it dangerous?"

"No," he reassured her. "And it will bring us even closer together. The intensity of our love will never die out."

She wanted to—because he wanted to, and she wanted to please him. Then, as she listened and studied, she came to understand what was required and what would happen —and she began to want it for herself too. She realized his reasons for wanting to take the step, and she began to feel the same. It would let her love him even more intensely— and forever.

So she said yes. Her reasons were selfish. So were his. They both wanted to preserve something delicate, something flowering. They wanted to freeze that perfect penultimate moment and stretch it from here to infinity.

Wide-eyed and innocent, they were *too* much in love.

* * *

What happened was this: first they gave her sodium pentothal to put her to sleep. Then, after she had fallen asleep, they gave her another anesthetic, a local one; they lowered her body temperature and put her in an ice bath. They shaved part of her head and peeled back a portion of her scalp. Carefully, they cut a hole in her skull. And they implanted a device.

It was a thing of colloidal plastics; it had been grown layer by layer in a process that was part photographic etching, part chemical engineering, and overall somehow akin to organic growth. The device was powered by ions that it took from the red blood cells which pass through it, and it modified the electrical impulses of the brain to which it was attached. One of the output leads went directly to the pleasure center.

They sewed up her skull, and they brought her temperature back to normal, and they then wheeled her into the recovery room.

Then they did the same thing to him.

The devices were identical in function. They were little computers with dual-coded transceivers tuned to each other; each one took information from certain sections of the brain. Each one had outputs to certain others, notably the pleasure center. The devices were two halves of the same circuit; they gathered information, they coded it, and they exchanged it.

The effect on the lovers was telepathic—no, *empathic*. The tiny plastic monitors tuned them to each other's rhythms, made them incomplete without each other.

There were adjustments to be made, of course. Her glandular rhythms were not the same as his; his emotional cycles were not always compatible with hers. Sometimes they had headaches.

When this happened, they had to go back to the doctors. The master computer would be patched into their circuit, and the problems would be analyzed. The big machine knew their special code frequencies, and it could reprogram each device into more careful alignment with the other.

This process of reprogramming and adjustment went on for many months. But they didn't mind; their love was total. It was ecstasy unlimited. They were closer together than they had ever been before.

Now they were tuned to each other. They were ready to take the next step.

They returned to the doctors, and they were strapped to tables. Needles were put into their arms and into their legs. Plastic tubes fed into their lungs and into their bladders. Wires were connected to their heads and to various parts of their bodies. But they knew nothing of this, for they had already fallen asleep. . . .

Asleep. In a timeless world of light and color, modeled in music and structure too complex to follow. It was a fluorescent world of yes and no, of existences and nonexistences, intense glowing planes against ultimate blackness, references without textures—had there been eyes to see it, they would have slid maddeningly across the glimmering surfaces. The colors swirled and changed. Somewhere a monitor circuit triggered, and somewhere else, another circuit began the laborious process of uniting the two entities as one.

The bodies breathed. Regularly. Slowly. With a steadiness that no human impulse could have originated. The chemical balances were perfect; they had to be for the machines to function. Bit by bit, two souls were joining; two flickering consciousnesses were becoming closer than any two had ever been before.

He was becoming she, and she was becoming he. They would be one person sharing two bodies—and if these two bodies died, they would exist without them in the mind of the computer, or they would find new bodies. But the important thing was that they would never be apart.

Never.

A single tear welled up in his right eye. A matching tear appeared in her left.

A technician noticed and wiped them away, but whether they were tears of joy or unhappiness, no one would ever know but these two.

Long after the adventure had been forgotten, long after their bodies and the bodies of the doctors who had ministered to them had crumbled into dust, they still endured; the two of them lived as the flux of patterns within a mighty complex; their existences were fantastically more varied than any living human being could have conceived. Their wonder was bright and their love was intense and endless.

They were not alone. There were others, hundreds, thousands, millions of others, all of whom had chosen not to die, but to live on in this curious glittering web. But these two were special—not because they were among the first, but because they were curiously different from the rest.

"For one thing," explained a master technician to his apprentices in a far-removed century, "these two patterns are identical. They act, react, and respond in unison to every imaginable impulse or set of impulses. For that reason, we're sure that they're only monitor patterns maintained in the matrix as a control for all the other patterns. Certainly, it would make no sense to duplicate any single individual this way; there's no purpose for it—but there is a purpose for monitors and self-comparison controls. This year we expect to add at least three million patterns to the hereafter matrices. We have to keep our transmissions errors below one in every one billion bits. That's why these monitor patterns are so important.

"One of the first things you learned in information theory is that information held in storage tends to decay; but the whole purpose of the hereafter matrices is to prevent decay of the personality patterns of the individuals within. We use these two monitor patterns for that purpose. . . ."

The master technician droned on, lost in his lesson and unaware of the vast changes that had come about in the world; he was only a victim of it too, not a master.

He perceived himself as a floating silver sphere; that was his identity module, a sensory device which did his traveling for him. The students were lesser modules, colored to show their status and identity. The bodies, if any, were removed elsewhere, floating in weightless tanks of nutrients.

The interface between man and machine had become so total that it no longer existed—man and machine were two parts of the same entity, a vast many-faceted being. The range of possible experience for the human mind had become unlimited.

This was a world where sex was an electronic experience, programmed for maximum impact. Love was unnecessary. This was a world where electronic telepathy allowed all minds to be one. Love was a perversion. This was a world where bodies were only inefficient storage units to be replaced as soon as possible. Love was a psychosis. Physical coupling no longer existed, mental coupling had been forgotten, and pair bonding was an unknown process.

In his glorious reach for godhood, man had been liberated from his body; and with it, he had been liberated from all the bloody-animal experiences that went with it. Love was unknown.

"But these are human patterns, aren't they?" asked an apprentice. "Aren't they aware?"

"They're *pseudo*-human patterns," corrected the master. "But I understand what you're asking. Yes, they're aware—but it's a theta-two awareness, a false awareness. Originally, these two patterns had been tied together with a comparison and correction circuit—that is, they monitored each other and adjusted continually. But we eliminated that centuries ago, and also removed some of the memory inconsistencies, which had been allowed to appear in each. We couldn't erase the crystals completely, of course, but we could reprogram them. Now, instead of each pattern looking at the other, they look only at themselves, and each thinks it's seeing its opposite number. So you see, they aren't *really* aware at all—and even if they were, they wouldn't mind. After all, they're happy, aren't they?"

A TRUE BILL
A CHANCEL DRAMA IN ONE ACT
by
James Blish

Preface

(As its subtitle indicates, this play is intended to be performed in a Christian church, not on stage. For best effect, it should be a substitute for a regular service, without prior warning to the congregation (except, perhaps, posting its title as if it were to be the subject of the day's sermon). For this reason, the actors who join in from the floor should not be heavily made up; usually the quarters are close enough so that stage makeup is unnecessary for anybody. The planted actors should be well scattered, but all in positions allowing easy access to the aisles.

A True Bill was written for a Little Theater group called the Rogues' Gallery and played during the Easter vacation in fifteen churches in 1966. The churches, in the Maryland/Virginia/Washington, D.C. area, ranged from High Episcopalian to an all-Negro Baptist congregation in a city slum. After the play was over, the genuine minister in charge asked the congregation to remain and discuss what they'd seen with the actors, and such groups were invariably large and lively. At no time did we encounter anyone who had taken offense either to the surprise or to the play itself, and as word got around, we got more invitations than we could accept. In lieu of selling tickets, we asked for half of the day's collection (except in the slum church, where we played for nothing).

We had no Asian to play the Judge, but we did have a Negro—admitted to the group, I'm happy to say, when several of the more prejudiced Southerners among us yielded gracefully to a majority vote—and we asked him to do it. It is a major role, and he had had absolutely no prior experience; but he was the first of all the main characters to memorize all of his lines (our lawyer blew his few lines in a new and different way at each and every performance), and he turned out to be magnificently versatile and convincing.

I have indicated simple music cues for the church organist. As it happened, we had three audio-cum-music buffs (including the author) in our membership, so we rigged up a quite simple sound system and taped incidental music, including a prelude, from phonograph records. I shan't say what pieces and excerpts we used, for if you have the resources, you'll find it more fun to choose your own. For the gun we used the obvious, a rented starting pistol; I'd expected this to be noisy, of course, but the actual sound of the shot under church acoustics made even the actors jump, and they at least knew it was coming.

Should you rehearse in a quiet residential area, better have the Corporal say "Bang!" when the shot is supposed to come, or be prepared for police inquiries. (This also saves money on cartridges.) It's even more important to have one rehearsal in each new church you play in, for church layouts vary widely; we hit one, for instance, that was fan-shaped and had no central aisle, and so required a completely different disposition of the entrances from the back and of the bit parts in the audience for the mob scene.

This is the first appearance of the play in print. For performance rights, please address me at Treetops, Woodlands Road, Harpsden (Henley), Oxon., England.

James Blish)

To Anne McKenzie
and the Rogues

CAST OF CHARACTERS
(in order of appearance)

THE CAPTAIN	A MARCHER
THE CORPORAL	MAGDA
THE SERGEANT	A DOCTOR
A MINISTER	A LAWYER
THE JUDGE	A SCIENTIST
TEEN-AGE GIRL	A HOUSEWIFE
TEEN-AGE BOY	A COLONIAL
A POET	MARY

Time: Today
Place: A courtroom

[*Prior to the opening of the service, the* MINISTER, *the* MARCHER, *the* TEEN-AGE GIRL, *the* HOUSEWIFE, *the* TEEN-AGE BOY, MAGDA, *the* LAWYER, *the* DOCTOR, *the* SCIENTIST, *the* POET, *and the* COLONIAL *take places here and there in the pews.* MARY *should also be seated, at the back of the church. They are all in contemporary costume except* MARY, *who wears mourning weeds of no particular period.*

[*The service opens as usual and proceeds to an offertory or meditation during which the organist plays "Sheep May Safely Graze." As this ends, the* CORPORAL, *in fatigues and helmet-liner, wearing a .45 automatic and a brassard marked* PROVOST, *escorts the* CAPTAIN *down the center aisle. The* CORPORAL *is a young man, slouching and feral, but precise in his purely military courtesies. The* CAPTAIN, *almost as young a man as the* CORPORAL *but carrying his responsibilities heavily, wears a summer uniform and has a briefcase in one hand.*

[*Both stop at the head of the aisle and exchange salutes. The* CORPORAL *does a right-face and walks back out, his face expressionless. The* CAPTAIN, *once out of the* CORPORAL's *range of view, stares after him and shakes his head ruefully.*]

CAPTAIN [*softly*]: Whew.

[*The* CAPTAIN *goes to the central bench, opens his briefcase and removes from it a gavel and a folder of papers, both of which he places carefully on the lectern in the pulpit. He then returns to the bench, looks briefly out at the congregation, and extracts from the briefcase more papers and a pair of reading glasses, which he dons. He sits down and begins to read.*

[*The* CORPORAL *takes up a position of parade-rest at the rear of the church. Any latecomers will have to push past him; he does not yield for them.*]

CAPTAIN [*reading aloud, but to himself, almost by rote*]: . . . Witnesses must previously have sworn to uphold the Constitution, if any, of the provisional government or other authority currently recognized by the Occupying Forces . . . Officers and counsel of courts appointed by the Occupying Forces are deemed to be gentlemen and invested with the dignity of existing local law, if any, by act of . . . Ah, it's no use. It makes no sense. I feel sick, that's all. If I ever get out of this flea-bitten pocket-handkerchief of a country—

[*Enter the* SERGEANT, *a matter-of-fact career man perhaps ten years older than the* CAPTAIN. *He too is in summer uniform but wears a side-*

arm like the CORPORAL'*s. Since he is armed, he remains covered—that is, he keeps his hat on— throughout the play. He marches down the aisle to the front of the bench and salutes.*]

SERGEANT: Reporting for duty, sir.

CAPTAIN [*remaining seated, but returning the salute*]: It's you again, eh Sergeant? How long have you been on duty, anyhow?

SERGEANT: Since they cut them three agitators down and carted 'em off, sir.

CAPTAIN: At ease. Ugly, wasn't it?

SERGEANT: It's always ugly. But they was only out to make trouble for the rest of us. These gooks will put a knife in your back as soon as scratch, and never mind whose side they're supposed to be on. At least them three won't bug us any more.

CAPTAIN: It's not over yet.

SERGEANT: I see it ain't. Excuse me, sir, but just what the hell *are* we doing here? I thought the trial was over three days ago.

CAPTAIN [*ironically*]: Sure. What we've got here now is an inquest. It's a custom we imported ourselves.

SERGEANT: Never heard of it.

CAPTAIN: Neither did the gooks till we barged in on them. In the old days, those three would have been strung up, and that would have been that. But now it's got to look legal. There's been a death by violence—three deaths. There were reporters from home there, four of them. They'll all tell different stories, but they'll call it either mob rule or a military execution unless we give the people a chance to decide for themselves what it was, under one of their own judges. You can see we've got quite an audience already.

SERGEANT: That's crazy! Excuse me, sir, but we ordered those guys strung up, ourselves, in the long run. This inquest thing could wind up with us being the defendants.

CAPTAIN: Well, that's part of the point of it.

MINISTER [*from audience*]: Give us back our dead!

CAPTAIN [*forgetting for a moment that he's not officially supposed to be in charge here*]: Quiet out there! Who's that?

[*There is no answer.*]

SERGEANT [*after the pause*]: Sir, that's what I meant. This is a bad time to stir 'em all up again. There's some kind of mob collecting *outside* the building, too—all talking at once—some of 'em carrying posters. They're working themselves up to set fire to the library, or stone the embassy, or some other damn thing like that. The reporters'll love that, too.

CAPTAIN: I know it. It can't be helped. Just keep your eye on the people here, and whenever you spot somebody speaking up, get him up here. We'll put him on the witness stand and see how loud he shouts from there.

SERGEANT: But . . . Yes, sir.

[*The* SERGEANT *begins to prowl back and forth before the front pews, sternly eyeing various people in the audience. The* CAPTAIN *puts his glasses back on and resumes reading.*

[*Enter the* JUDGE, *a small man with much professional gravity, which, however, tends to wilt slightly whenever he has to recognize the existence of the* CAPTAIN. *He walks slowly toward the pulpit. His entrance produces a slight murmur from the audience. The* CAPTAIN *looks up.*]

CAPTAIN [*sotto voce, to* SERGEANT]: Psst. The judge.

SERGEANT [*coming to attention himself, and barking at the audience*]: 'Ten-SHUN!

[*The* CAPTAIN *tries to flag the* SERGEANT *down, but it is too late; all the other members of the cast in the audience have come to their feet, and after all, the* CAPTAIN *is standing too.*
[*The* JUDGE *climbs embarrassedly to the pulpit and sits down.*]

JUDGE [*to* CAPTAIN]: Uh—thank you. Everyone may be seated.

[*This is superfluous, since everybody has already sat down again except the* CAPTAIN.]

CAPTAIN: Thank you, sir. [*He too sits.*]

JUDGE: I presume we may proceed?

CAPTAIN: Of course, your honor.

[*The* JUDGE *picks up his gavel, looks at it nervously, and then hits the pulpit with it with ear-splitting enthusiasm. The* SERGEANT *grins; the* CAPTAIN *tries to ignore the noise.*]

JUDGE [*to audience; fluently, but with a faint trace of an Asian accent—overlaid, if possible, by an equally faint trace of Oxford*]: Hear ye, hear ye, hear ye. Order in the court, please. This court is now in session, please, yes? We are met here by order of the provincial governor, and by permission of the Occupying Forces, to hold an inquest on the deaths of the three persons who deceased up on the hill day before yesterday. Since this is not a usual procedure in our country, you should understand that the governor and the Occupying Forces wish to make certain that the deceasing was in accordance with law and with the will of everyone concerned.

If it was, then the case is closed. If it was not, we will consider further how to proceed. [*He shoots a sidelong look at the* CAPTAIN, *who tries to nod unobtrusively*.] We have asked all the possible witnesses to come here and testify. All of you gathered here now constitute what in democratic countries is called a—a Star Chamber?—an *umkali imtomronat*—

CAPTAIN: A Grand Jury.

JUDGE: —a Grand Jury. And your verdict, whatever it may turn out to be, will be called a True Bill. Thus, if you decide that the Occupying Forces executed the three men unjustly, you may return a True Bill of murder against the officer or officers who ordered the execution. [*Somebody in the audience snickers. The* JUDGE *ignores this, but the* SERGEANT *glares in the direction of the sound*.] Or, if you find the deceased to have been criminals or anti-democratic elements, you may return a True Bill of legal deceasement or justifiable homicide. Or perhaps you will find the incident properly only death by misadventure. We will explain these terms to you as we go along.

Now, are there any questions?

MINISTER [*from audience*]: Just give us back our dead. Don't make martyrs of them.

JUDGE: You may be our first witness, sir, yes?

[*Nobody stirs.*]

CAPTAIN [*to* SERGEANT]: Bring that man up here.

JUDGE: Yes, if you please.

SERGEANT [*to* JUDGE]: Sorry, your honor. I still can't see who it is. [*Aside, to* CAPTAIN] If any one of 'em actually comes up here, I'll eat my rifle, bayonet and all. That's how gooks are. First they ask you to do their dirty work. Then they hide behind the nearest rock and holler that you did it wrong.

[*The* JUDGE, *at first at a loss as to what to do next, cocks an ear toward the* SERGEANT.]

CAPTAIN [*aside*]: Maybe we did. [*Noticing the* JUDGE'*s regard*] Shut up.

SERGEANT [*not hearing the order, already responding to the previous three words*]: There ain't any *right* way to do dirty work, except to do it fast. Otherwise, too many guys buy it.

JUDGE: Buy what, please?

SERGEANT [*still to the* CAPTAIN]: Buy a farm. Six feet. Gets planted. Hell, sir, *you* know. [*The* CAPTAIN *is trying to make him shut up by a combination of frowning and sheer telepathy; the* SERGEANT *is simply further exasperated by the young officer's naiveté*]. Killed.

JUDGE: Let us hear some more about this. Will you take the stand, please?

[*The* SERGEANT, *realizing that he has talked out of turn, looks helplessly at the* CAPTAIN, *who stands formally and faces the* JUDGE.]

CAPTAIN: Your honor, the Occupying Forces will be pleased to testify. We hope that other witnesses will follow our example.

[*The* SERGEANT *sits in the witness chair provided.*]

JUDGE: Will you identify yourself to the court, please?

SERGEANT: I stood guard over the prisoners at the trial, your honor. And afterwards, at the execution.

JUDGE: All by yourself?

SERGEANT: No, sir. I had three PFCs with me. Good men.

JUDGE: That remains to be seen. Did any of the condemned talk to you? In particular, the ringleader?

SERGEANT: Oh sure, he talked to everybody. The usual gas about brotherhood that everybody spouts around here. It sounds like religion, but your honor, once you've banged around in little wars like this as long as I have, you'd better believe that it's politics.

JUDGE [*very politely*]: Do you find it easy to tell the difference?

SERGEANT: No, sir, that's just what I was saying. In gook countries, whether it's politics or religion, it all comes out to knives in the back. Where we come from, nobody kills you for being against the administration, or belonging to the wrong church. But around here, they'll string you up by the thumbs if you don't agree with anything they say. You've just got to get in there fustest with the mostest.

[*The* CAPTAIN *is trying to catch the* SERGEANT'*s eye, in increasing anguish at the noncom's bluntness, but without success.*]

JUDGE: [*still more politely*]: Is that what he said?

SERGEANT: No, sir, but that's what he meant. He could of been you, sir, or me, or anybody, except that we had the firepower and he didn't. That's all brotherhood meant to him. It's all it means to any of these agitators.

MINISTER [*from audience*]: He never hurt you! He never hurt anyone!

CAPTAIN [*looking fruitlessly about the audience for the source of the voice*]: Quiet! You lost your turn!

JUDGE: If you please, Captain . . . the point is perhaps well taken. I never heard that the man did anyone any harm. He was certainly not a soldier—only a carpenter. And even by the age of thirty-three, he had never written a book. He only talked.

SERGEANT: Sure. That's all any of 'em do—until you turn your back. Then somebody on your side buys a farm, and there's nothing left to do but split up his gear and get on with the job. He ain't going to miss any of it, and neither is the supply sergeant.

CAPTAIN: Your honor, I'm afraid my sergeant's testimony must be a little baffling. I believe he's told the essence of his story.

JUDGE: I find it interesting. Tell me more, Sergeant, about this division of spoils.

SERGEANT: Oh, it's just a custom, sir. Share and share alike. For instance, this ringleader—I got his greatcoat when we cut him down. [*The* CAPTAIN *wipes his forehead and stares carefully off into space.*] It was all fair and square; I played show-down, sudden-death poker for it with my squad. Of course, between you and me, sir, they knew better than to win against me—I'd of loused up all their rotation points if they had. [*Suddenly not quite sure the* JUDGE *will get the point*] Only a gag, your honor.

JUDGE: What did you want his coat for?

SERGEANT [*trying to mend his fences*]: Only for a story, your honor. You know, sir, like when one of your kids asks you what you did in the war. Not that this hole is much of a war. Another guy in my squad won his hat; you couldn't wear it back home, it looks like some sort of owl's nest—but it makes a good story, too.

JUDGE: How many children do you have, Sergeant?

SERGEANT: I think I got one, if he made the date. He was due three months ago. I don't have the word yet—mail call's been pretty slow lately.

JUDGE: Thank you. Stand down.

[*The* SERGEANT *leaves the stand and resumes his post next to the* CAPTAIN.]

CAPTAIN [*in a fierce whisper*]: You damned blabber-mouth!

SERGEANT: You ordered me to testify, sir.

MARCHER [*from audience*]: Give us back our dead! Don't let them defile our homes! Stop police brutality! End the occupation!

[*The* JUDGE, *reading, pays no attention.*]

CAPTAIN [*to* SERGEANT]: Now what? Between you and them, I'd six times rather be shot at.

TEEN-AGE GIRL [*from audience*]: Make love—not war!

[*The* TEEN-AGE BOY, *the* POET *and the* MARCHER *join in, clapping rhythmically.*]

BOTH TEEN-AGERS, POET, MARCHER: Make love, not war! Make love, not war! Make love, not war!

[*The* TEEN-AGE GIRL, *encouraged by this support, begins a sort of dance in the center aisle. The* JUDGE *raps sharply for order. The* HOUSEWIFE *reaches out and yanks the* TEEN-AGE GIRL *back to her seat.*]

SERGEANT: You may be shot at yet, sir. They're working themselves up to something down there. There's a thin guy in a beard who's been marching round and round the building ever since the earthquake, carrying a big sign. He's got maybe a dozen other pickets with him, and all kinds of ragbaggy kids trailing after them.

CAPTAIN: What do the signs say?

SERGEANT: You've got me there, sir. I don't read gook lettering so good. Could be INRI, or LSD, or NASA, or anything. It don't make much sense no matter how you look at it.

MAGDA: [*from audience*]: But I loved him!

[*The* JUDGE *looks up.*]

JUDGE: Magda, I know your voice. Come up here. Captain, please have your man fetch her. [*He points.*]

SERGEANT [*to* CAPTAIN]: She's only one of the local pros. They come out and howl at all the funerals. What does *she* know about anything?

[*The* CAPTAIN *gestures sharply and the* SERGEANT *goes down into the congregation to* MAGDA. *He escorts her to the stand and helps her sit down, his expression ironically patient.*]

JUDGE: Magda, I know you, but we need to identify you for the written record. Tell me then, did you know any of the prisoners?

MAGDA: I knew the king, town father.

JUDGE: Your honor.

MAGDA: I knew the king, your honor. Not the thieves; only the king.

CAPTAIN: Does she mean the ringleader?

JUDGE: If you please, Captain . . . Now, Magda: What did you know about him?

MAGDA: I love him, town—your honor. I would have taken him into my bed. I would have charged him nothing. But he made me whole, instead.

SERGEANT: [to CAPTAIN, *sotto voce*]: Them joy-girls'll say anything to please a customer. Sometimes I forget what a clean woman sounds like.

CAPTAIN: [*sotto voce*]: Shut up.

JUDGE: But what do you know? Have you nothing else to tell us?

MAGDA: He warded off stones from me. He made me whole. And now they've killed him. He was a king, and I loved him, and now he's dead.

JUDGE: Yes, we know. Thank you, Magda. You may go.

[MAGDA *rises and makes her way uncertainly back into the audience. The* JUDGE *turns a page.*]

SERGEANT: [to CAPTAIN, *watching her go*]: That's how it goes—bitch, bitch, bitch. You come halfway around the world to give these gooks a hand, and they charge you fifteen dollars for a warm weak beer, and a dirty song with no tune and words you can't even understand. That's soldiering for you.

CAPTAIN: *You* don't gripe much, eh? . . . [*He suddenly sees someone he recognizes in the congregation and springs to his feet.*] Your honor, if it please the court, I see the physician of the deceased in the audience. At the trial, he testified—

JUDGE: Yes. He declared all three of them insane. Bring him forward.

[*The* SERGEANT *darts into the congregation and fetches back the* DOCTOR, *who sits down in the witness chair, settling his ruffled feathers.*]

JUDGE [*soothingly*]: We welcome an expert witness, Doctor. Please tell us: What is your present opinion of the sanity of the deceased—in particular, the ringleader?

DOCTOR: The usual psychic masochist has a strong martyr complex. Having been weaned too early, he feels that he was punished in infancy for some unknown crime, usually called original sin. In revenge against his mother, he desires to show the mother that he can produce his own substitute for milk and be independent of her. Thus he becomes an artist, or a prophet. That will be twenty-five dollars, please.

JUDGE: We are not quite ready for the fee yet, please. Doctor . . .

SERGEANT [*sotto voce, to* CAPTAIN]: I can get around in gook language as far as the john, but half the time I think they don't know themselves what they're talking about.

JUDGE [*continuing previous speech, over* SERGEANT]: . . . just exactly what does that mean, in layman's terms?

DOCTOR: I mean simply that the patient was harmlessly insane and should have been released into the custody of some competent person. All three of them badly needed trained help.

JUDGE: It will be observed, sir, that we have passed beyond that stage now.

DOCTOR: As was quite predictable. In due course, the psychic masochist, having found that art or religion do not substitute for mother's milk, defeats his own ends, punishes himself and commits suicide. Such people are no danger to society and should be kindly institutionalized.

SERGEANT [*as before*]: These kids have got more religions than a dog has fleas.

JUDGE: Thank you. Stand down.

DOCTOR: Please pay the nurse when you go out. [*Exit.*]

SERGEANT: Boy, I could use some sack time along about now.

CAPTAIN: Can you sleep?

SERGEANT: Any time, any place. I learned long ago just to drop where I stood. Nothing bothers me any more.

JUDGE: Who wishes to appear next, please?

LAWYER [*from audience*]: Why should we coddle murderers and parole them, and at the same time let the subversive thinker undermine the family, and our whole society? Why imprison the active criminal and praise the thought-criminal?

JUDGE: Come forward, please.

CAPTAIN [*sotto voce, to* SERGEANT]: Who's that?

SERGEANT: Dunno. Some lawyer, sounds like. [*He leaves the bench and resumes prowling before the front pews.*]

LAWYER: The man who destroys a way of life is a thousand times as dangerous as the man who destroys one life!

JUDGE: No testifying from the audience, please—

SCIENTIST [*from audience*]: As a scientist—

SERGEANT [*spotting the* SCIENTIST]: Aha! [*He grabs the* SCIENTIST *by the wrist and pulls him out into the aisle.*] It's up to the witness stand for you, me lad.

[*The* SCIENTIST *frees himself and walks with dignity up to the witness stand.*]

JUDGE: Now then, sir, just what *is* your interpretation of these events?

SCIENTIST: As a scientist, I feel that there's a great deal of imprecise thinking going on at this meeting. Today we live in a world where an act of nature, or an act of war, threatens us all with many megadeaths. We should be objective enough to stop and think about what a tolerable number might be.

MARCHER [*from audience*]: Anyone for megadeath?

SCIENTIST: In this context, the execution of just one potential criminal is hardly worth thinking about.

POET [*from audience*]: After the first death, there is no other.

MINISTER [*from audience*]: Some say that God Himself is dead.

SCIENTIST: That would be only what we call a mini-death.

TEEN-AGE GIRL [*from audience*]: This God bit is a grown-up racket. Our generation doesn't mind a little religion here and there. But if the wrong people take it up, well, sure it's dead.

TEEN-AGE BOY [*from audience*]: Yeah!

DOCTOR [*from audience*]: Some have to die that others may live. That's the nature of social therapy.

TEEN-AGE BOY: Oh, that's the nitty-gritty, baby.

MAGDA [*from audience*]: I loved him. He made me whole.

DOCTOR: Thirty pieces of silver, please.

LAWYER: Bury them all. The guilty must pay.

HOUSEWIFE [*from audience*]: But don't you think he might have brought food prices down? He seemed like such a nice young man.

TEEN-AGE GIRL: Oh, mother, *please*—you're embarrassing me in front of my friends!

HOUSEWIFE: Well, dear, I was only asking—

[*The members of the cast in the audience (except for* MARY, *the* CORPORAL *and the* SCIENTIST) *are now on their feet arguing with each other, and begin to filter out into the aisle. The* SCIENTIST *starts out of the witness box; the* SERGEANT *moves tentatively to stop him.*]

SERGEANT [*calling to the* CAPTAIN *over the mounting hubbub*]: The natives is restless—ain't that how it goes, sir?

[*The noise gets louder. The* JUDGE *bangs his gavel. The* CAPTAIN *looks up at the* JUDGE, *and then beckons to the back of the church to the* CORPORAL.]

COLONIAL [*from audience*]: This is a travesty! Get that bloody wog off the bench!

[*The* COLONIAL *makes for the chancel, waving his umbrella. The rest of the cast in the audience follow him, shouting and gesticulating. The* SERGEANT *tries to hold them back, jostled from one side by the* SCIENTIST, *who is arguing violently with the* MINISTER, *the* POET, *and the* MARCHER.]

CORPORAL [*shouting from his post*]: All right, break it up! Break it up, gooks! The show's over!

[*The noise gets louder still. At its climax, three loud bangs from the* JUDGE's *gavel are followed, after a beat, by a shot fired by the* CORPORAL *over the heads of the mob. All the mob actors scurry to their seats, including the* SCIENTIST.
[*Dead silence follows, during which the* CAPTAIN *and the* SERGEANT *brush themselves off and try to recover their equanimity.*
[*At the same time the* CORPORAL, *still holding his pistol aloft with one hand, has seized* MARY *by the scruff of the neck and is propelling her down the aisle.*]

SERGEANT: There's my corporal. That's the end of that.

CAPTAIN: Somehow I doubt it.

[*The* CORPORAL *reaches the chancel area and throws* MARY *toward the witness box. She falls on the steps with a stifled cry. The* CORPORAL *turns slowly, faces the audience, and blows smoke off the mouth of his pistol like a TV cowboy. He looks the audience over arrogantly.*]

CORPORAL: They scatter like sparrows. Show a little muscle and that's all you need. [*He turns, holstering the pistol.*] Hello, Sarge. Oh, hello, sir. [*Salutes negligently.*]

[*The* CAPTAIN, *appalled, ignores the salute and kneels beside* MARY.]

CORPORAL [*continuing previous speech*]: I nabbed one for you. [*He kicks* MARY *explanatorily.*] She claims she's his mother.

[MARY *cries out.*]

CAPTAIN: Are you ill? Come now, it'll all be over soon. In a little while you can go home.

MARY: You ... killed my son.

CORPORAL [*to* SERGEANT]: Sure, that's what they all say. She probably just wants his coat or something like that. In this lousy desert, there's only one dirty rag for every three of 'em.

JUDGE: Mary ... would you tell us about it?

MARY: Don't touch me. Let me weep.

CORPORAL [*swinging around to* MARY *and seizing her shoulders*]: Get up in the chair, you, and speak politely.

CAPTAIN: Let her alone. Go back to your post.

CORPORAL: Yessir. [*Aside to* SERGEANT] What's the matter with him, Sarge—getting soft on the gooks?

SERGEANT: Shaddup. Anything you need to know, I'll tell you.

CORPORAL: *Sure* you will. You're missing half the fun, though, Sarge. There's a cute broad down there, hanging around just waiting for some action. A lot neater than this one [*jerking his thumb toward* MARY].

SERGEANT: Beat it.

CORPORAL: Okay, okay. But just don't tell me any big story tomorrow. [*He looks scornfully toward* MARY.] Huh!

[*The* CORPORAL *goes back up the aisle, swaggering, and pausing to eye* MAGDA. *The* CAPTAIN *tries to lift* MARY *to her feet;* MARY *shakes her head and clings to the earth. The* JUDGE *watches them all without expression.*]

MARY: My son . . . my son . . .

CAPTAIN: Mother, if I can help you—

JUDGE [*abruptly*]: Captain, I leave the witness in your charge, and declare a recess. [*He raps once smartly with the gavel, leaves the pulpit, and retires swiftly.*]

[*The* CAPTAIN *jumps to his feet and tries to follow.*]

CAPTAIN: But, Your Honor!

[*The* JUDGE *has vanished. After a baffled pause, the* CAPTAIN *returns to* MARY, *lifts her gently and helps her stumble to the bench, where she crouches, still hiding her face.*
[*The* CAPTAIN *paces, at a complete loss. The*

SERGEANT *stands at parade rest at the other side of the chancel.*]

CAPTAIN: Now what? [*There is no answer.*] . . . Sergeant?

SERGEANT [*coming to attention*]: Yessir?

CAPTAIN: What did you think of the trial? Not this one —the other one, day before yesterday?

SERGEANT: No screwier than this one. [*He relaxes a little, responding to the* CAPTAIN'*s informality.*] Trials is all alike, sir. He didn't get a fair deal. Who does? He didn't break any of their laws, not that I could tell. It was just a put-up job. This judge looks all right, but that other guy—he was ours.

CAPTAIN [*with a worried look toward* MARY]: Ours?

SERGEANT: You know what I mean, sir. We said he was some kind of agitator, so his own people handed him over to us. We said he was stirring up trouble with the other gooks.

CAPTAIN: Well—wasn't he?

SERGEANT: Sure he was. Brotherhood and all that jazz. But that's just what they all say. We was just makin' some damn kind of example of him.

CAPTAIN: I had the impression his own people didn't like what he said, either. They seemed pretty glad to get rid of him.

SERGEANT: Well, I don't know why. He didn't say anything these preachers don't say all over this part of the world. All he said was that he was a messenger from God and wanted to bring everybody peace. What's wrong with that?

CAPTAIN: A little blasphemous, don't you think?

SERGEANT: He didn't blast us. He didn't blast nobody.

CAPTAIN: Do you think he came from God?

SERGEANT: That's none of my business, sir. He didn't come from Capitol Hill, that's all I'm supposed to care about.

CAPTAIN: Do you believe in God?

SERGEANT [*after a pause*]: Well, I do and I don't. Excuse me, sir, but what god are you talking about?

CAPTAIN: Well—the one he was talking about.

SERGEANT [*promptly*]: No sir. I don't. He'd just got hold of one of those local, one-goat gods they all have in these little holes. Out farther east, when those people talk about God, they make you listen. I wouldn't buy his kind of god for a minute. As a prophet, he was just a cheap imitation, compared to—excuse me, sir.

CAPTAIN: No, go on. What's to apologize for?

SERGEANT: Well, sir, if you don't mind, you're kind of a young man. I've been in the army for twenty years, and I've seen a lot of gods. I've seen a lot of agitators like him, too. So I can kind of compare 'em. You're an officer, but you haven't seen as much of the god business as I have.

CAPTAIN: Oh. A connoisseur.

SERGEANT: No, sir, a career sergeant. That's my profession. But if you're asking me about gods, well, I've seen better ones than his. He was a good guy, more or less, but he was putting us on. That's what the gooks strung him up for.

CAPTAIN: Hmm. [*He looks around; then, in a lower voice*] I had the impression that *we* strung him up.

SERGEANT [*a little sullenly*]: You gave the orders, sir. *I* strung him up, sir.

CAPTAIN: You should have knocked my damn block off instead.

SERGEANT: I didn't get all these hash-marks for hitting superior officers—sir. And I'll tell you this, sir; that one up on the hill ain't the first god I knocked off, and he won't be the last. Maybe some day I'll see a *real* god, and he'll knock *me* off before I can get to him. A real god ought to be able to keep his chin covered. I bayoneted *this* joker like a sheep; what kind of a god is that?

CAPTAIN: What kind do you want?

SERGEANT: One that'd knock me down and read the Articles of War to me when I step out of line. Not a sheep.

CAPTAIN: And what about the baby?

SERGEANT: What? I don't get you, sir.

CAPTAIN: The son you're waiting for. How'll he manage without a father? Or suppose your tough god decided to kill him off, too? Some gods eat them.

SERGEANT [*stiffly*]: Excuse me, sir, but I don't think that's very damn funny.

MARY: My child. Oh dear my child.

MINISTER [*from audience*]: Bury the dead.

MARCHER [*from audience*]: Justice is love!

DOCTOR [*from audience*]: A clear case of bad toilet training.

LAWYER [*from audience*]: The end justifies the means.

TEEN-AGE GIRL [*from audience*]: It's only a racket.

TEEN-AGE BOY [*from audience*]: Don't blow your cool, baby.

COLONIAL [*from audience*]: Stop this travesty!

HOUSEWIFE [*from audience*]: Lower food prices.

CORPORAL [*from his post*]: Break it up now down there! Break it up!

MAGDA [*from audience*]: He made me whole.

SCIENTIST [*from audience*]: What are the facts?

POET [*from audience*]: An end to killing!

CORPORAL: Shaddap, all of you!

> [*As before, the offstage voices mount to a tumult; they should repeat their lines from both this scene and their preceding scene, ad lib. At the climax there is a full fortissimo diapason chord from the organ, and the* JUDGE *reenters.*
>
> [*The noise at once dies down to silence. The* JUDGE *resumes the pulpit. He seems a good deal taller, more sure of himself, more imposing than before.*
>
> [MARY *raises her head and looks up at him.*]

MARY: I bore him. I nursed him. I warmed him. I housed him. And now they have taken him away.

I covered him. I sang to him. I petted him. I fled with him. And now they have taken him away.

*[This speech gradually takes on the quality
of a church solo, chanted rather than sung.]*

Deep in the desert, I cherished him. I listened to him
lisp, to him talk, to him stammer, to him preach, to him
make blasphemies, in the very House of God, and oh, I
was terrified, and oh, I loved him! And they hated him,
and I was so afraid.

[Organ continuo rises softly under.]

I tried to hinder him, I got in his way, I was ashamed. I
thought he would disgrace me—he would speak to anybody, even those loose women who followed him—and
then, and then, they hung him! Oh living God, they hung
him! What had he done? What had he ever done? Even
the sheep and the cattle breathed on him when he was little! Kings came to him in his dreams! And oh, you should
have seen the stars staring down from the cold!
But step by step, word by word, he went from me, because he wanted to be a king. Someone had told him he
would be a king. I—felt in my womb that he would be a
king, but no, no, not a king on a gallows-tree!

[Reprise.]

I bore him. I cherished him. I bowed down to him when
he left me; and all my mighty masters, I weep for him, and
for you, who have taken him away. . . .

*[The CAPTAIN and the SERGEANT listen, en-
tirely oblivious to the JUDGE.]*

CORPORAL *[from his post]*: Ah, the hell with that. He
got what was coming to him.

SERGEANT *[taking one step, as if against his will, toward MARY]*: Uh . . . excuse me, ma'am . . .

MARY [*turning to look at him*]: Who are you?

SERGEANT: Nobody. I killed your son.

CAPTAIN [*shooting a swift glance at the* JUDGE]·
You're talking out of turn, Sergeant.

SERGEANT [*ignoring him*]: I killed your son. Myself.

MARY: Why?

SERGEANT: That's my trade. It's my career. It's what I
was brought up to do. I'm a professional. I'm good at it.

MARY: At murder?

CAPTAIN: Sergeant, shut up. That's an order.

SERGEANT: In a minute. I've got a question. I want to
know, did I kill a god?

MARY: No. Only my son.

SERGEANT: But—he was a god. Wasn't he? Wasn't he?
Didn't I help turn him into a god? Tell me I did!

MARY: He was a man.

SERGEANT: Didn't I help him sacrifice himself? All
these year-kings have to die. I seen it happen in all kinds
of countries. They have to die so they can become gods.
Didn't I help? Didn't I? Please, didn't I?

MARY: No. He was only my son. He was not proud.
He was not rich. He was not scholarly. He was not a king.
He was made of dust and blood, the same dust and blood
that I was made of. If there is a god, that's what he's like.
And if there are people who can love and obey him, they
too are dust and blood. That's all I know. If my lovely son

was a king, then . . . you are a king, soldier. And Captain, so are you. And . . . [*in sudden terrible sorrow*] and everyone, except my son up there on the gallows-tree.

CAPTAIN: We are all murderers.

SERGEANT: I know . . . but I keep hoping—

JUDGE: Is that your verdict?

CAPTAIN [*looking up, startled*]: I beg your pardon?

JUDGE: It is not mine to give. I asked: Is that your verdict?

CAPTAIN: Your honor, it's not up to me to reach a verdict. This is your court.

JUDGE: No more my court than yours, and everyone's. I can only return the verdict that you give.

CAPTAIN: I don't understand.

JUDGE: Mary . . . are you through?

MARY: My life has just begun.

JUDGE: Sergeant, help her out.

[*The* SERGEANT *gently helps* MARY *to her feet. She stands at last, tall and dignified.*]

CORPORAL [*from his post*]: Hey, Sarge, where the hell are you?

SERGEANT [*guiding* MARY *slowly down the aisles*]: I dunno. But I'm on my way.

CORPORAL: Well, hurry the hell up. It's getting dark.

SERGEANT: That's funny. It looks like dawn to me.

[*They exit slowly; the other members of the cast in the audience watch them go. The* CAPTAIN, *too, looks after them, and then backs up to the* JUDGE, *puzzled and half angry.*]

CAPTAIN: Is that all?

JUDGE: It is all that counts.

[*The* CAPTAIN *and the* JUDGE *exchange a long look. Then the* JUDGE *leaves the pulpit and exits slowly. The* CAPTAIN *starts after him, then changes his mind and goes back to the bench, where he pauses to think. Then, shaking his head, he mounts the pulpit and retrieves the gavel and the papers he had put up there in the first place. He sits down at the bench and mechanically begins to stuff everything back into his briefcase. He pauses almost immediately, however, and looks blindly out at the congregation.*]

CAPTAIN: I'm never going to be able to explain this to the people back home. Is there nothing else to say? Doesn't *anybody* have anything to say?

[*There is quite a long silence. The* CAPTAIN *puts his head into his hands.*

[*Off stage, a long, heavy rolling sound begins, becomes louder and louder. The members of the cast remaining in the audience look up and around, trying to locate its source, finally focusing at the back of the church. The* CORPORAL, *too, is looking around; finally he is staring out the exit.*

[*Belatedly, the* CAPTAIN *looks up, alarmed. The* CORPORAL *lifts his hands as if to ward off a blow.*

[*The sound ends in an apocalyptic crash.*]

CORPORAL: The stone! [*He claps his hands to his face. His voice breaks.*] The stone, THE STONE!

[*Ten-second blackout. As the lights all come on at once, the organ bursts fortissimo into the "Et resurrexit" from the B Minor Mass and continues it more softly as a postlude.*]

IN A CROOKED YEAR
by
Gardner R. Dozois

Why call out or cry
when the generals I've fought with
all my life
are similarly attacked.
    —Aram Boyajian

Soldiers may grow a soul when turned to fronds,
But here the thing's best left at home with friends.
    —Wilfred Owen

"They're trying to kill me," Yossarian told him calmly.
"No one's trying to kill you," Clevinger cried.
"Then why are they shooting at me?" Yossarian asked.
"They're shooting at *everyone*," Clevinger answered.
    "They're trying to kill everyone."
"And what difference does that make?"

    —Joseph Heller

In a fiercely mourning house in a crooked year
   —Dylan Thomas

I
Spring-Winter

The valley was aflame behind him. Behind him, his companions burned and smouldered like fitful tallow candles, and the flames of their burning stained the night sky with dancing scarlet and molten gold, ghostly chemical green and white-hot blue, blotting out the stars. The smoke cloud straddled the valley like a shroud, writhing and churning, welling up in great silent bubble-bursts of explosions, lanced with sudden flame and held together by a shifting web of silver fire. Wind whooped and howled by him as the night was sucked into the blazing heart of the fire-storm. He took another step, wincing as pain slashed up through his shattered leg—clumsily splinted three days ago in a shabby field hospital filled with dying men and desperate medics, somewhere near where Pittsburgh used to be—and stopped to gasp for breath, swaying and fighting unconsciousness. The harsh light of the fire-storm washed and wavered across his face, alternately lighting it brilliantly and plunging it into deep shadow, like the fickle glow of a great neon sign.

———————◆———————

It is almost beautiful, I think, swaying, feeling the sick, dogged pounding of my heart, hearing the labored rasping hiss of my breathing. The light of the fire-storm dances and dazzles, forming tumbling, shifting patterns of light and dark, sending liquid, humped shadows jigging around the steep mountain walls of the valley. I squint my eyes to slits against the glare. The metal crutch bites into the soft flesh of my armpit as I lean my weight against it. How many days? Pittsburgh was what, two, three, surely not as long as four days ago? No, no more than three, but we walked so long to get here, and I counted every breath in every mile. Three days? I shake my head slowly, feeling the soggy night air resist the motion like water or thick molasses. There are thick silver cobwebs being wrapped around my brain, layer by smothering layer, and someone's packing my eyes with cotton batting so that I see fuzzy. I draw my hand across my forehead, trying to brush away the cobwebs, but they are curling and fluttering like injured moths inside my skull, and the motion makes me ill. My time sense is shot. Three days? What after Pittsburgh? Walking and flames, ruined buildings like shattered teeth, bodies, and there was a fog that killed two men. Cows lying bloated and black, mottled with curdled purple. Sirens, and a great sound of people wailing—or did I dream that? The silver chalice with the wine, but I dreamed that too I think, huddled into myself at night for warmth, and the cool woman of mist who touched my face with ice—I dreamed that too. There are no women anymore. Three days! The commander says there's an enemy paratroop unit in this area, but the lieutenant says how do you know since there's been no communications with headquarters for three days maybe they're dead up there maybe the enemy's dead and he starts to scream they're dead they're all dead we're dead and the commander tells him to shut up. We're going to stay and fight, he tells us as we walk, because that's our duty as fighting men whether the rest of the goddamn world is there or not. But there was mud, too much mud; it wanted to suck me down; it wanted to absorb me, flow over my eyes and close them. And there was blood and I couldn't stay. Three days. My head nods and I nearly fall, recovering myself with difficulty.

The fire-storm rolls and surges across the valley battlefield below. I did not want to run away, but I am tired and the moths won't get out of my head. I *didn't* want to run away. Believe me, I shout, but the noise is lost in the roar and dull cough of flames. What did you do in the atom war, Daddy? I say, and snicker weakly, my rib cage rising and falling with the strain of breathing. Someday, as I sit in my someday-house with my sweet someday-wife by my side, my someday-children will ask me that question, and I will draw on my pipe (Pipe-smoking is more distinguished than cigarette puffing. Must remember to cultivate it; someday.), and I will nod my head wisely and I will say, why, I did nothing, nothing but try to survive as best I could and try to keep out from under. The bastards can't make us do this, it'll be our decision to make if the time comes, we used to say to ourselves late at night, we secret pacifists, we barracks intellectuals, trying to compromise ourselves as little as possible, only *just* enough to keep us out of the prison camps, but not an iota more, no sir. So what if we pretended to go along w h the others, so what if we obeyed orders and kept our mouths shut, we still had our minds, didn't we, and we were still *us* deep inside, weren't we, and at the final moment, when it came right down to it with no return, the decision was still ours, wasn't it? Nobody could *make* us do it, the decision is ours, we said, not knowing that there was no decision to make, that any such elemental decision had been made for us a long long time ago.

So I left. Goddamn it, I shout, swaying. So I ran away while you stayed to fight. So you're dead and I'm alive. Does that make me a coward? Does that make me some kind of leper? Goddamn it, you're *dead*. You've no right to censure me anymore. The echos of my weak shout die, and I turn away choking, swallowing a sob. The flames laugh at me with a high, saw-toothed snickering.

------------◆------------

Anger cleared his brain, enabled him to turn, put one foot in front of another, stumble weakly through the night. Somewhere ahead there was a cave; he had found it late this afternoon as he fled from the gathering battle in the valley, only to be drawn back after nightfall by the final cataclysmic volley of low-yield tactical nukes. Somewhere there was a cave. He focused on that thought, narrowing his consciousness to concentrate on only that one idea, banishing all else from his mind. There is a cave ahead. Take a step. There *is* a cave ahead. Take another step. Keep the leg muscles pulling and pumping and don't think. Just keep moving, always keep moving, never stop. Never stop for a second. And never think of anything but your foot lifting, moving ahead for another step and another step. He sagged against the crutch and dragged himself away until the fire-storm sank behind the hill and was only a red glow tickling the underbellies of the fat storm clouds that had gathered overhead.

The night hooted joyously around him, superheated air baking his skin. Take a step—swish, foot through tangled tall grass; crackle-snap, twigs and small branches breaking under the metal toe of the crutch; snatch a breath, take a step, breathe. Gradually it became automatic, a mindless rhythm, so that when the cave mouth did finally yawn from the shadows, the shock of sudden discovery pulled him sickeningly awake out of a walking doze, and he stumbled and fell on the sharp gravel of the cave floor.

He floundered for a moment, trying to push himself back up from the ground with the syrupy dream motions of a slow-motion ballet, and then he relaxed and let his head sink back into the dirt. He breathed in great shallow rattles, too weak to twitch, and felt the world slip away. After the long nightmare of effort, sleep was almost an anticlimax.

In sleep, he found himself on the battlefield, groping through fire-lanced smoke, through oily, grittily-churning darkness. Sparks and yellow flame vomited into the air from every side, swirling into nightmare dervishes. A crescent wave of pale fire swept through the billowing smoke toward him, devouring as it came. He cowered back, but the fire passed through him without harm, without warming his skin, as if he were protected by an invisible wall of insulating glass.

The ground shook and bucked underfoot, rolling and

groaning as it was raped by continuous barrages. He fought for balance against the nauseous heaving of the land, straining to see through chaos. He knew that there was something here he had to look for, something that he had to find. He knew that it was vital that he find it, but somehow he couldn't remember just what it was. He stumbled foreward, searching, and not knowing what he searched for or why.

It was no longer day or night on the battlefield, but a sort of hellish twilight. It was impossible to see the sky; the sky was now a churning mass of bloody smoke a few feet overhead, laced by the smell of hot iron and the permeating reek of burning flesh. He passed a shattered vehicle, armor plates curling and blackening like withering leaves. Smoke swirled away like a curtain, giving him a glimpse of a man lying on his back, one hand spread wide near the knee that he didn't have anymore, his eyes wide open and staring, although he was undoubtedly, irreparably dead. This wasn't what he was looking for, he realized, and he hurried away.

More explosion ripped and stabbed through the roaring, red dark. Everybody is dead now, he thought calmly, and it's only the atomatic machines that continue to fight, mindlessly. It's a war of machines now, and the machines are fighting each other relentlessly through the fiery night, like tinker-toys that are slowly running down but cannot stop until they do run down. There was a roaring whistle overhead, like a berserk freight train in the sky, growing louder, growing nearer: a homing nuke.

It landed close, beyond the ruined vehicle, and the concussion wave blew him away like a feather in a jetstream, sent him rolling away over and over again across the scattered ashes of his friends, but he felt no pain. The flash of the fireball fused the sky to quartz, but he was not burned. Death wailed around him like an evil whispering rain, but he was not touched. He began to cry, weeping as a child weeps and not knowing why. Ashes pattered down over him, burying him, wrapping him in the security of the tomb. But he knew that he had to keep looking until he found it, so he shrugged himself free. He floated to his feet and started off again, leaving no footprints in the debris and ashes.

It had become very quiet on the battlefield. Except for an occasional echoing cough as a gas tank exploded in the dark, and the constant, sinister chuckle and hiss of flames, all was still. He swam through suffocating silence. They're all dead now, he thought, everything's dead now, even the machines. Even the machines are dead now. He felt a sudden unexplainable pity for the machines, and a sorrow, and gnawing shame that he had pity enough to spare for them when he hadn't even cried for his friends in his deserted unit. But it wasn't the machines' fault. Was it fair to create something solely to kill, and then try to tell it not to? But whose fault was it then? Someone had to take the blame, someone must be responsible for it, someone must suffer for this ultimate sin. But of course; that was what he must be looking for: the one who was responsible for it, the one who would have to pay.

Ahead, something moved suddenly through the smoke, coming closer and closer, moaning mournfully. He found himself screaming without sound, beyond sound. The thing moved closer through the hushed, smothering dark. It was the ghost of a machine, he knew it. An iron ghost, a grinning skull all of rubber and wires and printed circuits, with waving cables like smoke and an evil red glow behind its quartz-and-glass eyes. It was the ghost of a dead man, walking with eyes open and fire in its hair. It was Death, a slobbering, groping Death personified out of the slime of its own field.

It was a man. It was a man, staggering, reeling, with the tattered remnants of a familiar uniform floating around him. It was the enemy.

He clawed at his crutch and stared, his fear ebbing to be replaced by an uncomfortable, confused vacuum. The enemy floundered backwards, trying to get away; he was covered with blood and breathed in racking sobs. They stared at each other, unconsciously circling slowly while their filmed eyes locked, like mad wounded dogs too sick even to fight.

But gradually, as they circled, the enemy began to grow

larger, his steps became firmer, the bloodstains melted away from his uniform, the jagged tears in the fabric re-knitted themselves smoothly. Immaculate and frightful now, the enemy circled arrogantly, his shoulders hunching predatorily, his step becoming a stalk. Even the enemy's outlines had altered subtly, flattening and broadening out, turning him to a gross juggernaut of inhuman strength. The enemy circled closer, his back humping, his legs bowing grotesquely into crooked toadlike pillars of bunched muscle.

The enemy snarled at him—lips riding back to reveal long, yellowed fangs, razor-sharp and flecked with fresh blood—snatched at his belt and drew a heavy weapon from a battered holster. The enemy swung the weapon up to bear and took steady aim, the churning red highlights of the fog glinting murkily from blued steel. The muzzle yawned blackly at him, pulling his eyes down and down, swallowing them, gobbling his vision. The enemy pulled the trigger.

He awoke screaming, bathed in cold sweat. And in spite of exhaustion, it was a long time before he slept again.

———————◆———————

The birds are singing as I stir, long and clear and liquid. It is morning. I writhe on the dirt floor of the cave as they sing. I open an eye slowly, slowly, peeling back the eyelid with ultimate care. A shaft of bright sunlight stabs the eye, thrusts a blazing spearhead deep into my brain. I scream matter-of-factly, try to move. My shattered leg scrapes against a rock. I scream from the gut this time, every part of my being in the scream, which lashes out through my throat, taking the top of my head with it. The world is yanked out from under me like a rug.

When I wake up again it is raining, a long, gray drizzle. It's impossible to tell if it's day or night. I lie listening to the soft pockata-pockata, pitter-pat of the rain until the cold begins to creep up through my body, gnawing at the marrow of my bones. I worm to the very back of the cave and curl up into a ball as best as I can without hurting my leg. Tiny riverlets are winding snakelike through the gravel and pebbles of the cave floor and are touching me, patting at me like soft, intimate hands. The water begins to pool and soak into my clothes, to soak into my shivering skin. It feels like blood, seeping in instead of seeping out. I clutch my coat tightly around me. I listen numbly to the rain bouncing and ricocheting off the rocks, gurgling down the hillside, dribbling and sliding down along the walls and plopping softly as it splashes against my body. I don't remember falling into unconsciousness again, but suddenly the sun is shining, and the birds are singing, and it is morning. I moan softly as the sun burns my flesh.

I stir and sit up slowly, stopping every so often to put my head between my knees. For a long while I just sit there, leaning against the stone and just breathing: breathing great hungry gulps, breathing tiny gourmet sips. The people in Pittsburgh don't breathe anymore. I breathe more slowly, thinking of the time I watched dawn wrap its web of golden haze around a white church steeple on Easter morning, and a bell had moaned far away and I had nudged a flat pebble gently out of the sheltering earth with the scratched brown toe of my shoe. After a while I can think of other things besides breathing. I stir again and move around some more, squirming cautiously. How long since the battle? Christ only knows, if He's still up there; I don't. A day maybe? Two? But I'm sitting in my own filth and I am very weak. Three days? My time sense is shot. It can't be three days. My bones feel like they're made out of chalk. I drag myself to my feet, using the crutch as a lever. I feel the fierce pull of the earth on every atom of my body, up through the soles of my feet and along my sagging spinal column to my swaying head, trying to drag me back down with bonds like iron glue. I stagger, catch myself with the crutch and push myself erect again. I breathe carefully for a moment, trying to regulate my thudding pulse, and then I start to inch slowly and determinedly toward the cave-mouth, blinking in the gloom and half-shadows. I reach the cave-mouth, rest for a second, and then thrust myself outside.

My world explodes like a magnesium flare.

Reeling, I slam blindly back against the hot, sun-drenched stone and cover my eyes with my hands. Too bright. Almost undetectably, I inch my fingers apart, just a hair. The dazzling white light of a clear summer's morning crackles at me. I wince and flinch back instinctively but keep spreading my fingers slowly wider until my eyes gradually adjust to the kaleidoscope glare. The world swims into focus. Green, green dancing and swirling and shimmering all around me as the tree-covered hillslopes toss and ripple in the wind. And the blue bowl of sky arching godlike above the gabled hills, so bright that it seems to sear my retinas. After days of gray semidarkness in the cave, the sudden explosion of light and color that is the world sears me emotionally and leaves me trembling. The colors can almost be felt; I can sense their shifting patterns on my eyelids even when I screw my eyes shut in sudden panic.

I open my eyes again and let the colors rave at me, drinking them, touching and tasting their subtle, oscillating textures. I am afraid that the world will absorb me, drown me in its intensity until I become just another light wave spinning and vibrating along the color spectrum, or at best a single leaf nodding its head among the vast sea of living green.

Quivering, totally open, totally vulnerable, I struggle to ride out the emotion-storm. Slowly—the rate at which my starved nerves and shriveled senses try to swallow—the world slackens, becomes less ravenous. The intense, almost sexual, flood of emotion that had possessed me and buffeted me helpless begins to drain away, and a tree is once again a tree instead of a flaming emerald fountain.

I look out across the serene hill country, across the marching miles of trees, and tremble reflexively. Above the gnarled crest of a faraway hill, a hawk circles high, wings on fire. It is the only thing that moves in all of this bright empty land. The silent country gibbers at me, and each tree across all the lonely miles has its own whispering, sighing voice; but they are not human voices, and I am alone. But alive. But I am still alive. My hands caress the hot stone softly, almost defiantly. I am alive.

———————◆———————

As he rested against the stone, the empty land was split by a cruel scream of triumph. Above, the hawk wheeled, swimming the rolling blue river of the air, skimming the suddenly virgin sky with burning wings. He watched the hawk in fascination, seeing it as an avatar of mindless tenacity. It was once again king of the air; Idlewild was dust. All it had had to do was wait a few generations until the fiercer clockwork cousins had gobbled themselves up. I had won by evolution. *Was* intelligence a survival trait? Megalopolis was, as dead as the Pyramids, but the hawk continued to hunt according to a million-year habit. That kind of blind, racial patience frightened him. Was there an equation to balance intelligence and suicide? Was Armageddon the inevitable price of penicillin and the Unified Field Theory? If men were hawks, then no Homer, no Michelangelo, no Beethoven, no Aristotle, no Shakespeare. But there was a 150-mile smoking hole from Boston to New York. How do you argue with a hole? How do you argue with a hawk?

Sun splashed and glinted from the hawk's steel talons, its iron beak. The land turned slowly beneath the feathery belly, spun by whistling wings. The hawk's bloody eye had decided on a field mouse, binocular vision riffling the menu of the forest. The hollow death banked, climbed for altitude, hovered. For a moment it hung, held by hunger, then it swooped.

He tried to follow the hawk as it dived, and found that the world was blurred and faded around the edges of his eyes; he was still weak from loss of blood. As he turned his head, a bird sang in a nearby tree. He froze, the wind lightly rippling his hair. Instantly, as if a switch had been thrown, the world was gone, and the only thing that remained, the only focus for his attention, was that warbling, liquid singing. Hunger flattened his stomach against his ribcage, fluttered it like a sick butterfly up and down his spine. The bird sang again. He searched desperately, straining his eyes until they watered, and finally saw it hopping along a low branch, shaking its bill from side to side in the dappled sunlight.

Saliva filled his mouth, nearly choking him as it trickled down his throat like bitter, oily glue. His hand went to the pistol he still wore at his belt, a response so automatic it didn't even touch the surface of his mind. Clumsily, he tried to unbutton the heavy flap that kept the weapon in its holster. His fingers fumbled and slid helplessly over the glossy leather of the holster. He was too weak to unbutton the flap. He slumped against the stone and clawed weakly at his hip, hot needles jabbing his stomach and brain. His numb fingers bumped against the tiny metal catch of the flap, once, twice— On the sixth try he grasped the catch, held onto it as desperately as if it were a woman, twisted it as violently as if it were the neck of the enemy.

Taking a rattling breath, he touched the cool handle of the pistol, drew it. The bird hopped another foot out along the branch, rustling the cool leaves. Hardly breathing, he shoved off the safety and raised the gun with both hands, steadying himself by leaning back against the sloping rock. The bird chattered and scolded at the morning, preening its feathers. His aim wavered, then steadied. Gently, gently, almost lovingly, he caressed the trigger.

The pistol roared, tearing itself from his weak fingers and clattering to the ground near his feet. The bird exploded like a small feathered bomb. A sudden, shocked silence roared across the hills. A singed feather floated briefly above the branch and then settled toward the ground. For a second, the world seemed to hold its breath, waiting motionlessly while the sun circled high above, and then the trees began to sigh and whisper again down the mountain slopes, louder and more fiercely than before.

Nobody can make me do this, he thought automatically. He shuddered, muttered a weak obscenity, and turned away. He retrieved his pistol, jammed it into his holster, and lurched across to the tree, trying not to fall.

Blood and matted feathers were strewn along the ground under the branch for a considerable distance; a high-velocity slug at that range had not left very much. He fell to his good knee and probed into the mess, rustling feathers with his stirring fingers. Goddamnit, there must be *something* left. A fat, black fly circled, settled contentedly onto a pool of blood, rippling its scarlet surface. He vomited, bringing up nothing but a trickle of bitter bile.

When his retching had shuddered into sobs, he crawled painfully away from the dead bird and sat hugging his knees, trying to unsnarl his nerves. There were other ways to hunt, other things to hunt. He would survive. His eyes instinctively rose to the low crest of the next hill. Beyond was the valley battlefield; very possibly there were valuable supplies that had survived the fire-storm and that he could salvage, supplies that might make all the difference between survival and death. He shuddered, feeling his teeth clash and grind together in nervous reaction. Oh God, were there any of them left out there, waiting for him, waiting to punish—

He jerked his thoughts harshly away, struggling to control his trembling. He would survive. He had not sinned. He had survived: they hadn't. Survival was not a sin. And he would survive. For a while he would rest, and when he was able, he would return to the valley under cover of darkness to scavenge. He faced the thought with reluctance and with a strange terror. He didn't want to go back there. The terror was illogical, and he tried to drive it away, shaking his head. There was no danger. He would be safe. He had *not* sinned.

He crawled to his feet and limped aimlessly away to search the nearby scrub for something to eat. He had little luck. That night he slept fitfully, the acid knife of hunger beginning to twist under his ribs.

In the days that followed, hunger grew worse, grew sharper, grew more stabbing, until he felt its knife swell into a swallowed swordblade intent on hacking its way out from inside. Hunger robbed him of his sleep, drove him aimlessly into the night, deprived him even of the luxury of exhaustion. Though he beat the area around his cave in widening circles, somehow he never went near the valley battlefield; even hunger was not yet strong enough to break his unreasonable, horror-tinged reluctance.

One afternoon, he came across a scuffled trail in the dirt that could have been human footprints. Or it could have been deer sign; the track was blurred, and his skimpy woodcraft was insufficient to tell. He stared dully at the scuff marks, wondering what would happen if there were another human at large in the area that he was already beginning to think of as his. He tried to figure possibilities and consequences but was too fuzzy-minded to concentrate. Intelligent thought was becoming more and more impossible; the inescapable pressure of starvation shattered abstract association-trains as quickly as they were formed. He tried to calculate the number of days he had gone without food and found that he couldn't remember how long ago he had awakened in the cave. He thought maybe he should be more worried about his inability to remember, but he was too wrapped in numbing lethargy to care. Time had ceased to exist, except as a measurement for increasing hunger.

Later that evening, he found a large earthworm under a rock and swallowed it, still alive and wiggling, without even tasting it. This gave him a glimmering of an idea, and he began to search a little more logically, overturning rocks and ripping strips of bark from dead trees and stumps. He gobbled beetles, snails, caterpillars, worms, even flies if he could catch them. He came upon a small bush dotted with berries and stripped it clean without caring if they were poisonous or not. Another time, a gobbled root made him vomit helplessly for hours. Once he caught a grass snake and wept in thankfulness, caressing the supple, leather-dry body. He skinned it as best he could with his military knife and ate it raw, licking blood from his fingertips. With the dulling of the sharpest razor-edge of hunger, he began to think about traps and snares for the first time, wondering if he could make them out of strips of his clothing, wondering how to use them and where.

A few days later, he noticed that his teeth were rotting out.

Dead men visited him that night, naked and bloated, with pale liquid fire dripping like pus from their hollow, empty eyes. They hissed at him in voices like lapping flame and tried to speak to him, but he could not hear their words.

———◆———

At last, as I knew I would, I return to the valley. I come creeping over the low hills, a sly, furtive shadow melting through the waiting darkness. The night presses down on me like a thumb, wrapping me in soothing, satin blackness. The only sound is the slight squee-swish of my metal crutch and the off-key keening of a tumbling night wind. A dark cloud-bank looms and contorts above like a tortured elastic mountain, eccentrically lit by a pale moon that occasionally burrows into it and snaps shadows by their tails across the sky. I am invisible as I climb the hill, and I am afraid of my invisibility. If the rock falls in a desert where there are no ears to hear, does it make a sound? Can a man be invisible when there are no eyes to see him?

But there are eyes. I realize this with a shock, my mind stumbling out of the mesmerized groove it has been wearing for itself. Two red eyes float momentarily to the side of the path, like smouldering cigarette butts burning through the black fabric of the darkness; they disappear as the night sweeps them off. A faint, musky reek bites into the soft flesh of my nostrils. It is an animal, I think; it is only an animal. I shudder, rubbing a hand along my arm, feeling prickly gooseflesh. I will not believe in demons. A nightbird moans among the trees, falling away from hearing. There are no demons. Please. Don't let there be any demons.

I creep forward again, feeling the soft weight of eyes. I fear the pressure of the eyes, yet I fear invisibility more because it implies that there is no one to see, that I have been singled out, that I am alone. Something locked within my skull whimpers hysterically and scratches to get out; I try to ignore it, trembling. If there is never anyone in the desert to hear the rock falling, then how can you ever be sure that there is a rock to fall? Or a desert, for that matter? Doesn't the observed phenomenon take place precisely because there is someone there to observe it? How do you know the tide comes in if you're not there to see it? Maybe it gurgles off to play cards with the boys every once in a while when it knows there's nobody checking up on it. Why should the sun bother to rise in the morning when nobody's around? It could sleep late and nobody'd be the wiser, especially not that bastard first sergeant. I begin to laugh and choke it back down. It is not a good laughter.

I sense the next thought coming and scuttle faster to avoid it, but it squeezes relentlessly up from my subconscious anyway and oozes like cloying oil across the surface of my mind. Can a man exist when there are no other men who know of his existence? In time, will he not fade away like a deity whose worshipers no longer believe, disappearing Cheshirelike and leaving not even a smile behind to mark his going? I am invisible, I whisper to the night, because there are no men left to see me. Eyes flashing ahead again, these larger, bounding away quickly. But I can be seen. There are eyes that can see me, but they are not human eyes. I am invisible, but I can be seen. A paradox. I giggle to myself, crouching and swaying, clutching at the fraying edges of my sanity. Imagine, I'm a paradox, and at my age. I've made a mark in the world. I laugh. I stagger up over the crest of the hill. I pause, suddenly and shockingly sober, and I listen, straining.

———◆———

There was a sudden rustle of tall grass, small shadowy forms exploding by. He threw his arms up before his face and cowered back with a moan. His thoughts surged disjointedly in a dozen random directions. There are no demons, he whispered, clinging to that. A darting scarlet shadow appeared in the wake of the small things: flash of tiny bright eyes, grass shaking and reforming down the length of hill behind as a running body tunneled through it like a fleshy torpedo.

There are no demons, damnit. He cautiously lowered his arms. Those were rabbits and a hunting fox. A wailing in the sky, passing overhead. He began to tremble uncon-

trollably. That was a bird, a bird. There are no flying demons either. There are only animals now. He began to cry
silently, without volition, as if it were a thing that someone
else was doing while he watched.

Alone in the night, he cried and rocked on his heels and
wondered why he wept. There was no reason to cry. He
would survive, and there were no such things as demons.
There were no demons or gods or ghosts or angels anymore; they had died with the race, deserted an empty
earth. In fact, there were not even any people or machines
anymore. There were only animals now.

This thought annoyed him for some perverse reason.
The end of the world had come and gone; ipso facto,
nothing should be left alive. He listened to a crackle of
breaking twigs down the slope, the sound fanning a spark
of anger. Fireflies drifted along with the liquid night,
blinking in and out of existence. Suddenly and intensely,
he hated them. The animals were still alive, and the birds,
and the trees and grass. It wasn't fair that they should be
alive after Armaggedon. Somehow it made humanity seem
transient and unimportant, and he didn't want to have to
think about that.

Memory whispered something about the meek inherit-
ing, and he grimaced. If man *had* to destroy himself, he
could at least have taken everything else with him and
saved face. It was unpleasant to think that the world could
go on existing without man. He found that he had always
naturally assumed that the world would fold up like a stu-
dio bed when man was through using it, that the sun and
the stars would shut themselves off, that the universe
would be dismantled like a stage set when the play is finished and the actors gone.

Maybe it's because of me, he thought. Maybe the world
is being maintained for me because I'm the last man left
alive, and when I die, the universe will run down *then*.
Maybe I'm what's keeping everything going. Maybe I'm
responsible. He giggled, feeling an uneasy, unexplainable
guilt. There were no people left anymore. Suddenly he felt
like a traitor; but the reasoning behind that slipped away
every time he groped for it, and it made his head hurt.

He remembered (though he couldn't remember from where he remembered) that he had to find the one who was responsible, the one who would have to pay. He clung to this, using it as a motivation to go on. He risked another cautious look around.

Huge red eyes blinked at him from the crook of a tree: an owl, visible as a white ghost against bark. He felt a sudden flare of unbelievable hatred for it. What was the morality of a universe that let an owl survive while the woman who had slept beside him was dust? How could you reconcile that with any sort of logic, how could you live with that? Who was to blame for that huge an injustice?

Breathing in great rasps, he snatched his pistol from his holster. The owl blinked at him unperturbedly, its head seeming to swivel on its neck. He holstered the pistol slowly, vaguely ashamed. That was the reflex we could never get rid of, he told the owl. But we came close. We almost made it out of your cycle of tooth and claw, eat or be eaten. We almost did. We took a calculated risk. We gambled that empathy could balance intelligence, and we lost. We just couldn't get rid of that part of you in us, that's all. We couldn't love enough. We couldn't stop being predators. But we came so damn close to breaking the circle. And you never even tried. The owl stared at him disinterestedly. You never got to the moon, he told it, you never could have conquered the stars. The owl wasn't listening.

He turned away, shivering. Faces crowded into his mind, the men in his unit, but already the features were blurring and memory wouldn't bring them into focus. He thought for a while of a certain woman, but even that face was blurred, and he fought to suppress panic. He closed his eyes and remembered the owl; it was in sharp focus. The owl is alive, he told himself puzzledly, aware of things that he didn't want to think about shifting under the surface of his mind. That's why it's in focus. It belongs here; it survived. It shares the guilt, a voice said. He shook his head, wobbling it back and forth like a pendulum. He stood up, stretching cramped muscles. He remembered the

blurred trail he'd found. Maybe they were human footprints, somebody else left alive. Maybe it would be a
woman. That thought panicked him more, and he buried
it. Even thinking of someone else being left alive made
him uneasy, made him angry and afraid. Why? He rubbed
nervously at a leg cramp.

He began to limp slowly forward again, feeling the tidal
ebb and flow of panic, shoulders hunched, head tipped at
an odd angle, fingers scrabbling aimlessly, eyes strained
wide, still listening intently to nothing.

------◆------

There is a new kind of silence coming into the world.
Listen to it, the silence; can you hear it? There are no
man-made sounds, no buzz of engines, no clatter of
wheels, no chiming of church bells, no honking of horns.
Listen, there are no shots, no screams, no weeping. Listen,
there is no music, no laughter, no soft sighing. Mankind is
gone, and its greatest legacy is silence. For ages, man has
filled the world with the echoes of his building and de-
stroying, his wars and loves and living; but now he is gone,
the echoes are dying, and there is a new kind of silence
coming into the world. Listen. The silence spreads and
multiplies molecule by molecule, smothering even memory
under a soft fall of feathers. Listen. If I should scream
now, jetting my soul into the absorbing, muffling air with
a single wailing cry, there would be no human ear around
all the ravaged world to listen. Listen. The dying crackle
of the fires that eat smoulderingly at the Cities of Men is
the last sound that the human race will ever make. Listen;
the silence is very loud.

------◆------

The place where the human race had died was marked
only by a green chemical glow. Clouds of phosphorescent
fog had gathered softly in jagged shellholes, sending wispy
trailers rolling out across the blasted land, flowing
over and around the dead like water tumbling polished

bones on a river bottom. The crystal stream that had wound through the valley was a shrunken trickle, scummed with black. He paused on the outskirts of the place, anger ebbing, hushed and awed by the cathedral silence. Here the last men had died, he thought, somehow never questioning the fact that they were the last. He knew, after all, that he was the last man alive, and he had been the only survivor of this battle. He took a slow step. Here two full battalions had clawed at each other with every insanity in the modern arsenal; each side conquering with weapons that destroyed everything alive with impartial fury, turning the technical designation of victory into a moot point. He cringed back instinctively. He didn't want to go out onto the ravaged place, but he had to; he needed clothes, he needed weapons, he needed ammunition. Whimpering, he crawled forward, avoiding the green fog.

The blackened ground was feathery and crusty under his feet, making a slight scrunching noise and spitting up swirling puffs of ashes under the pressure of his boots. He realized that he was walking ankle-deep through human debris, and he felt the vomit sloshing hot against his clenched teeth, a little seeping through to touch the insides of his pale lips; he swallowed it with difficulty, forcing himself to move. Don't breathe; oh God don't breathe the ashes. He half ran to the side, circling the perimeter of destruction, leaving an irregular trail of staggering footprints in the ashes. Somewhere there must be something left. His thoughts wore a bloody groove deeper into his brain. Graverobber, graverobber, deserter, sin. Unclean, hissed a muffled demon voice from his subconscious, as strangled and incessant as a jack-in-the-box screaming for release from its padded container. He thought of the night as a bloodshot eye, following him with relentless, evil hunger. His shoulders hunched, waiting for the punishment, waiting for the blow that would crush him flat like an offending insect. Why did you escape? Unworthy? Coward, rumbling somewhere in his stomach. Alone, bubbling and leaking from his nose in a sob. They are coming to get you. He stumbled on, staggering crazily away from a marching finger of fog. They are coming to get you.

Glint of metal ahead, dark forms, vaguely human, lying scattered across the ground, twisted, broken, and contorted, looking like flies caught in amber or ants frozen into a cooling stream of black asphalt. He paused, feeling his stomach twist far away in another universe. The edge of the fire-storm: these bodies were intact, though scorched. He looked at them, monuments in human flesh to concrete stupidity, and strangely, he felt the trembling, feverish madness drain from him, leaving only uneasy fear. They made it all right somehow, they made it real. He could worry now about how much ammunition he needed to steal, what kind of clothing he needed, and not think about them coming to get him, about them hiding just beyond the gabled hills and waiting to pounce. He could play at survival now and be the calculating pragmatist. Robinson Crusoe must survive regardless, never think of touching a jagged seashell to your throat. The universe wasn't unraveling; the corpses made it real. He had seen plenty of corpses. And there were always plenty more people to churn into corpses. Don't think of that, he told himself uneasily.

He bent over one of the still figures, forcing his mind onto the problem at hand, the problem that was cold under his hand, the problem that stared accusingly at him with empty eye-sockets, the problem that was tacky to the touch. There are always plenty of logical ways to solve problems.

Strip the corpse of valuable gear, put it into the blood-stained field pack, lash the field pack to your own back. He did so, watching his hands move detachedly, as if they belonged to someone else. Safety matches, waterproof; good. Into the pack. More ammunition. Jam it into the pack, jingling against an extra knife and some canned food-concentrates. He struggled to strip the clothes from the body; the clothes resisted him, slightly tacky, sticking to cold flesh. Rigor mortis had set in, and the limbs were awkward to move. Slit the clothes carefully at the seams, resew them later. Clothes and, yes, sewing kit, into the pack.

He was tugging at the boots when something changed in

the atmosphere of the night. He became aware of the silence again, like the sound of great dark wings beating over the hushed battlefield, like the sound of the patient breathing of those who waited behind the gabled hills. He straightened, chills snarling along his nervous system. He felt his breath come faster, felt his fingers curl into taut fists, felt his body stirring, his blood pounding hotly. Why? The half-naked corpse gleamed white as an ice sculpture in the shadows. He laughed shrilly, on the ragged edge of hysteria. Homosexual necrophilia? No, this is a ghost memory—this is the dreadful, half-pleasurable anticipation of a child hiding huddled under the porch and waiting for his father to find him, knowing that he had done something wrong, and knowing that he will be punished and that he has no place to run to, and that he wouldn't dare to run away even if he did have a place to go. Blood roared in his ears. Why? Look up— He screamed, choking it into a gurgle after the first shrill note. The stars were looking at him. The tumbling night wind had finally swept away the clouds, and the stars were very sharp and bright, and they were looking at him. They will *see* what you are doing and they will know and they will come to get you.

Feeling naked and unclean, he crouched close to the ground until the panic drained from him. He became as limp as a crumpled piece of cellophane. The stars have been there for a long time, and they always watch and say nothing, and they never come to get you, no matter what they see. They are content to let men solve their own problems. He blinked at the stars, wondering. For how many ages had the hungry eyes of men turned up at night to watch the stars and dream? And now there were no men left to watch the stars, and no dreams. So the stars were invisible too, and soon they would realize it and blink out, turning the night into the dusty inside of his own skull.

He looked back down at the corpse under his hands. He felt nothing, no sorrow, no pity, no empathy. He could be afraid, the fear churning his stomach, afraid of death, afraid that they would come to get him. But he couldn't cry; he couldn't work up the overwhelming sorrow, the sense of loss, which he knew he should feel. It all seemed too far away, too unreal. It seemed too small a thing to cry about.

Why was that? Surely that wasn't right?

He diverted his thoughts, uneasily aware that there was something unnatural about his inability to mourn. As penance, as a substitute for grief, he began to lash himself into a cold fury. He climbed slowly to his feet, the anger building, looking for a scapegoat, something to divert his attention from himself, something to lash out at. His eyes rose back to the icy stars. He snarled, a reaction as old as the jungle womb of the race. Hey God, sir—he shouted aloud, dramatizing himself, puffing out his chest—are you there? Can you hear me, huh? There's been a death in the family. Called Gotterdammung. Didn't you know? He giggled, a touch of real hysteria seeping in. He began chanting the funeral mass in a wailing, sing-song voice, breaking up, dissolving into snickering laughter. Shit, if I'd known sooner, I'd sent you an engraved invitation so's you wouldn't miss anything. RSVP, baby. He swayed back and forth, the field pack dangling from his hand by the strap and swinging in time with his body like a cloth pendulum. He was play-acting, pretending emotions that he could not feel, but it was fun. Did you enjoy yourselves, all you bastards? he shouted, no longer sure whom he was talking to. Did you all have a real good time? He shouted louder, grimacing fantastically, putting a little soul into it. Did you get a kick out of it? D'yhear? D'you hear me? He was enjoying himself now, feeling grand and glorious and tragic. He reared back and screamed at the sky, daring it to answer.

The sky didn't say anything.

After a while, he decided he'd done a good enough job and went back to stealing the boots.

II
Winter-Spring

I sit in darkness, leaning against the rock, and it is cold. The night is wet; the soggy air pressing against my face, running its velvet fingers along my spine, making me tremble. The cold rock sucks warmth from my flesh, turning it into smooth marbled stone, and that is a good thing, because then I will not move and they will not see me and come to get me. I sit very still, trying to become a rock. I am a rock, heavy and hard, pressed deep into the wet, sheltering earth. I am invisible. If I move, they will come to get me. I must not move because then I will be seen, and I am invisible, so I must not be seen, no. I am a rock, crouching. There is an earthworm tunneling under me, rubbing slimily against my inviolate, hard smoothness, pressing up, straining to break through the surface, but I sit immovable on it and block its passage and single it out and make it alone. I will not fade away because I am solid now and no one will come to get me because no one ever bothers to get rocks. I am a rock.

The field pack dangles loosely from my marble hand, swaying slightly with the motion of my breathing, banging against my knee with the steady, sonorous tap-tap rhythm of a dead hand knocking against the lid of a coffin. But I do not breathe because I am a rock; I do not hear. Rocks do not have to have crusted blood under their fingernails. It is good that rocks do not have hands or smell the air filled with the corruption of death.

It is early morning, and it is misty, and the mists are pearly wet. They look like white shrouds and they wrap around me and creep rustlingly up over my eyes. But rocks don't have eyes and they can't come to get me. False dawn thrusts a pale blue wing over the horizon. I watch it as a rock watches, patient and safe, watching with every surface, every inch, of my polished marble body, not caring.

The light fades into deeper, textured darkness, the night

holding its breath, pausing for a beat in the steady rhythm of time. There is a single star on the horizon, very bright, very low. It is watching me, waiting for me to move so that it can tell them and they can stride forward over the gabled hills to get me. I do not move. Slowly, a veil of velvet air slips aside on the horizon, and the sky becomes a degree lighter. The bright star fades, struggling. It is becoming invisible; soon it won't be able to see me. I sit patiently, wrapped in earth, feeling moss growing on my smooth side.

A bright red wound opens on the horizon, blood seeping horizontally out along the sky. Above the creeping finger of dawn, a tawny golden-orange glow spreads up the curving sky, setting the heavy clouds afire, staining and diluting the jet black of night. It is lighter, spreading branches of trees around me visible now, etched black against the pale golden sky, abstract silhouettes. The light grows, and I can make out the texture of the bark, see the whorls and ripples in the wood. The branches turn purple, then blue, shading toward brown. The bright star has disappeared, lost and drowned in the bloody wash of morning. Shadows make twining, shifting patterns on the ground, elongating rapidly as the sun climbs. The mists are fleeing, lashed by light. Color bleeds back into the world, chasing grey. Warmth and light beat gently against my face, heat melting my stone into flesh, translating me. I am safe.

The sun heaves itself above the horizon, swims up along the sky. I move slowly, hesitantly, stretching stiff muscles. The air is blue and clear and fresh, cold as crystal water. A web of morning sounds crackles around me. The grass is heavy with dew, and mists retreat uphill, swirling and parting around my crouched form.

I drop the field pack to the ground near my feet, fumble at it with numb fingers, come up with a package of cigarettes from a dead man's pocket. I nudge a cigarette into my mouth, clumsy with cold, waste a precious match. I suck in the hot smoke, feeling it filter down through the pores and cracks of my body, loosening it, dissolving the molecular chains that bound it into rock. The sun is high

now, nestled among fiery pink clouds. I drag at the cigarette. For the first time, I think that it may be okay to live.

The thought is hesitant, shy; I have not allowed myself
to think of the future before. The smoke in my throat is
like burning leaves. Why can't I live? I can survive. It is
even worthwhile to survive. The marching miles of au-
tumn trees shiver in response to the sun's caress, suddenly
flash with bright life. I puff; this is nice. Life is still worth
living after all, even without people. I realize that I will
survive, and the knowledge is soothing to my mind,
smoothing the jagged edges of my thoughts. I sit bathed in
the morning, at peace.

———————◆———————

As he rested on the stone, slivers of rock suddenly exploded into the air a few inches from his hand, stinging
him. A sharp echoing crack! rolled around the hills, shuddering slowly into silence. He stared in unbelieving horror
at the new powdery scar on the surface of the stone. More
rock exploded near his hip, the sound of a richochet lash-
ing away through the trees, shredding leaves. Another flat
coughing crack echoed! cruel in the morning hush.

He forced his legs to uncoil, grabbed the field pack and
dived behind the large rock he had been sitting on at the
edge of the forest. He flattened close to the stone, pressing
against the grass. His metal crutch was crushed under him,
jabbing against him and sending tiny fingers of pain darting across his body. The grass was wet against him. His
mind was blank; he couldn't comprehend what was happening.

Another shot slapped the stone above him, the bullet
skipping away through the tangled leaves. He peeked
around the edge of the stone in time to see a bright muzzle
flash from behind a hollow fallen log halfway down the
slope of the gentle hill. Stone pinged! nearby.

His mind churned, thoughts tumbling in haphazard procession. One thought emerged from the welter: it is the
enemy down there, trying to get me, trying to kill me. A
memory he couldn't identify flashed a picture of the

enemy into his mind: immaculate, bestial, a hunched figure stalking him with inhuman arrogance and strength. Automatically, he drew his pistol, poked it around the edge of the stone in the direction of the hollow log and fired. The roar of the gun rattled his teeth. He heard bark tear soggily. He suddenly smelled the reek of hot oil, and there was a shiny empty shell lying on the dirt near his elbow. He had killed near Pittsburgh, a swift firefight under a broiling sun, and the dead eyes had stared at him without seeing, and the neatness of geometrical shells in the dirt had been an ultimate mockery. Time seemed to slip and waver, blurring crazily, past and present and future mingling horribly into an insoluble maze, an endless circle.

Not again, he screamed silently, not again. There was crusted blood under his fingernails. Not again! He triggered off two wild shots in the general direction of the hollow log, heard stone sing and shiver above in reply as the enemy fired back; and then he jammed his pistol into his holster and crawled frantically into the forest, keeping in the shelter of the boulder and dragging his crutch and the field pack clumsily along behind him.

He wormed his way deeper and deeper into the sheltering forest, sliding down steep inclines on his belly, puffing and struggling on knees and elbows up tangled hills. The meadow fell away behind and was lost. He kept crawling, his flesh torn and bleeding from the clawing underbrush. Far away he heard two more shots, faint with distance; the enemy had not yet seen through the ruse.

Finally he stopped, invisible under a dense thorn thicket. He curled in exhaustion, gasping, wincing at the thorns that tore his flesh, leaving drops of red blood on the shiny black wood. Jammed against the thorns, he writhed, and his lips formed words silently, puffing against the air. The bastards, he whispered, not knowing whom he was accusing, the bastards—

He found that he was having more difficulty thinking. Sometimes it was even hard for him to tell when he was awake.

I stretch cold fingers toward the crackling fire, straining, flesh as absorbent as a sponge, sucking up heat. Blue wood-smoke curls around me, stinging my nostrils, framing my head, making a pearly halo. The wood spits and moans as it is eaten, as it is translated into smoke, just as my flesh stiffens slowly into stone with the approach of night. I press closer to the fire, drinking heat. If there is enough heat, enough light, I will not have to turn into a rock to hide from the watching darkness.

Outside, it is dusk, the sky being slowly translated from whorled granite into smooth, secret ebony. As I watch, a few fat snowflakes squeeze like lazy teardrops from the slate grey sky, drifting and swirling like tiny dancing diamonds among the bare dead branches of trees. It is the first snowfall of winter. I watch it drown the falling sun on the horizon, blank it out with churning white. I can no longer see the gabled hills that rim the world. Will they sneak up on me under cover of the storm, tear me with their cruel talons? I feel my flesh turning to safe stone at the edges of my body.

I watch, straining through the snow. Everything is very quiet, pressing in. Far away I can hear the slow crackle of the Cities of Men smouldering beyond the horizon. I wonder what warms its hands at those fires? My cave is high, high on the shoulder of a hill, and I can see all the world from here without it seeing me. I am invisible.

The snow dances, pirouetting, pressing its soft mouth wetly against the jagged mouth of my cave. I can see down the throat of the storm now, and deep within its shifting velvet body, a face forms from the flying snowflakes, built up layer by layer out of a million individual crystals, a crazy-quilt face with staring empty eye-sockets that slowly fill up with white snow, which looks like silver fire. Go away, I scream at it, go away.

It speaks, hissing at me, its lips billowing and expanding with the wind, its crawling tongue flickering. I shake my head, trying not to listen to its whispering. It wants me to do something with my pistol. The snow drives me back against the rear wall of the cave. Go away, I scream. The face hisses. I am invisible, and I do not need you, I do not want you. I don't want to hear what you say. You can't tempt me because I am a rock. The snow howls. Go away. There is nothing left to tempt me with, the world's treasures are ashes. I am the only one left and I am invisible. The face chuckles, lips pursing and writhing, whispering, whispering. I won't listen, I scream, I don't have to listen. I've got to find the one who's responsible. I've got a mission. The snow lips laugh at me, puffing.

Suddenly surrounded by the cold echo, I think of spring and blades of grass, but I will not think of that. Symbolism was in books, and all the books are dust. Spring was a dream; winter is the reality. Outside, the face wails plaintively, evilly, whispering.

You stupid bastard, I scream, why don't you give up? Why don't you go away? You're an anachronism too. The world doesn't need you anymore, you stupid bastard. There's not even anyone left to tempt anymore. Go away!

But the face doesn't go away. The lips shape the words, but I will not listen to the trickling whisper. The fire is gutting, dying. My hand touches the butt of the pistol, wrapping around it, but then the fire dies and my arm turns to stone, the paralysis seeping up through my body, translating my flesh into a safe, dappled marble.

And as the sun blinks out on the horizon and I become a rock, I hear a gunshot, faint with distance. Far away, the enemy is hunting among the high hills and the soft dead fall of snow.

The shadows came on him at midnight, rousing him from his long, stone thoughts. Who are you who are you, he screamed at the hunched waiting darknesses. Shadows darted around the cave, leaping and contorting. I didn't do it I didn't do it, he gibbered, cowering on his knees, I didn't mean it I didn't want it nobody wanted it. He laughed, tearing his throat. Nobody wanted it, please, nobody wanted it. The shadows screamed at him, knocked him over, straining to absorb his blood into their hollow selves. Oh God, he moaned, twisting on the floor, *did* we want it to happen? Did we want it to happen, all of us, secretly want it to happen? Did I want them to die, all the people I've known? The shadows clustered closer, and he almost thought that he could make out faces, recognize the longing darkness. He screamed. No I won't look. I won't. He thought of all the people he had known, numbering them, and as he spoke each name silently in his mind, a shadow darted in response from the dark corners of the cave and tore his flesh like a black thorn. He wailed mournfully. I wanted you dead, but I didn't know that you would have to *die*. Please go away please go away. The shadows rolled over him, tightening convulsively around him like misty talons. They were female shadows now, velvet darknesses all with long, rippling hair and bright, gleaming eyes. He felt his body stirring in the night, and he thought a certain name and sobbed—no, surely I didn't want you to die too—but the shadows twined around him and pressed him helplessly flat to the floor of the cave and tore away his sheltering clothing, making him naked and unclean. The soft female shadows buried him then, hissing sibilantly and touching him with probing hands of mist, their eyes gleaming in the night. He felt his body stiffening in response, and as the shadows wrapped him in warm, contracting darkness, he leaped and moaned and thrust, bucking like a mating salmon, trying to pin down the shadows, trying to hold them against him, trying to touch misty flesh that melted and flowed through his straining fingers, hammering and rolling, grappling with elusive shadows, which enfolded him and yet stayed just out of reach, until he gasped and screamed hoarsely, the hot pulsing madness draining from his flesh. He slumped spent and crumpled in the ashes of the cold fire. His body wet and trembling, sweat drying in the cold night air, he shuddered into feverish sleep, ravished by old dreams, raped by shadows.

———————◆———————

I watch the sun go down and I shift the knife in my hands. I must wait for the exact moment, or it will not work. The snow has been piled deep around the cave for many days, and I cannot get out to hunt. My ribs stand out nakedly through my parchment-thin flesh. It must work. It will work.

The sun sinks lower. There is a huge rubbery worm behind the painted horizon, and it swallows the sun every night, swallows it down to its spongy, chambered belly where they do filthy unclean perverted things so that the sun is belched forth in the morning pale and exhausted, unable to melt the prison snows. I know the signs, I know the signs well. They are unclean and they must be stopped. They are perverts. I will make the worm let go of the sun, and the sun will rise flaming strong and melt the snows and translate my cold stone into flesh and make me clean again, and I will not have sinned or have blood under my fingernails.

A weak feathery rustle under my hands. I have a bird there, a bird I trapped in a snare. I have pinned it to a board, crucified it there still living. It is an instrument, a sacrifice to free the sun.

The sun nears the horizon.

I press my knife slowly into the bird, the cold steel sliding into its flesh. There is blood on the steel, blood matting the feathers. The bird screams and thrashes, and I pull the knife out a little, slowly, probing oh so slowly for its life, letting the steel explore its body.

The bird screams again, throwing itself wildly against the rusty nails that pin it down. I control what it feels, I can make it writhe, I can make it twist. It is the controlling that counts, the burning focus of passion and hate. It is love. Love is touching and sharing, love is stirring emotion, making another feel what you feel. This is love, the steel snickering into flesh and the bird writhing, sharing my passion, I feeling its pain. There are all kinds of love.

I am not alone because I can still touch something else.

I can still make something else feel, and I will not think that I am alone. And the emotions are so strong that they are broadcast, sent out across all the world. The worm behind the horizon feels what the bird feels, and I can make the worm let go of the sun by hurting the bird. Everything, every living creature all over the world feels what the bird feels, and so they are all writhing under me and my passion covers and conquers the world.

My excitement grows, but I must wait until the sun is gone, I must wait until I have hurt the worm as much as possible. The knife probes. The bird's struggles are weakening. The sun is suddenly gone, vanished into the worm's gaping gullet behind the horizon. I drive the knife home to the hilt. The bird strains against the steel, gasping, dying, and I gasp with it in sympathy and sorrow and love. There are all kinds of love.

When I have finished, I push the messy remains of the bird to one side and return to the fire. I take one of my last food-concentrate tins from the field pack and begin to work it open with the bloody knife. I will survive. The sun will come in the morning and melt the snows, and I will survive.

The stars are out sharp and bright in a clear winter's sky, but I am inside my cave and I do not think they can see me. I watch the black bulk of the gabled hills rimming the world, bright in the moonlight, and I do not see them watching, so I do not think they will come to get me. I will not have to become a rock tonight; the fire is bright. And I don't think the shadows will come for me tonight; fighting the worm has left me drained and shaky. The most important thing is to survive. Do not listen to the whispering. I inch closer to the fire and spoon food concentrate into my mouth, licking spilled crumbs from my hands. What is the enemy doing? I wonder. I imagine the enemy doing things and feel a faint spark of returning excitement. They are all perverts. I must kill the enemy. He is the one responsible. He is an agent of those who hide behind the gabled hills. While he is here I am not unique.

I scrape the bottom of the tin for more food, the metal rasping loud in the night. I am not an ordinary man. An ordinary man would have gone insane under the pressure, he would have been driven mad by the thought that he would always be alone *don't think of that*. I have managed to retain my sanity in spite of the fact that I am the only one left *don't think of that*. I will not listen to the whispers, I will not listen. It is not easy to stay sane, but I will keep up the struggle, unlike the enemy. The enemy is insane. Crazy people are unclean. They are all perverts.

Suddenly I feel like crying and I don't know why. All the world outside is hollow and empty *don't think of that*. I will not listen to the whispers. Time is a maze and all the roads lead to the same place, over and over again. You cannot get out, you cannot ever get out. I feel eyes watching and I look up in fear, thinking of the enemy. But I see a flash of a liquid fiery eye peering hungrily over the rim of the world, and I know that they are thinking of coming to get me.

I think of them heaving themselves up from behind the gabled hills, towering monstrously into the night sky, scaly bodies gleaming in the moonlight, striding forward to get me, crushing trees under slimy webbed feet, and I am afraid. I am invisible, I think, and you cannot come to get me. I begin to turn into a rock, growing into the ground, turning cold and hard and opaque, my blood curdling into veins of streaky quartz. I am not an ordinary man.

———◆———

At night as he slept, twitching uneasily and curled against the cold, dreaming stone dreams of the granite veins that run madly through the secret body of the earth, he would sometimes return to the battlefield in his mind's eye, seeing the white drifted snow that covered the blasted ground like a feathery shroud.

And at such times, he would imagine that the scattered bits of machines—broken pistons, shattered flywheels, twisted springs—were stirring slowly under the heavy snow with a horrible kind of life, stirring and crawling toward each other, groping blindly. He could see the resurrected parts inching and worming over the frozen ground, meeting, fusing together, until a sinister, mismatched machine began to grow, self-assembled, swelling part by part until it bulked huge and bloodstained in the night, a pulsing mountain of junk. Then, shattered, misshapen, held together only by some inhuman will, it would begin to drag itself painfully across the hills toward the cave, oil seeping like dark blood from the fissured surface, the bent needles of meters flickering behind cracked glass in time to a metallic heartbeat, knotted black wires groping to find his throat, and he would wake up, screaming.

And every night of the long winter it would creep closer across the high hills, rattling and shuddering and clanking and groaning, and he would begin to listen a little more closely to the whispers.

———◆———

I cannot remember my name. This is not fair. I have not been well. The world is frozen outside. The snow never melts and I cannot get out, and I find it hard to think anymore. I cannot remember my name. I have it right on the tip of my tongue, but every time I try to say it, it slips away and I cannot remember. I know that I did have a name once. It began with a D or a B. It could have been a G. I cannot remember. This is not fair. Everyone should be able to remember their own name. But I have not been well.

———◆———

The thing crept closer that night, churning through the frozen earth like a blunt plow, leaving a ruler-straight furrow in the ground. There was a red glow somewhere deep in its bowels, the smouldering glare seeping fitfully out through cracks and rivet holes, and battered gears whirled and spun and clicked nakedly inside the hollow iron skull, gleaming in the moonlight.

———◆———

I don't know where I am and I don't know how I got here. I can't remember. The cold outside is like knives. It is always white. There is no color, there is no light. There is only the pale grey of polished stone. I am curled in a cave and there are high gabled hills pressing in all around but they make me afraid and I will not look at them. I do not know how I got here. I remember something, I think, warmth, vague comforting blur, mother? wife? but I cannot remember and even as I say the terms their meaning fades. I know who I am and I know about things like that, but I find it hard to think anymore and I can't remember.

There is nothing but white outside. A voice tells me that there is green underneath, but I think that is a dream. There are so many dreams. They get tangled sometimes and come over and over again and I can't tell them apart. There was a fire in the valley and eyes that could not see, but I think that that was a dream. There is no valley and there is no green because I am a rock, and I have always been here, growing from the ground and dreaming of these other things. Rocks dream too much.

I always feel like crying now and I never know why. I remember that no one wanted this, but I cannot remember what *this* is or who the no one was. There is another voice echoing, which says everyone did want this, secretly wished for it to happen, but I don't know what happened or why, although it makes me sad when the voice says it. I also know that the bastards can't make me do this, and I whisper this again and again because I know it is important, although I don't understand it, and I laugh each time I say it because I remember that it is funny, and that you're supposed to laugh at funny things, although I don't know why.

There was a house and bright flowers and I went to school and I played catch in the sunshine, but I know this is a dream and I wrap it in stone and smother it. There is just me and the whispers. They are trying to make me forget that I am a rock, but I will not listen. The other things are dreams and unclean.

I dreamed once about a war and an army, I think, and I say the words again but they mean nothing to me and I know urgently that they should and I try to catch it but it slips away like misty flesh. We had causes and missions and reasons, and the causes were very important, but I can't remember them anymore because it is too cold. I remember that the causes were very important and worthwhile, but I cannot remember what they were. I cry and try to remember them so that I will know why it is always cold and I cannot get out, but they always slip away, and so maybe they aren't that important after all. They are dreams too.

I try to remember my name and I try to say it, but my shriveled tongue gags me and all that comes out is a retching sound. I cannot remember what a name *is,* although I know that I must keep on trying to say it because it is important too. There are many important things and emotions and images tumbling in my mind, but they have no order and they blur and melt into each other and I cannot untangle them. They echo away into darkness before I can grasp them, and their churning hurts my mind. Rocks do not have minds, and so they should not have to have them hurt all the time. I know this is logical, although I cannot remember what logic is. Flash of a face in the mind I do not have, dissolving quickly, flesh melting into shadow, and I know that I loved her once, although I don't know what love means.

But these are all uneasy dreams and outside. I am inside and safe. The only sound is the slow crackle of moss growing on my sides. I am a rock, and rocks should not dream.

———◆———

By early spring, the thing had crawled so close that he could hear the rattle and thump of its broken wheels against the flinty ground at night, hear the ponderous scrape-slide as it dragged itself relentlessly through frozen mud toward the cave. Every night as the dying winter spiraled toward summer, he would crouch at the back of his cave and trace its jangling progress through the darkness and scream again and again, soundlessly, and only the beating pressure of his silent screams kept it from lumbering into the moonlit clearing before the cave and rolling horribly into sight, and only the mindless rhythm of his ancient, stone thoughts kept him from listening to the acid whispering of the shadows.

———————◆———————

The snow is retreating before the sun, leaving soggy footprints, and I laugh and splash my hands delightedly in the steaming black mud outside my cave. It is early morning and the sun is trembling on the horizon. The winter is nearly over. For more than a week now I have been able to burrow beneath the wet ground uncovered by the fleeing snows, finding slugs and grubs to eat, getting my strength back. I have been ill, but now I am well. I have broken the worm behind the horizon and made him give me back the sun and I am happy. Someone once told me that God is dead, but I am not; I know because I brought back the sun.

I fumble until I find my crutch, and use it to lever myself to my feet. My bones feel as if they are made out of chalk, and I can hardly stand. I stumble from the cave, wincing at the bright sunshine, drinking the loud colors. For a moment I feel hollow and afraid, and I think that this has all happened before, but I can't remember when. I shrug away the fear; nothing can harm me. I brought back the sun. A hawk wheels above, wings flashing in my sun, and I watch it dive.

I stumble very slowly down the sloping path away from the cave, letting my feet guide me. All around me I hear the rustle of my servants, my children, running through the bare underbrush, staying discreetly out of sight and waiting for my commands, eager to serve my will. The stark trees bow to me as I walk, waving their branches in salute. The sky arches above, clouds shifting and sculpting themselves obediently in response to my changing moods. The rocks cry out with a million joyous voices as I stride by, crushing them underfoot, and they cry louder, happy to be crushed.

I trip on the rutted path, recover my balance. I am not

. an ordinary man. A lesser man would have broken under the strain of winter, a lesser man would have gone insane. A lesser man would not have been able to make the worm let go of the sun. I am not an ordinary man. I am God, and God never worries about the blood under his finger-nails.

The pool at the bottom of the hill is free of ice for the first time in months. I was once a rock, and rocks can drink urine and chew leather for moisture, but now I am God, and God should drink water from a pool. Laborious-ly, I lower myself to my good knee and bend over the pool to touch cracked lips to the water.

I jerk back in surprise and fear. There is someone in the water. I lean slowly forward again.

There is a face in the water, flickering choppily as it is rippled by tiny wavelets. The face is ancient and wrin-kled, cracked by a million deep-etched lines, the flesh as stained and coarse as old leather. The hair has turned brit-tle and white, the luster and texture of straw. The eyes are sick, yellow and bloodstained, sunk deep into the head and smouldering hollowly. One eye has a nervous tic, which makes the face look as if it is winking obscenely at me. The teeth are rotted and black. A tangled beard, brown, streaked with white, caked with dirt and spittle, covers the neck and chin, stretching back to blend into the shaggy mane of hair. The face is almost invisible under a thick layer of grime and blood and dirt, and it looks very frightened.

I am frightened too, and angry that someone should be in my water, and I start to command it to disappear, but as I do I see its lips move too, and I watch as its lips shape the words *the bastards* and I hear the puff of my own voice saying the same thing, and then I know that it is me, and I scream.

I twist away from the pool, trembling, shoulders hunched against the blow that will crush me flat. Shudder-ing, I inch back to the lip of the pool, stretching one hand toward the face, afraid to touch it. A kind of sob snarls along the back of my throat. I trace the deep lines in my face, tug at my brittle hair. It's only been a year, God it's only been a year, but it's been a crooked year and I can't untangle the dreams.

I scream again and pound the water with my fist, scattering the face into dancing fragments, sinking it with a ring of widening ripples. I lurch to my feet and stagger away, feeling the face reforming in the water behind me, feeling it leering at my back. I will not look at it again. I will not believe it. I begin to run clumsily, jolting my bad leg, thrashing my way among the naked trees. I am not so sure that I am God now, and I am beginning to be afraid again. The trees tug and snatch at me, branches raking like claws. I hear a ponderous rustle and crunch of underbrush far away, and I know it is the thing sliding down the hillside behind me, hunting me down now that I have left the sanctuary of my cave. I whine in fear, saliva gurgling in my throat.

I run faster until I break from the forest into a clearing and hit a lingering snowdrift and slam heavily into soft mud. I lay still in the sucking mud, breath whistling and rasping between my teeth. I raise my head cautiously, peering through waves of pain and a veil of hot tears. Sudden nausea and fear bite into me like talons, and I choke back the thin bile that is all I have to offer as vomit. I have returned to the battlefield.

I cower, watching my hand go forward as of its own volition and brush aside some of the snow covering the ground. The ground is still blasted and black, but now it is laced with green, new grass pushing its way hesitantly up through the barren ground. I touch the ground, feeling its wetness and chill, feeling how it dries and grows warm as the sun bakes it. The grass is vivid against the pale drabness of my skin. I wonder whether to laugh or cry. That blind life should come groping again in the wake of death is so beautiful and horrible that I cannot bear it, and I sob, grinding my forehead against the mud.

The whispers are very loud now. I cannot break out of the maze, I cannot break the circle. I cannot get out of the crooked year. None of us ever could.

My fingers brush the butt of my pistol, stroking the cool

metal, and I am dimly aware that the thing and my crutch and my pistol and the bombs that raped the valley are all connected and related through some twisted corner, some crazy crossroads of the maze, all instruments for dreaming.

The whispers are threatening to tumble into inescapable words when a long shadow falls over me and I hear a heavy body force its way from the forest behind me.

My scream tears the tattered fabric of the world, ripping my throat raw. It is the thing looming over me to crush me grind me smother me, absorbing me tracelessly into its broken iron body. The shadow swells, blotting out the sun. I scream and scream, feeling bones crack, muscles pull tight, my taut body arch *they are coming to get me they are coming to get me they are coming to get me* and the pistol is in my hand and it explodes again and again and I am screaming and I hear something else scream faraway and the pistol roars and the echoes wash through the sleepy morning and the pistol clicks and the pistol clicks and it is empty.

I drop the pistol and I am on my feet screaming and trying to run, but I do not see them, and I do not see the thing. There is only a dirty bundle of rags crumpled on the ground a few feet away.

I stop screaming. The silence is loud.

I moan nervously and stumble forward, dropping to my knees. The bundle of rags is a human figure, lying on its back, staring blindly toward the rising sun. There is fresh blood welling through the tattered uniform. It is the enemy.

I watch as the enemy's lips writhe and twist, bubbling, and then grow still. How long has it been since I've heard a human voice, and how long will it be now? Hesitantly I touch the enemy's face; his flesh is already growing cold. His face is dirty and battered and frightened. It looks a lot like the face in the water. It is slowly smoothing, relaxing into death. I didn't mean it, I didn't want to do it, and I know that I am lying and I sob. I touch the enemy's callused hands with a callused finger.

I try to turn into a rock and find that I can't anymore.

But I think that I can see my flesh starting to fade, losing color and becoming transparent, and I know that I may soon be permanently invisible. I am crying, and tears cut channels through the grime of my face, and I cry for me, and for everybody and everything. I cock my head and listen to the greedy silence and feel for a heartbeat. There is none. My hands are covered with blood. I am alone. I try unconsciously to wipe the blood off on my pants, on the new grass.

The whispers have taken flesh. They are very loud and bright, and they roll in letters of marching fire and iron through my mind. I know what they want, and I know why. I have found the one responsible, the one who has to pay. I am very tired. I grope for the pistol, lift it from the dew-wet grass. I cradle the pistol in my lap and begin to load it. There is one way out of the maze, one way to break the circle. It's the way that has always existed, the way of love, of empathy.

As I lift the pistol, I reach over with my free hand and close the enemy's staring eyes, gently brush the hair back from his forehead. My heart swells with tenderness and sorrow, and a certain strange exultation. I press the cold muzzle against my temple. There are all kinds of love.

The sun rose hot and clear that morning, and a flock of returning birds sang it a hymn of beating wings and liquid exultation. The sky was a pale fresh blue and it was filled with sprawling, fluffy clouds that flamed into molten gold when the sun burrowed among them. Far away, a hawk screamed at the morning. It was going to be a beautiful day.